The first real Indian raid arrived just before a hard rain, taking everyone by surprise. Leah was in the tower, when eight hostiles came charging on horses from a wood, galloping toward Fred and Simon who were plowing a field. Leah saw them and yelled, leveled a rifle at them and fired.

Fred shouted to Simon, abandoned his plow, and ran for his rifle. Simon pointed a pistol at the leading brave and fired.

"Get outa there," Leah yelled and fired a second rifle.

Fred fired into the midst of the attackers, then turned and ran as Dud hurried out from the palisade with a pistol in each hand. The Indians had scattered but were still charging and whooping shrilly.

Dud shouted, "Shoot at the horses! Put 'em afoot!" He fired one pistol then the other as Fred and Simon raced toward him.

Jeff galloped past Dud yelling, "Reload!"

ACROSS THE RED RIVER

Arthur Moore

FAWCETT GOLD MEDAL • NEW YORK

Library of Congress Catalog Card Number: 90-93050

ISBN 0-449-14626-X

Manufactured in the United States of America

First Edition: August 1990

Oh wilderness were paradise enow. . . .
                                        Omar Khayyám

To everything there is a season, and a time to
every purpose under the heaven.
                                        Ecclesiastes 3:1

Chapter One

JEFFREY Becket halted the bay at the entrance of the old town cemetery and got down slowly. He glanced at the dark sky, where a crystal-like glitter of stars filtered through the trees. A flock of swift-moving birds wheeled across the far horizon and he felt the long, stark silence of this place.

It was late and he'd ridden from the farm that evening for one last visit. His parents, Amos and Eudora, had been buried here several years before the new cemetery had been opened on the far side of town. Leaving the horse at the weathered gate, he walked along the thread of road, up the gentle slope of hill between the rows of gray stones and leaning headboards.

He would not rest here, when it was his time. Pulling off his hat, he walked to the center of one row and faced two rain-streaked headboards. A faint, cold mist rose to shroud the smoke-gray trees. It had rained that afternoon but now it was clear overhead.

HERE LIES AMOS BECKET 1783–1836, LOVING HUSBAND AND FATHER. Amos had come down with an internal problem the local doctors had not been able to diagnose or treat. He had not lasted the winter.

His mother's board read: EUDORA ANN BECKET 1788–1839 BELOVED WIFE AND MOTHER. Eudora had not been strong since the last daughter had come into the world eight years before. And though she had never said a word to that effect, it seemed to everyone that joy and life had gone out of her with Amos's passing.

Upon her grave Jeffrey laid the wildflowers he had picked on the way. "We're going west in the morning, Mother. All of us send our love. And I guess we won't be coming back anytime soon. Rachel is fine. She would have come with me but she had so much to do. . . . We bought us a new wagon—well, it's new to us. It's sturdy, with well-seasoned wood and falling tongues. Rachel bought an iron stove with a boiler, a dutch oven, and we've got a pretty good tent. I think we're going to be all right.

"We're talking about going as far as Texas, but that ain't been decided. I know you always wanted to go out to Texas, Pa, so we'll be thinking about it."

Jeff looked at the sky again. A breath of air lifted the distant tree leaves and mottled clouds drifted slowly across a hunchbacked moon. Amos had talked about the move for years, but he had never been able to un-mire himself from debt or from the fatherhood that had blessed him with seven children and tied him to his plow.

But now it was 1840; a fateful year, Jeff thought. He was twenty years old, and if he did not pick up stakes and go right away he might never be able to. His three brothers, Matthew, Toby, and Nathan, and his older sister, Sarah, were all settled with wives and a husband, and rooted. His younger sisters were not adventurous and would marry in due course.

And in another year Rachel, his wife, would undoubtedly be large with child. This was the time to go.

He said, "I sold my land to Matthew. He had a good crop last year and paid me off in seeds and money. I bought a Hawken rifle and some bolts of cloth for Rachel and we got two mules. So don't you fret about us, Mother. There ain't anything going to stop us and we're going to build a life."

He looked round him and at the cold sky once more. There was a flurry of sound, a clatter of horses from the hard-packed road far below. He put his hat on. He would probably never come this way again.

"Good-bye, Mother. . . ." He stooped and fussed with the wildflowers, then stepped back. "Good-bye, Pa." He took a deep breath, turned, and went down the grassy slope to the horse, tears starting in his eyes.

He was a big, strong young man, very like his father when Amos had been twenty—so all the older folks said. Perhaps Jeff was quicker in hands and mind; he'd had more schooling, three years in fact. He could read very well and do his figures. Amos had been able to add a column of numbers but he'd had to make his mark when writing.

Mounting the bay, Jeff rode away without looking back. He and Rachel would sleep in the house once more, then leave most everything behind except necessities. Matthew had said he'd sell what furniture he could, then pull the house down and chop up the wood and cart it away, burning the rest to make room for more crops.

As most were, they were poor as church mice, but Jeff knew that things would improve when they found better land. Their little plot in Arkansas was fair, but very far from the best. They had barely scratched by on it and never put away anything for bad times. And there was no way they could buy better land. No one would sell on a promise.

Sarah and her husband, Matthew, and the others had long since acquired land a few miles south and east and were apparently content. But, Jeff thought, they have no dreams, and no willingness to abide hardship until things changed. Jeff's dreams did not soar, they were of the land, but they were something to reach out for, and he knew they would come true.

Over a period of a year they had met to discuss a move west. Jeff and Rachel, the Hurleys, the Caines, and the McAdams family. Charlie McAdams was Rachel's father, and he advised them all to stay where they were.

"You know what you got here. You don't know what you'll be getting into. It could be a lot worse. . . ."

Fred Caine was eager to go. He was pushing sixty and no one could be more unhappy with his lot. He and his wife, Louise, had two sons, Simon and Joel. Simon was nearly eighteen and Joel fifteen. Joel had decided to stay; he was sweet on a girl in Durand and hoped to marry her. He was apprenticed to the local blacksmith and had no interest in land. For a year he had been living in the blacksmith's house, so the parting would not affect him.

Simon was the one who was constantly in trouble. A moody, resentful lad, he was difficult at best to get along with. . . .

Rachel had never been captivated by the plan, nor was she totally against it. She had listened when they had had their discussions, arguing about this or that eventuality. She spoke only when her opinion was sought. Most times, she said, her husband spoke for her.

She was tall for a woman, with dark hair and eyes gray or hazel by turns, according to the light. She had a rather long face with a wide mouth, but a very comely face in all. She was a woman of very little real humor but much practicality. She would not have described herself as being hardheaded, but things were thus and so. Some could be depended upon, others not. Her husband, she had decided long ago before they were married, could be depended upon. So that when he made up his mind, she had no objections.

When Jeff had received the seed sacks and the hard money from Matthew he said to her, "Make a list of the things you need and we'll get them in town."

He had bought harness and tools and a better plow. She had laid in sugar, salt, flour, bacon and meal, coffee, vinegar, rice, and some quilts, extra clothes, and a few medicines. When they left Durand behind they knew that prices along the way, if they came to trading posts, would be sky-high.

Jeff had decided not to buy oxen to pull the wagon. They owned two mules, both in good condition; they would do. They had no cattle or milk cows to drive, but Fred Caine had several.

When everything was ready and packed, the tarpaulin stretched across the load, it was time. It was a hushed morning of cold sunshine veiled by a silvery haze, with no breath of air stirring. Jeffrey tied the bay on behind the wagon and waited patiently as Rachel went once more into the silent house. She stood in the center of the little room they had called the parlor, looking at everything—and nothing. This was where her new husband had brought her to live. And now, so soon, they were leaving it behind—leaving everything behind. The heavy, dark furniture, the pump that Jeff and Dud Hurley had installed for her in the kitchen, even the bed they had slept on. They had taken only what could be put into boxes and bags, and not much of that.

When they found a new home she would have to collect new things. The menfolk would have to fashion new furniture somehow—cut down trees to saw them into wood lumber—after they built the houses to live in. She sighed deeply, thinking of living out of the wagon.

And it frightened her a bit that they were going to move into the wilderness. But Jeffrey, she knew, was looking forward to it.

She walked through the little house and went out to the wagon. She looked back once as they drove away.

Chapter Two

JEFF Becket rode to the rise of ground in a dazzle of sunlight and halted under a copse of trees that leaned away from the wind. He stretched and gazed round at the horizons. The sky was a deep blue, paling far ahead, passing from blue to green then a misty white where it merged with the shadows of hills barely seen. In between were dark green swaths of color, probably forests, with patches of brown and yellow that were weedy fields.

Below him, only a few miles away, a winding garland of green threaded its way through the coppery-brown earth, and closer he could make out the dusky green-and-white winking leaves of cottonwoods.

There was water there, a good place to make camp for the night. He turned the bay and rode back to the distant wagons.

Fred Caine came out to meet him, a wiry, skinny man in a dirty checked cotton shirt and patched jeans. One of his eyes was gone, a pale cataract glazed over it so that he constantly cocked his head as if to see better. Fred had been the one who had talked for and organized the western move in the first place. His oft-stated reason was better land. But everyone knew he quarreled bitterly with his neighbors.

Jeff and Dud Hurley had discussed Fred many times, wondering if they should let him accompany them. They decided after much back and forth to take a chance. Between them they would be able to handle Fred.

"There's a creek up ahead," Jeff told him. "Five, six miles." He glanced at the sky. "Be gettin' dark about the time we get there."

"You see any redhides?"

"No. No trails either."

"Ummm." Fred squinted back at the wagons. "We ain't movin' faster'n a three-legged goat."

"I'll ride around the tail." Jeff turned the bay. Fred was nervous about Indians. When they'd left the last town behind the old-timers had said the Comanch might be active this year. . . . "Good grass, all the way to Mexico."

They had seen none at all, but of course everyone knew that the ones you don't see are the ones that hit you when you don't expect it.

Dud Hurley's wagons were bringing up the rear. He had two, a heavy farm wagon with three-inch iron tires bolted on, and a lighter buckboard. His wife, Leah, drove the buckwagon. They had recently been married, a year ago come July, and had no children, yet.

Dud was a big man, although shorter than Jeff, with tawny blond hair and blue eyes, and a disposition that hated to see bad in anyone, even Fred or Simon Caine. Leah was short too, strong and round-faced, and very outspoken. She said the sharp words for both of them, though Dud tried to shush her. A man knew where he stood with Leah.

They were traveling a wide, shallow valley and Jeff rode away from the wagons, circling around, his eyes missing nothing, narrowing into the sunshine. Indians, if they came, would possibly slip up behind the last wagon. That was his suspicion, knowing at the same time that Indians never did what you expected. The old Indian fighters said that if you thought an Indian was doing one thing . . . he damn well was doing something else.

Leah wasn't straggling. Her buckboard was up even with Dud's heavy farm trap, and they were gabbing. Jeff waved at them, lifted his rifle, and Dud nodded and lifted his. He was watchful.

Jeff rode on, making a wide circle about the little train. He saw Rachel looking at him, a blur of face, and waved to her. Rachel waved back and Jeff reined in, his eye caught by movement in the trees several hundred yards off to the right. He slid the Hawken across his thighs and pulled back the hammer, his heart beating faster all of a sudden.

Then a deer left the brush and turned away from him to disappear again into the trees.

He took a breath and let the hammer down slowly.

They had left the farms behind a week ago to head into the setting sun, three families in all and five wagons, seven people.

Arkansas was a long way behind them now.

The families weren't exactly sure where they were headed. The maps they'd perused were very sketchy and inaccurate. The vast area was unsurveyed, and might never be. Many people had only the vaguest idea of where they lived, whether Oklahoma or Mis-

souri or Arkansas. . . . Jeff was sure of only one thing: When they
crossed the Red they would be in Texas.

Of course they could not be positive which river *was* the Red.

But it didn't matter. They wanted land they could both farm and
raise stock on, near water and near forests for lumber. Which territory didn't matter. Dud Hurley said they would know the place
when they came to it.

They had lived near the town of Durand, and travelers who had
come from the west had said there were hundreds of likely spots to
settle, exactly what a man needed to set his family down. However,
they all said too that there were the Comanch to worry about. . . .

But they were four riflemen, all good shots, even Dud. And the
women could shoot and load as well. Rachel was a good hand with
a pistol. Jeff had taught her to use one while they were courting,
only a few months ago. And Dud had said that Leah was a surpris-
ingly good shot.

They reached the winding creek before dusk. The gold of the
evening was slowly fading as they formed the wagons into a kind
of square. Because the square was too small to hold the travelers
and their animals comfortably, the stock were led into a rope corral
near the water where they could be driven inside quickly.

Dud got out a shovel and dug a pit for the fire and the women
began to prepare the evening meal. It was simpler, they had found,
for all to pitch in and make the meals communal affairs, because
there were so few mouths to feed.

The men discussed the coming night. Fred said, "We're getting
into Indian country. . . . Maybe we ought to double the guards."

"We're going to lose sleep that way," Dud said.

"You rather lose sleep or lose your hair?"

Simon asked, "You think they know we're here?"

"Hard to say," Jeff said, "not seeing any. But it's smart to figure
they do."

The night passed without incident. After breakfast next morning
they crossed the little creek and continued west, navigating by the
sun.

In hours they had left the flatlands behind and entered low,
wooded hills, following winding valleys, often in sandy washes that
would become raging rivers in winter.

Fred Caine rode along the line of wagons, back and forth, telling
everyone to stay alert, while Jeff and Simon scouted ahead. Halting
the bay on a gentle slope where brown grass crackled under the
horses' hoofs, Jeff froze.

There, on the next slope, maybe two hundred yards away, a

naked, painted Indian on an angular sorrel appeared. The rider trotted around an outcropping and then disappeared.

Jeff's heart hammered for a moment. He looked toward Simon who was gazing at the far hills. Lifting the Hawken, Jeff slid his thumb to the hammer and yanked it back. Simon saw the movement and said, "What?"

Jeff said softly, "Indian." His gaze swept the surrounding hills. Nothing moved, but where there was one Indian there might easily be a hundred.

Simon whispered, "Where you see 'im?" His eyes were huge.

Jeff looked toward the slope once more before turning the bay. "Let's go back. Easy now. I think he saw us."

Simon fingered his rifle. "You think there's more of 'em?"

"Yeh. He was wearing paint." Jeff nudged the bay. "We best be gettin' back."

Simon turned his horse quickly and Jeff grabbed the bridle.

"Go easy. If they're watching, don't let 'em think we're in a panic. Ease back nice and slow. Don't look around like that!"

"I d'want an arrow in my goddamn back!"

"You figure to stop one by watching?"

Simon growled. "Maybe I can see it comin'."

"No, you won't. Time you see an arrow it'll be stickin' out your belly." He urged the bay horse. "Come on."

He led the way, walking the horse as if nothing in the world were amiss and Simon followed, still grumbling. If he and Simon were killed or captured, the others in the wagons would have no warning of an attack—and would be outgunned to boot.

Jeff listened for sounds: hoofbeats bearing down on them, or the nasty thwack of an arrow into flesh, the report of a rifle . . . but the hills were silent. Not even a bird chirped. Was the silence more ominous?

Jeff recalled the tales of old-timers in Durand. Plainsmen had a healthy respect for horse Indians, and a hatred as well because the savages tortured their prisoners to death. The Kiowas were the worst . . . and they were close.

As the trail made a bend, Jeff glanced behind them. No one followed that he could see. If the Indian had been the point, out in front of a war party, it would take him time to get to the others and organize an attack.

Simon said, "I see dust."

In a few moments they could hear the wagons, wheels lumbering and bumping, jarring pots and pans and spines. None had springs. It was often better to walk beside them than ride.

Fred Caine appeared and Simon suddenly spurred ahead yelling, "Indians!"

Instantly Fred halted the wagons.

It was the wrong thing to do. There was a higher flat area just ahead where the hills widened. The flat was covered with short brown grass, an ideal place to corral the wagons—just in case. Jeff pointed to it, "Get those wagons up there! Quick, dammit! Get moving!"

Fred cocked his head. "You see Indians, Jeff?"

"Yes—move those wagons!"

Fred shouted at him, "Simon says you seen *one* Indian!"

Jeff ignored him, racing to the rear wagon. As he reached it he spotted the Indian galloping toward it. He caught a glimpse of Dud Hurley's pale face. Jeff reined in, raised the Hawken, and fired at the Indian's horse, watching it stumble.

Dud yelled something and fired his pistol. Leah, in the buckboard, was slapping reins, shouting at the horse, as the wagon gained speed. Jeff rounded her wagon and two Indians charged out of the whirling dust. He leveled the pistol and fired at the first. The horse went down in a wild tangle of legs. The second horse, too close behind, ran full-tilt into the first.

Jeff spurred after the wagons, frantically reloading the pistol. Dud had pulled aside, allowing Leah to go past. He had the reins wrapped around a wrist, both hands on the rifle, looking for a target. Jeff dashed past, reining in beside Rachel. She was white-faced, a pistol in her lap, biting her lower lip as she followed one of the Caine wagons. She was all right. She gave him one swift look then concentrated on the mules.

In minutes the wagons gained the flat. Fred and Simon fired almost together at something—then Fred was getting the wagons into a square with the stock inside.

Jeff circled the wagons at a lope and came back to his own. An Indian on a gray horse approached from the trees and shook a coup stick as Jeff leveled the pistol and fired at him. But the Indian was too far away and soon disappeared. It was suddenly quiet. Jeff walked the bay into the square and dismounted by Rachel, holding her for a moment. "All right?"

She nodded. "Just scared to death. . . ."

"We'll be all right now. There's only a few of them." He reloaded the Hawken and laid it on the wagon seat so he could reload the pistol. Damn, if they only had some pepperboxes. The store in Durand had none because no one asked for them, according to the storekeeper.

He glanced down the slope. There were two dead horses there in the weeds. It was probably a small party of eager young men, who apparently did not have firearms, and were glad to get out of the camps and raid what they could find.

There were half a dozen arrows stuck in the sides of the wagons. He went around then, asking if anyone had been hurt, and miraculously no one had. Not even the stock had been touched. They had been lucky.

"I saw two up close," Dud Hurley said. "They were young ones. No organization. They just came charging in, hoping to find us asleep, I suppose."

"They lost one I know of," Jeff replied. "And one damn sure hurt."

"Fred shouldn't have stopped the wagons. It turned out all right, but it could have been a tragedy."

"Spilled milk," Jeff said, but he felt the same. And it was Simon who had caused the trouble, spurring ahead, yelling "Indians." *That* could have been really bad, throwing everyone into a panic.

"It was too close," Jeff said later to Rachel. "Luckily it was a bunch of young ones, probably on their first war trail. They did everything wrong. They could have hurt us bad."

"Will they attack us again?"

"I think they'll try to crawl up close tonight. They don't want to face rifles in daylight. Indians don't want to get dead any more than we do."

During the afternoon a few arrows came sizzling in to whack into wagon sides. The Indians were still out there, probably boiling over . . . but the arrows did no damage.

Dud said, "They're mad as hell."

Simon fired half a dozen times at movement in the far brush, till Fred finally told him to stop wasting ammunition.

Fred spoke to Jeff, never once apologizing for stopping the wagons earlier. "You figger they'll charge us tonight?"

"I think they'll try to slip up quiet."

"Then we'd best build up fires for light."

"I'd keep some small fires going, outside the wagons, with coal oil handy to toss on the embers. We might be able to surprise 'em."

"Damn good idea," Dud said.

They dug a deep pit for the cook fire and the women hurried to finish a meal before it got dark. After they ate, the fire was doused so it would not silhouette anyone.

Afterward they crawled under the wagons, watching the shadows blend into the dark. Small birds flitted in the thickets across the flat and then were quiet.

They built small fires outside the wagon square, four of them, each with a can of coal oil nearby. Then there was nothing to do but keep the fires going—and wait.

Hours passed.

Leah Hurley said, "Maybe they went away."

Dud disagreed. "That's what they want us to think."

Jeff lay under the wagon, rifle and pistol in front of him, eyes missing nothing. Rachel was behind him with her pistol, ready to reload for him. No Indian can come close, Jeff thought. The brown grass, an inch or two high, is no cover at all. But he recalled an old plainsman saying an Indian could hide behind a single blade of grass. It was not encouraging.

The night grew old. Were the Comanch going to let it pass in peace?

Then he thought he saw shadows change. He blinked his eyes— was he getting tired or was something out there? He squinted and looked just to the left of the shadow, not directly at it. Was it a figure on the ground?

Slowly he reached for the can of coal oil. He heard Rachel's quick intake of breath. He splashed the oil on the coals—and in the sudden bright light saw three painted faces, eyes round in surprise. Then all three yelped, getting to their feet.

Jeff fired at point-blank range with the rifle, grabbed the pistol, and pulled the trigger, hearing the others firing. Then the light was gone and he yelled, "Reload, reload!"

Rachel handed him her pistol and he heard her say to herself, "Powder first, powder first," as she reloaded the rifle.

But they were gone.

Dud came to the wagon. "Think they went this time?"

"Hard to tell, but I think we hit two or three."

"They're not running into luck. Maybe they'll figure their medicine is bad."

"I hope so."

"God willing," Dud said. He consulted his silver turnip watch, flipping the lid up. "I make it another two and a half hours till sunup."

"Well, let's keep everybody awake. They can sleep tomorrow."

"Yes . . . agreed." Dud turned away and Jeff heard him talking to the others.

The Indians aren't likely to try the same thing again, he thought.

They may have had enough already and are riding off, licking their wounds, carrying their dead.

He lay quiet under the wagon, the Hawken poked through a wheel and resting on a spoke, the pistol at hand. The others around the little square lay quiet too. Now and then he could hear the mutter of voices, but mostly it was still.

And the night fled toward dawn.

The Indians returned as the first gray streaks of day began to lighten the sky. Jeff put his ear to the ground, feeling the distant drumming—hoofs!

He yelled, "They're coming again—on horses! Get down, get down!" He looked for Rachel. She was stretched out flat on the ground behind him, eyes wide and round, a powder horn clutched in one hand. He gave her a quick smile and drew back the hammer of the Hawken.

They rode screaming and yammering onto the flat, and arrows slammed into the wagons. Jeff fired the rifle into their midst, grabbed up the pistol, and fired again—then they were gone.

A horse lay kicking and screaming in their wake till someone put a bullet into it. Jeff looked around at Rachel. She was sitting up, dutifully reloading the rifle, her face pale as milk; she was scared to death but carrying on. He pushed back from under the wagon and slid an arm about her.

"They won't be back. It's all over."

She relaxed into his arms with a great sigh. She said in a small, broken voice, "Will it be like that . . . ?"

He said slowly, "I wish I could promise." He kissed her cheek. "But nobody's hurt."

She dabbed at her eyes, looking quickly toward the others, then took up the powder horn again. Everyone was talking at once, scurrying about. Dud climbed up on a wagon to scout around, but he saw nothing. The Indians were gone.

Jeff saddled the bay and rode out, circling the little camp. There were two dead horses in the thick brush and one in the grass in front of the wagons. He came across the remains of several fires farther away, with gnawed bones strewn about, but nothing else.

He walked the bay to the highest point near the camp and gazed around, hunched against a cold wind. Leaves, lifted by a spiraling breeze, drifted past him. Far to the north were the charcoal streaks of mountains. Beyond the camp were clumps of dark pines and toward the end of the little flat trees grew, with leaves shining like silver coins. But the redskins were gone as swiftly as they had appeared.

They rested for half a day, puttering and sleeping, and finally got moving again after a midday bite.

They traveled for four days without incident.

The party finally came to the river, halting on the banks as the winds scuffed the water.

"How the hell we gonna get across that?" Fred asked, of no one in particular.

"We'll cross," Jeff said.

Chapter Three

"It's got to be the Red," Fred Caine said. "What else?"

The river was not where their map said it should be, as far as they could tell. It was a big, slow-moving current, deep green in places, with slate-colored surfaces and smoky browns here and there, with the sun splintering on distant ripples.

They followed the water for several days, taking soundings with a rope tied to a rock, looking for a way to cross and finding none.

Fred said at last, discouraged, "The other side's the same as this, ain't it?"

No one could argue that.

Jeff was sure they could cut down trees to make pontoons for the wagons, to float them across. The river was obviously low and in no mood to fight them.

But as they discussed this idea, they came to Handy's Place. It said so on a crude sign: HANDY'S PLACE   JAFE HANDY, PROP.

Handy was a lout of a man, big and uncouth, dressed like a ragpicker, smelly and dirty. He had an Indian wife and a pattering racket of kids, black-haired, sullen, and noisy.

"Where ye come from?" he asked. Jeff thought Handy had strange, greedy eyes and hair so long, it might have been gathered up from a threshing floor.

"Arkansas," Fred replied. "This here the Red River?"

"Yeah, it is. You ain't fixin' to settle hereabouts?" Handy did not seem glad to see them.

"No, we're not," Fred said. "We aim to cross over."

Handy seemed relieved; his mouth pulled back over ragged teeth. "You kin cross 'bout a mile." He pointed. "They's a ford. The river's low right now so y'all won't have no trouble with them wagons."

His house was a heavy log cabin that appeared to sag in the middle. It squatted on a bit of high ground like a badger. It had two chimneys and a single plank door, propped open. Dud went near it and turned away, his face contorted. It smelled of nameless things. An ordinary man could not survive inside.

Handy's wife appeared in the door for a moment, doubtless curious about the strangers. She was a dappled pudding of a woman with black hair hanging down her front. She had a stolid gaze in a stone-brown face; she looked at them and was gone.

There was also a large pole corral containing several horses and mules, a barn of sorts with a sign painted in axle grease above the doors: SALOON. Handy sold whiskey by the bottle or the barrel. He went into the barn and came out with a wooden box and set it on a counter made of planks on two barrels.

"Bar's open, folks," he said. He took bottles from the box and lined them up. "Drinks, one dollar."

"One dollar!" Fred said.

"You know 'nother bar within a hunnerd mile?"

Fred snorted, then examined a bottle. "You make this-here poison yourself?"

"Shore I do." Handy poured a dollop into a tin cup and pushed it across to Fred. "Give you a taste free."

"Don't do it," Dud advised. Handy glared at him.

Fred looked into the cup suspiciously, then tasted it gingerly and made a terrible face. "Jesus God! That got a bite like a catamount!"

Handy beamed. "Shore has, ain't it?"

Fred backed away. "No thanks, Handy. I got my stomach to think of. You put too goddamn much rattlesnake in that stuff."

Handy scowled, looked at the others, and sniffed. He piled the bottles into the box and lugged it back into the barn, muttering to himself.

They held a short meeting and decided to go on along the river to the ford. Handy's Place had a smell that followed you around, Rachel said. She would not be able to eat a thing if they stayed anywhere nearby. Everyone agreed with her.

When they had reached the ford, Jeff rode across and back, the water barely up to his boot soles.

The wagons crossed with no trouble and they camped on the far side under the trees; the land was flat, with clumps of trees scattered like hen feed; there was plenty of firewood. The women went downstream a way and bathed in a pool as Jeff and Dud rode out a half mile or so, seeing no one.

The land was probably under water in winter—it was low and flat—the reason Handy had not built his house near the ford.

"He wasn't sorry to see us go," Jeff said to Dud. "I'll bet he sells that rotgut to Indians."

"Yes. No wonder those redhides are wild, if they drink that juice. His liquor would give the pope the jim-jams."

Jeff brought out the map after supper. It showed a town called Pommer, somewhere in the area. It also showed several rivers they had not seen. Crossing the Red meant they were in Texas, Dud said.

"It'd be nice if there was a signpost."

In the morning they continued south and west and Jeff rode ahead, scouting the land, looking for an area that would provide crops, and trees for lumber, and be near water. Several times Jeff reported a suitable area, but Fred insisted things would be better farther on.

Now that he was moving, Fred seemed to want to continue. Almost, Jeff thought, as if he were afraid to stop. And he was touchy about it, so Jeff did not argue and let him alone.

The Caines, Fred and Simon especially, were a moody lot. His wife, Louise, was under Fred's thumb, never seeming to have an opinion of her own, so she was seldom consulted. Fred was sometimes a reasonable man, but he could also be very quarrelsome.

Rachel asked, "How far are we going?"

"Until we find the right place," Jeff said.

"I've already seen it twice."

He chuckled. "But Fred hasn't. And you know how stubborn he is."

"Why do you and Dud allow it?"

"Because he may be right. And if he isn't, we can always go back."

She smiled and kissed his cheek. "Don't look for Eden here on earth. It may not exist. Besides, we're all tired of living out of wagons."

They reached the town of Pommer the next day. It did stretch the imagination to call it a town. In other places it would have been called a hamlet. It was a small collection of houses, stores, shacks, and canvas shelters all set down haphazardly on a flat, treeless plain.

The wagons rolled in as the yellow dust of the afternoon gilded the light. The town seemed built around the largest building, the general store, which had living quarters above. The sign proclaimed: GEN'L MERCHANDISE, G. TITUS PROP.

A few porch idlers stared at them as they pulled up in front of the store, and Titus came out to the boardwalk. He was a tall, lean man, bald as an apple, with specs perched on the bridge of a generous nose. He wore a once white apron over a dark shirt and pants and had a wide smile. He hooked his thumbs in the top of the apron.

"Where you folks headed?"

"Well, we're open to argument," Jeff told him. "We're looking to settle."

Titus beamed on them. "There ain't nothing we would rather see than good settlers, sir. Where y'all hail from?"

"Arkansas."

"Well, you're in Texas now. I trust you c'n tell the difference? Don't the air smell fresher?"

Dud laughed and stepped up on the porch. "It does for a fact." He put out his hand. "My name's Dud Hurley. You're Mr. Titus?"

"Folks calls me Jerry. How do, Mr. Hurley."

"And folks call me Dud." He pointed. "And this-here's Jeff Becket. His wife, Rachel, is in the wagon there. Over there's Fred Caine and his wife, Louise. That's Simon by the mules." He stepped down. "This's my wife, Leah."

Titus nodded to each of them. "I'm sure glad t'know you folks. Y'all plan to cabin hereabouts?"

Fred said, "You may be the man to ask. You hear of a good place for us?"

"Y'all farmers?"

"No," Dud said.

"Yes," Fred replied and looked at him.

Titus smiled. He pointed south. "Over thataway, maybe ten, fifteen mile, is Dead Hog Crick. They's forest and fertile land there, both. You won't find better in this big corner of Texas. I advise you to go look at it."

"We will," Dud said quickly.

"You'll thank me for it," Titus assured them.

They went inside and bought staples from Titus and then camped outside of town by a running creek. Over supper Rachel said, "Dead Hog Creek? Can't we change the name?"

"A rose by any other name," Dud said.

Jeff agreed. "I vote we change it—if we land there."

"Anything would be better."

Leah said, "Mr. Titus wants us as customers."

"Of course he does," Dud nodded. "But that doesn't mean he isn't honest. It would be foolish of him to tell us the land was good when it isn't. We'd soon find out. . . ."

Rachel leaned against Jeff. "Are we going to have a log house?"

He looked at her, the light tangled in her hair. "Probably. But it'll be warm in winter and cool in summer, and we can always add on to it."

"You mean we'll start with one room?"

"Yes," he admitted. "We'll have to put up a house quickly, 'fore the rains. But one day we'll build us a sawmill and then you can have a proper house."

"Well, whatever it is, I want a floor. You hear me, Jeff? I want a board floor. I will not live on packed dirt."

He squeezed her. "If I'd known what a lot of trouble you were going to be, I might not have married you."

She moved closer. "Yes, you would." She rubbed his thigh. "Wouldn't you?"

He squeezed her tightly. "I think it's bedtime."

Chapter Four

In the morning they left Pommer behind and went south, looking for the creek. They found it in the early afternoon, a placid stream, silver and brown with ripples glinting along the far bank. It wound slowly across the prairie, calm as an old man sitting in the sun, but with gray driftwood piled along the banks where it had raged in months past.

They halted to water the animals where cattails grew in profusion. Jeff rode ahead where a blur of dark green caught his eye. As Titus had said, there was forest land, too.

They camped that night in a curl of the stream, and as he watched the shallow, smoky drift of the current Jeff felt this was home.

Rachel felt it too. "I'm not going any farther," she said. "You can build our cabin right here, by the creek."

"Not here," Jeff said. "Up there, on higher ground, so we won't be flooded out this winter when the water rises."

"Very well, husband."

Dud and Leah agreed too, this was the spot they had been looking for. Leah, backed by Rachel, declared she was not moving another inch. Fred grumbled, but had to give in.

Before breakfast, under a curdled-milk sky, Jeff rode over tawny meadows as far as the dark tide of pines that marched down to the creek and across it. There was lumber for a thousand houses, and when the logs were cut it would be easy to snake them across the grass, or float them along the creek.

After Jeff returned and ate, he talked with Dud and Fred as he sipped coffee. Simon sat by them, listening. He was Jeff's age but not head of a family. He had no vote among them.

Fred wanted to pace off land and stake it. "We ought to decide that now and keep to it."

"How much land you want to pace off?" Dud asked.

"Well, say a half-mile square for each family."

Jeff's voice was even. "Do it by guess? None of us are surveyors. We could wait on that."

"By guess is good enough for now," Fred said, growling a bit. "We can survey it all later. I want t'know where my land is."

Dud shrugged. "I don't need a half-mile square of land. I'm not a farmer like you and I'm not going to try to be one. All's I need is enough for a truck garden to feed us."

Jeff said, "You get the same as us, whatever it is. If you don't use it, it's still yours. You can sell it one day if you want."

Dud made a face. "All right. . . ."

The stream ran fairly straight for several miles and they decided to claim land along it. Fred showed them a paper. A half mile was 2,640 feet, he said. "What if we pace off one thousand paces for each family?"

"That's more than a half mile," Dud said.

"Eight hundred paces then."

Jeff said, "A thousand is fine. There's plenty of land. Who will do the pacing? It ought to be the same person."

Dud replied, "We can draw straws."

Fred picked up some twigs and broke them off, then offered them to Dud and Jeff. "Long straw does it?"

Fred drew the long straw.

When they told the women, Rachel said. "Does that mean we'll live a half mile apart? Is that wise?"

"We ought to consider that one day there'll be a town here," Dud insisted. "Why don't we pace off a section to live in, and call it the town-to-be?"

"And all of us live in that section close together," Leah agreed. "That makes sense."

"It makes protection too," Jeff said.

Fred grumbled a bit, as he always did, but even he could see the sense in it. After some argument they paced off eight hundred paces along the creek and two hundred deep and called it, as Dud suggested, the town-to-be.

It was all level land, well above the creek. It took several days for Fred to pace off all the land and stake it as best they could without instruments. The stream ran generally northwest to southeast; when the pacing was finished, they drew straws for the parcels. Fred's land was thus on the north, Dud's in the center, and Jeff's on the south. Fred and Jeff could then expand more easily if they wished.

Nothing was said about the land across the creek.

* * *

All that done, the next order of business was shelter. Winter was on the way. Fred suggested they put up three houses at once.

"Three houses?" Dud said. "It'll take twice as long."

"And be less safe in the long run," Jeff put in. "We ought to build us one long house and divide it into three rooms."

"No, no!" Fred objected, his voice rising. "We got three families here!"

Jeff said, "Three houses'll be hard to defend. We're going to have Indian visitors, sure as hell."

Dud agreed with him. "They could cut off one house and kill everybody in it!"

"I want t'own my own goddamn house!" Fred argued loudly. "Dammit, that's why I come way the hell out here!"

"Cool off, Fred," Dud told him. "We're just thinking of the common good. It's a temporary thing."

"We ain't seen any Indians lately, have we?"

Jeff shook his head. "But they probably been looking at us. Anyway we'd be smart to figure they have. If we build one long house and divide it into three rooms it'll be stronger and we can help each other."

Fred continued to grumble, but was outvoted.

Dud asked, "Where shall we build it?"

"Right in the middle of our town-to-be," Jeff said, "where the bluffs are. That way we'll have the creek at our backs and water handy." There was a short section where bluffs, seven or eight feet high, ran along one bank.

Dud nodded. "Good. All right, Fred?"

Reluctantly, "All right. . . ."

They selected a ten-foot, heavy, straight log, hooked up two mules and dragged the ground, over and over again, where the house was to be built, leveling it. Dud tested the level with a pan of water.

When they were satisfied, they spent hours tamping the earth down, and that done, they decided where the northeast corner of the house would be and staked it.

The house should be lined up north and south, Fred insisted. It was custom. They let him have his way.

That night Fred tied a rope to the stake and lined up the rope with the pole star, driving a second stake so the rope was stretched as near north and south as he could make it. That line would become one side of the house.

They had no carpenter's square so, in order to find the right angle, Jeff measured off three arm's-lengths and tied a knot in the rope, then measured off four times that same length and tied another knot, then five times and tied another knot. In that manner he made a triangle and staked out the rest of the house's outline.

Next the large foundation logs were carried and laid into place. The most difficult task was notching the ends. The logs would have to fit tightly at the corners; it was a job that Jeff did best.

Hewing the logs level on one or both sides was grueling work. But it was necessary so that as little mud-caulking as possible would be needed. Some logs had to be split, and Fred set to this with a froe, a T-shaped chisel.

The house was laid out, thirty-six feet by ten. It would have three fireplaces, one for each room, for heat and cooking. Each room would have a plank door and one small window.

The house wall that would contain the doors and windows was the most difficult. It took hours and hours to saw through the green wood and peg the logs into place. The three rooms would be tight and small, as the women pointed out at once.

"There's hardly room for a table and a bed!"

"We'll make do with bunks built into the wall, one above the other," Jeff said. "The house'll keep the rain and snow off us and be easy to heat when it's cold."

"And be dark as the inside of a raccoon," Dud added.

"I want a board floor," Rachel said.

"It would take days to split logs for that," Jeff told her. "You can have a board floor next year. This year we get the house up. Next year we improve it. Maybe in three years we'll have separate houses."

Dud went looking for a clay bank and found one. He hauled loads of clay to the house, then started on the fireplaces. His father had taught him this skill, he said, when he was just out of shirttails.

"The throat of the fireplace is very important. If the set isn't just right, the chimney won't draw well."

He worked slowly. With a pile of fieldstones that had been collected by the women, a tub of clay and plenty of sticks, he carefully built up the fireplace. Into the fireplace he inserted pothooks, a crane, and as the women suggested, a shelf for the cook to use. When the first one was finished everyone was lavish in his praise.

He fashioned the two others in exactly the same way. They would last, Dud said, as long as the house stood.

He then started on the chimneys.

The walls went higher, and as they were built beyond reach it was necessary to skid the logs up with ropes, then notch them into place—all backbreaking work. The three windows were small and high up and would have to be paned with greased paper.

When they reached the roof line the men had to decide what kind of roof they wanted. Fred offered to make shakes, saying he had done it often before. Although Jeff feared that shakes would be more easily set afire in an attack, Dud supposed that a log roof would probably leak. He opted for shakes, and so it was decided.

Without metal hinges, they had to use thick leather straps for the doors. On their next trip to Pommer they would buy hinges from Titus. The doors were locked from the inside by bars. Simon was given an auger and showed how to bore a hole above each door. Then he threaded a cord through and fastened it to the bar so the door could be opened from the outside.

As Dud had predicted, each room was dark as night, even with a bright sun shining. But it was better than living out of a wagon.

With the roof finished, the house took on a different look and feeling. It was even closer inside the small rooms than they'd imagined. In the daytime Rachel would leave the door standing open for air and light.

Dud had a bottle of whiskey he'd brought from Arkansas and insisted they have a celebration to mark the building of the first house along the Eden River.

"Eden River!" exclaimed Rachel. "Are you renaming it?"

Dud was indignant. "I'm not going to live alongside Dead Hog Creek!"

Rachel sided with him. She had already mentioned Eden to Jeff, he reminded her. "How many for Eden River?"

Everyone was, except Fred who wanted to think it over. But they outvoted him. Eden River it was. Dud poured a bit of whiskey into each of their tin cups.

"We'll have to tell Jerry Titus of our new name."

"And put it on the map," said Rachel.

Chapter Five

THEY were careless. They had seen no hostiles and had grown neglectful. Even though they'd posted a guard, the morning after the little celebration a horse was missing. The animal had been taken out of the corral without anyone hearing or seeing. . . .

It seemed impossible, but there it was; the poles were down and the horse was gone. They were lucky the thieves had taken only one animal.

"We've been visited," Jeff said, staring around at the horizons. He examined the ground, but it was too trampled to follow tracks.

"What do we do about it?" Dud asked.

They looked at each other, then Fred said, "Build a tower."

"What? A tower?"

"Yeah, a ten-foot tower. It's easier than building a damn palisade."

Jeff spoke slowly, weighing things in his mind. "I think maybe we'd best do both. With a palisade we can keep the animals inside. The tower will let us see farther."

Dud objected. "But whoever's up in the tower might get killed there!"

"We can give him some protection so he'll be hard to see from the ground. And if we tie a rope to the tower he can slide down in a hurry in case of trouble, instead of using the ladder."

Dud asked, "Will the tower be any use in the dark?"

"On most nights," Jeff said.

Fred agreed. "You can see movement from up above." The tower was his idea and he was for it, but the palisade was another matter. "It'll take us all the rest of the year to build a log wall! The stakes got to go into the ground too."

"Only a foot or so . . ."

"And there's furniture to make. We going to sit on our butts all winter?"

"We can make the furniture inside, if it rains," Dud said.

24

Fred lost the argument, and they began chopping trees and hauling logs once more. The tower and palisade together were a huge undertaking. The palisade would need a fire step along its entire length, with ladders to get up and down. But it would provide safety and make it impossible for Indians to steal their stock.

However, they knew that the bigger they made the wall, the more guards they would need to man it. So they planned to barely surround the long house. After all, it too could always be enlarged.

When she and Jeff were alone Rachel asked, "How long are we going to have Indian troubles?"

"Nobody can answer that. We can hope the government builds a fort in the area one day. That'll help control 'em."

"The government doesn't know we're here."

He pulled her close. "I'm afraid you're right."

Storekeeper Jerry Titus, riding a fast roan horse, showed up toward the end of summer when the palisade was mostly up. He was delighted to see their progress.

"You folks are fixin' to stay!" He had brought a bottle of brandy he said, in case there was any occasion to celebrate something. The house and the other building were plenty.

He spent a few hours, gabbing and eating, telling everyone the news and the gossip. "A man named Van Buren is President. Don't know nothin' about him."

He also had a newspaper he had bought from a traveler who'd gotten it in Missouri. The paper said the country had just gone through a financial panic. That was not of interest to any of them, and no one had heard of Van Buren.

"Sounds like a foreigner," Fred said.

What was interesting to them was news of the wild Indians. Apparently they were active, and Titus was surprised their only brush with them so far had been the loss of a horse.

"But that palisade'll fix em," he said. "Horse Indians hate walls."

"We go armed everywhere," Fred said. "They know what a rifle can do."

"Don't underestimate 'em," Titus advised.

He pulled Jeff and Dud aside when he went out to his horse. "The Comanch raided a family over north two weeks ago. Burned 'em out and killed ever' last one, including two kids and a woman. You watch yourselves."

"What about you, riding out here in the sticks?"

With some pride, Titus showed them two big pepperboxes. The

weapons were in holsters slung over the pommel of the saddle, very handy. With his Sharps rifle he had a lot of firepower. "I can fight off any band of redhides armed with only bows."

Jeff's eyes lighted up at sight of the pepperboxes. He handled one like it was delicate gold, and Titus said he had another one for sale in the store and would save it for him.

"Thank you," Jeff said, squeezing the other's hand. "I want it."

They had not finished the palisade before the first rains came. But they had propped up the wall and during fair weather they worked on the fire step—which would be a platform built so they could fire over the parapet of the palisade.

They also made an outside oven, roofed it, and ricked up wood for the fireplaces, providing cords for each family. With the stock inside the palisade, they were ready for winter.

Jeff hunted during the winter months, bringing in deer and occasionally rabbit, so they were never without meat. He made two trips to Pommer before it snowed, buying staples from Titus and the pepperbox pistol he'd been promised. It was a two-action Ethan Allen with a streamlined bar hammer. Titus proclaimed it the fastest firing pistol ever invented. Now Jeff could get off six shots in as many seconds.

Beside the staples and goods, packed on a mule, he also bought small items for Rachel: a bit of cloth and lace, combs and a dress pattern, a box of pins. . . .

It was the winter when Rachel told him she was pregnant. "I missed my time twice now," she whispered one night in bed.

It took him a moment to realize what she had said. Then he hugged her—it was marvelous news!

She had counted it out and decided the child would be born next October, or close to it. She would begin immediately to make small clothes and fixings for his arrival. The baby would be a boy. She was certain of it.

She also began jotting down names, all boys' names. She was very partial to William, but Jeff favored Roy.

That winter Jeff adzed boards from logs and rough-planed them. He made a square table with four sturdy legs, two heavy chairs, and a frame for their bed. With an auger he made close-spaced holes around the four sides and threaded rope through the holes to fashion a taut netting.

Rachel sewed a tick, which they stuffed with straw. It made an excellent mattress—for a short while. The straw quickly formed hard lumps and the tick had to be restuffed.

The snows turned to slush and gradually left the ground. It rained off and on, but spring was in the air. The sun came out to glitter on the waters of the creek and a fresh wind pawed the clothes on the line that Rachel put out.

Suddenly one day they had a visitor. A man on a ratty-looking horse came to the edge of the creek, on the far side, and stared at them, shielding his eyes with his hand.

Simon saw him first and yelled, and Dud came out to look. The wide gate of the palisade faced the creek and usually stood open during the day. Dud walked through it and gazed at the man, then waved, shouting, "Howdy!"

The stranger lifted his hat, yelling back. "How you git acrost?"

Dud replied, "Never been across, 'cept on the ice in winter."

The other nodded, sat the horse for a few moments, then turned and rode away slowly. That evening Dud said, "There's a ford upriver somewhere—wonder how far?"

"You want to get across," Jeff said, "build a boat or a raft."

Leah asked, "Why you want to go across?"

"Never really thought much about it till today," Dud said and told them about the visitor.

"Probably some jasper three jumps ahead of the law," Fred said.

They planted an extensive vegetable garden, hoed it, weeded it, carried water for it from the creek, and were rewarded at last with green shoots.

Leah and Dud went berry-hunting and returned with vines they then planted along the sides of the garden. And that spring Fred began to talk about planting a crop. He cleared ten acres or so of his land and burned the weeds, scattering the ashes over the plot. But he had no seeds.

He knew that Jeff had seeds from the sale of his land to his brother Matthew. He hinted about the seeds several times but Jeff did not bite. Then he began to talk about how the three families ought to share and share alike. They were out in the wilderness alone, depending on each other, and it wasn't right for one to hold out against another.

Jeff said to Rachel, "That man is a no-good. Me and Dud should never have allowed him to come along with us."

"But he's here," Rachel said, combing her hair before bed.

"Now you've got to suffer him." She put the comb away. "I never thought you wanted to be a farmer."

"I don't."

She gave him a little questioning smile. "Then why not sell him the seeds?"

"I don't want any deal with Fred Caine that involves money or trade." He shook his head. "And I won't give him the seeds either. Is it my fault he didn't think ahead?"

"Shouldn't we all share alike?"

"Don't wave that Bible at me. Fred Caine has got to stand on his own feet, not on mine. He's old enough to know how."

"Yes, he is that."

"The man is agin everything until he's backed into a corner . . . and so is Simon. He's going to grow up just like his hardheaded father."

"What do you want to do—Jeff?"

He went to her and embraced her gently. "I want us to live peaceful and good. I'm going to farm if I have to, but I've got my eye on cattle."

"Cattle!" His plan startled her.

Jeff stopped her lips with a kiss. "I haven't talked it over with no one, not even Dud. But this looks like cattle land to me. I think one day there'll be a bigger and bigger market for beef. When you look at how the country is growing . . ."

"But where is the market?"

"Well, that's what I mean, one day there'll be a market. Before we left the old house I was readin' about folks driving cattle to market in Pennsylvania . . . so why not here?"

She looked at him in astonishment. "Drive cattle thousands of miles?"

Jeff sighed deeply. "I know. First there's got to be a railroad to drive to. But it's not thousands of miles. Kansas City can't be more'n five hundred miles north, as the crow flies."

She sat on the bed. "How'll you get a herd together?"

"Little by little." He smiled. "Cows have calves every year, you know."

"So I've heard."

He pulled off his shirt. "This's just between us, wife . . . hear?"

"Yes, husband."

Chapter Six

THAT summer they finished the palisade and the fire step, pegging most of it together. The area under the platform was excellent for sheds and tools and cribs for animal fodder. They also dug a well inside the palisade so water would not have to be carried from the creek.

The women wanted an icehouse, such as they'd seen and read about. "The creek freezes over in winter," Rachel said. "Why can't we save some of the ice?"

So outside the log wall, on the creek side, Jeff and Dud dug a deep cave, shored it with timber, and made a stout door that faced north. Next winter they would cut creek ice and pile it inside. Dud thought foodstuffs would keep, maybe halfway into the summer.

Fred Caine came to look at it, then dug his own icehouse, grumbling to himself about sharing and sharing alike.

In September Jeff laced a pack tree on one of the mules and rode to Pommer for staples and supplies. He preferred to go alone, he said, saying he could make better time. He had his rifle and pepperbox and did not fear hostiles.

A number of buildings had gone up in Pommer since his last visit, and more tents and shacks straggled on the fringes. Jerry Titus told him that new families were arriving, some driven west by the panic. Unfortunately those were mostly poor souls who had nothing at all. They lived in wagons and the menfolk begged odd jobs here and there to keep alive. The few who had savings had started in business.

Jeff and Titus sat around the belly stove, feet up on the ring, cracking walnuts and gabbing. The storekeeper wanted to know every detail of their lives, obviously taking great pleasure in hearing of their industry. After all, it had been who'd sent them to the creek in the first place.

"I knew you folks would make it, soon's I set eyes on you."

And Titus had much news. The country had a new president,

the hero of Tippecanoe, William Henry Harrison, elected by the
Whigs; it was the first time that party had won in forty years.

"What's that, Tippecanoe?"

"It was a battle," Titus said. "Harrison was a general in the
army then."

"That so? Who were we fightin'?"

"A bunch of Indians up in Indiana. I had a newspaper about it—
can't find the damned thing." He selected a thin cigar, rolling it in
his fingers. "What crops y'all puttin' in this year?"

"Not much. Corn and beans and yams . . ."

"Lissen. I can sell all the corn you bring me. Probably yams
too."

Jeff was surprised. He hadn't thought of that possibility. "You
can?"

"I can sell it outta this store or send it north where I got con-
nections. How you fixed for seed?"

"Plenty." Jeff nodded.

Titus grinned at him. "Then we c'n go into business. This's
damn poor farmland around here. Good for nothin' but weeds and
nettles. What you say?"

Jeff put out his hand. "Shake, partner."

He had no trouble on the return. It was only a three-hour ride in
good weather. He had been surprised at Titus's offer, and he knew
Dud would be delighted . . . even more than he was. Jeff could
never think of himself as a trader.

He had bought Rachel a string of beads of a reddish stone that
glowed in the light. Titus guaranteed that she would love it—and
he was right.

She ran to a mirror, then ran back to kiss him. She was especially
pleased, he knew, because he had brought her something for herself, and not just for the house.

Rachel felt very well, and looked even better. She was keeping
a careful record of the days since she had realized she was pregnant.
And in the middle of the summer she was rounding out. Leah
Hurley spent much time with her as they discussed the coming
event. Leah had no children, but she came from a large family. She
knew a great deal of what took place at a birthing.

Louise Caine had had two boys, but Louise was such a mouse,
afraid of making a direct statement of any kind, that Rachel decided
not to ask her anything. Leah thought her advice was probably
useless. Louise was likely to say whatever she thought her listener

wanted to hear. Long years with Fred had accustomed her to mousedom.

There was no doctor in Pommer. Jerry Titus said the nearest medical man was probably eighty miles away, in Hartigan. And even if Jeff took Rachel there in a wagon there was no way to know in advance if the doctor would be in town or out somewhere making his rounds—and not due back for a week.

However, Rachel was sure she and Leah could accomplish whatever needed to be done. After all, women had been doing it for centuries.

Jeff cleared five or six acres of land, as Fred had done, and hooked up a mule to the plow and turned the earth. Then he harrowed it and seeded it with sod corn. It was all he could do that year.

After work in the evenings, he talked with Dud. Sometimes they walked along the creek, Dud puffing his pipe or chewing the stem. Dud had little interest in farming, except to sell the proceeds. He farmed to live but he dreamed of opening a trading post. The dream did not seem likely to come true here, for lack of customers.

Dud had been born in New York state, in a little town near Lake Ontario, with Canada just across the St. Lawrence River. His father had been a teacher and his mother had attended a women's academy for several years, leaving it before graduation to get married.

Dudley was one of three children; the others were girls. Dud had been pushed to go into teaching but had resisted. He had left college after two years, saying it was not for him. Somewhere deep within him, his mother said, there was a rebellious streak. He hadn't wanted to settle down in an ordered community; he had wandered west in search of . . . something.

However, he had discovered early on that he was not fitted to be an adventurer. His nature would not allow him to seek violence as some did. It was not that he was afraid . . . but he was no Jeff Becket.

He and Jeff became fast friends, though seemingly they had nothing in common. Perhaps each had what the other lacked. Dud bought land near the Becket farm and tried his hand at raising crops—and eventually married Leah Elkins.

He said to Jeff, "People are crossing the creek farther north where it's shallow. If we had a bridge here, we'd see some travelers."

Jeff agreed that a bridge was an interesting idea. Of course they had no way of knowing how deep the creek was. In summer, when they went swimming, they usually stayed in the several coves. None were very good swimmers and the current was strong. . . .

To find the best spot for a bridge it would be necessary to go out in a boat with a rock tied to a rope to take soundings.

Dud said he thought he would draw up some plans for a boat and maybe build it himself come winter. He wanted that bridge.

As summer passed, Rachel was changing. Everyone talked of the glow in her cheeks, the glossiness of her hair and skin. She was large, and could wear only special clothes, but she felt marvelous, except for the daily sick feelings.

However, sometimes at night Rachel also had misgivings—which she kept to herself, staring into the dark. Some women did not survive childbirth, and she would not have a professional doctor to attend her. But she was strong and Leah was positive in her attitude.

"Look around you," Leah said. "Thousands and thousands of babies are born every day in the world. Your baby will be perfect . . . and so will you be."

It was what she needed to hear. Jeff seemed to take for granted that all would go well.

"Men," Leah said, "do not realize the importance of women. If men had to have the babies, the world would shrink in population."

In the waning weeks of summer they saw more travelers hurrying south, hoping to beat the rains. Jeff talked to a few. They were going home, they said, or they were drifting. Many were traveling alone, some by twos and threes. Usually they camped by the creek and were gone by sunup.

Fred Caine thought them a shifty lot, and he kept an eye on them.

Dud looked at them differently—speculatively. One evening, talking with Jeff, he suggested they go into a sort of partnership.

"Partnership? How?"

"I mean that you're the hunter. You go hunting, bring in venison, and I'll sell the meat to these pilgrims."

"I doubt if one of them has a copper in his kick."

"No, they won't have. But we can trade for something. You've hunted this region more than anyone. You know where to find deer. . . ."

"Well, if you think they'll have trade articles."

Dud smiled. "We can find out."

Jeff took the next day, saddled the bay, and went out looking for deer. He was gone only two hours and returned with a small buck.

He and Dud cut up the meat and stored it in the icehouse.

That night it rained, a gentle pattering to remind them of what was to come. The next morning the air was translucent but the storm was gone by midday; the sun came out, burning through a curdled-milk sky, and stayed for two weeks. A kind of Indian summer, Dud said.

During this pause of good weather, Dud traded all the meat and baskets of vegetables. He received a shotgun, bags of lead balls, powder, a few knives, and a silver watch. Spread out on a blanket it wasn't much, hardly a beginning, but Dud was confident.

"We got this from one bullet and a bit of digging. Next time you go to Pommer I'll go along and maybe we can realize some hard cash."

Jeff harvested the corn, piled most of it in a wagon, and made the journey to Pommer with Dud alongside, riding his gray. Jeff drove the wagon around behind the store and parked it near the back door, where someone had been breaking up wooden crates with an axe. He went inside to dicker with Titus while Dud took his trade items to the street.

By the time they were ready to return Titus had bought all the corn and had it stacked in a shed. Jeff received a little hard money and a heavy sack of seeds. He also loaded onto the wagon the sacks of staples and other goods that Titus had made up from the lists Rachel and Leah had given Jeff.

Dud showed up with a pocketful of cash and two well-worn but quite serviceable rifles.

They made a short stop in a deadfall for beer, comparing notes. They were both much better off than they had been; the trading was a success. It was always good to have hard money, Dud said. It often made the difference in a close deal.

They divvied up the profits and went home before dark.

The first real Indian raid arrived just before a hard rain, taking everyone by surprise. Leah was in the tower, taking her turn—the women took turns by daylight to free the men for harder tasks.

Eight hostiles came charging on horses from a wood, galloping toward Fred and Simon who were plowing a field. Leah saw them and yelled, leveled a rifle at them, and fired.

Fred shouted to Simon, abandoned his plow, and ran for his rifle. Simon pointed a pistol at the leading brave, holding it in both hands. When he fired the horse went down and he ran across the field toward Fred.

"Get outta there!" Leah yelled and fired a second rifle.

Fred fired into the midst of the attackers, then turned and ran as

Dud hurried out from the palisade with a pistol in each hand. The Indians had scattered but were still charging toward them, whooping shrilly. Two were down in the field and a horse was running off toward the creek.

Dud shouted, "Shoot at the horses! Put 'em afoot!" He fired first one pistol then the other as Fred and Simon raced toward him. He ducked away as a lance screamed by him and hit the wall with a deep thud.

Jeff galloped past Dud yelling, "Reload!" He headed directly toward the Indians, firing the pepperbox. They wheeled away from him, yammering, surprised by the quick-firing gun.

He swore at them; one brave was on the ground, his legs kicking. The others streamed away from him, entering the woods again.

Halting, Jeff watched them go and began to reload the pistol. That had been a close thing! The quick action by Leah in the tower had blunted the attack, and the pepperbox might have unnerved them. Probably none of them had faced such a gun before.

He rode back to the field and dismounted to push the fallen Indians with his boot. One had been hit twice, once in the temple. He was wearing war paint and smelled to high heaven. Jeff screwed up his face and looked at the second man who was facedown in the dirt, very dead.

The third brave died as Jeff stood over him. His eyes glazed over, staring up at the sun. Fred Caine came up beside him. "They after horses, you figger?"

"After whatever they could grab. Anybody hurt?" Jeff looked around at Dud, who shook his head.

Dud said, "What'll we do with the bodies?"

"Leave 'em out here," Fred growled. "They'll come and get 'em. Save us kickin' dirt over 'em."

Chapter Seven

THE baby arrived toward the end of October.

Rachel and Leah had cut diapers, a huge stack of them, from bolts of cloth Jeff had brought from Titus's store. They had also made a dozen little shirts from sacking that had been washed and left in the hot sun till soft.

Jeff had long since assembled a small cradle and put it aside.

When the time came close, Rachel had a bad night; a low backache would not go away. She could barely pull herself out of bed in the morning. The pain, she moaned, seemed to center in the small of her back, moving downward.

The pains were far apart, but she knew it was a matter of hours. She sent Jeff for Leah. "I think it's going to be today. . . ."

Leah came in a hurry and they put Rachel to bed again. The pains were coming faster. . . .

Hours passed as Jeff paced and worried.

The contractions became stronger as Rachel writhed, perspiring and stifling moans. Leah laid cool cloths across her forehead and Jeff paced the room till Leah shooed him out. "Go outside somewhere. There's nothing you can do here."

Leah had a pair of scissors ready, strong thread, and plenty of soft cloth in which to wrap the baby. While they were waiting, Louise showed up finally, asking if she could help.

The pains came together, merging into one enormous ache. Leah gave Rachel a bit of folded cloth to clamp down on.

And then it was over. Rachel felt everything become a misty, silvery haze. . . . There was still pain, but relief too . . . and then she heard the baby cry.

The youngest Becket weighed seven and a quarter pounds by Dud's scale. Leah washed him and wrapped him in the warm cloth and put him in Jeff's arms. "Hold his head up."

Rachel smiled weakly, seeing her son for the first time, and reached for him. Jeff put the baby in her embrace. "You were right, he's a boy."

"He's so tiny."

He sat on the side of the bed and brushed the damp hair back from her forehead, feeling much more shaken than he would admit. Rachel had gone through the entire ordeal alone, with nothing at all he could do to help her. And now that it was over, his hands shook.

Rachel named the baby Roy because Jeff liked it better than William. Leah suggested she put down William as the baby's middle name.

"Why would he need two names?"

Leah shrugged her round shoulders. "Lots of people have two names."

"Well, I think one is enough. When he grows up he can pick out a middle name if he wants one."

Caring for the baby took all of Rachel's time at first, until she learned how to divide her chores. But it was work she enjoyed. And Leah came to the door daily, wanting to hold the baby and feed him. She was eager for one of her own, she said. Dud wanted a lot of children. But despite all their trying, she had not missed her period once.

She said, "Dud says it's God's will, but I never thought God was small-minded. He gives babies to a lot of women who don't want them. I'd think He could listen to my prayers now and then."

Rachel smiled. "He's probably saving you for twins."

"Lordy! I never thought of that!" Leah put her hands together and looked up at the ceiling. "Please, God, don't give me twins!"

Jeff too was delighted with the baby and would sit and hold him by the fire while Rachel made supper or breakfast. He had carefully written the date and time of the boy's arrival in their leather-bound Bible, a book that had belonged to his mother and contained the facts pertaining to his own birth.

The baby's coming marked the last of the good weather for a month or more. It rained, then snowed, then rained again, and the creek rose higher than they'd ever seen it. But it did not reach even close to the palisade.

The days grew dark as the sun was muffled by lowering clouds. Jeff and Dud sat inside, and Dud introduced a new and fascinating game called chess. They sat over the board, by the fire, for hours on end, smoking and frowning. . . .

Little Roy slept in his cradle and the world seemed a very peaceful place.

When he got restless and the weather permitted, Jeff saddled the bay and rode out over the fields, or across the creek on the ice, just looking around. He found no sign of any human or horse, shod or unshod.

After the Indian attack Fred had ordered two pepperbox pistols from Titus, who had sent east for them. They had not yet been delivered.

During their chess sessions Dud talked now and then of his dream. He was thinking of building a room onto his house, making it a store or trading post.

Jeff said, "There isn't room for it."

"Well, we promised the women we'd build separate houses."

"What if your trading don't amount to anything at all?"

Dud made a face. "Well, I know it'll take a while. But I already talked to Titus. He'll sell me some goods at prices where I can make a dollar."

He's determined, and maybe that's half the battle, Jeff thought. He had to admit to himself that he too had a dream—of cattle.

In the spring more travelers appeared, wandering along the creek, some on horseback, some walking with pack mules, moving in both directions. Most said they were looking for a way to cross: was there a ford nearby? A very few, with possessions piled high in a wagon or cart, were looking for a place to stop and put down roots.

The first family to pause and talk was named Porter. They were four: a man, his wife, and two children, a boy and a girl. They owned a light wagon and two mules, and Dud showed them where they could put up a tent in the town-to-be area.

They camped near the palisade, rigged a canvas tent shelter, and settled in, saying they were thinking about staying for good. The man was a dark, rangy type with a gaunt, lined face and big, gnarled hands. He was a blacksmith by trade but had done a bit of farming. He had an anvil in his wagon and could build a forge. It was a skill none of them had. Both Jeff and Dud made the family welcome; Rachel and Leah both brought them corn and vegetables, offering to do what they could to make them comfortable. A blacksmith was desperately needed!

Porter's name was Angus. His wife was Addie, a stout woman who seemed very timid and withdrawn, but eager to please. When Rachel and Leah called on her she was flushed and nervous at having company in the ragged tent. But Leah quickly put her at ease, saying they had journeyed from Arkansas not long ago and knew all about living out of wagons.

The first evening the Beckets and Hurleys discussed helping the Porters build a cabin; they were set on convincing the blacksmith to stay. The cabin would have to be built outside the palisade. It would probably be out of the question to attempt to extend the log walls to include another family.

The palisade, despite its purpose of keeping hostiles out, was very confining. The women said it made them feel like they were in a prison.

"And besides," Rachel said for the hundredth time, "you promised us separate houses in three years."

"The trouble with women," Jeff said to Dud when they were alone, "is their memories. You tell 'em something and they never forget."

Dud agreed. "But we *did* promise. . . ."

"Yes. But if we build separate houses we'll have to tear down the damn palisade!"

Dud got out a piece of paper and made sketches. "We could open the palisade at one end. . . ."

"If we do that it destroys the whole idea of the thing! The palisade is a fort. What good is a fort that's half open?"

Dud grinned at him. "Well, you can't have it both ways. I'm afraid the palisade will have to come down."

"That makes us vulnerable."

"Yeah." Dud nodded. "Maybe we can talk the women into another year, if we mention Indians frequently."

Jeff smiled. "Talk about scalping, you mean?"

"Especially about scalping."

"All right. Now what about the Porters?"

"The only sensible thing is to help him build his house. We need him."

Jeff nodded. "Of course."

"I've already agreed to let him use part of my land to plant a crop or two. He'll pay me back with part of the produce."

"Then all we have to do is convince Fred Caine."

Dud smiled broadly. "Fred's got a lame wagon. I think he'll agree to help a blacksmith build a house. Fred is stubborn and shortsighted, but not stupid."

Dud was correct. It was the fact that Porter was a smith that made Fred agreeable. No community could survive without a blacksmith.

They took the mules and chains to the forest again and cut down trees, trimmed them, and hauled them to the site. The house went up before the summer had waned. Porter's twelve-year-old son, Jason, hauled clay to caulk the logs and the fireplace that Dud built. They also framed a shed behind the house that Porter would use as his shop.

And while they were at that work, Rachel reminded Jeff of his promise about her board floor. *That* took till the first rains to accomplish.

Fred Caine was sixty-five that winter and was feeling his age, especially when it was cold. Then his back acquired a deep-down ache that would not go away. It helped immensely to drink hot whiskey toddies and sit by the fire. Two or three toddies dulled the pain so he could sleep.

Originally he had come from Pennsylvania, a little town in the western mountains that had no school, only an elderly church deacon who gave reading and writing lessons. From him Fred learned to read simple sentences and to write his name, which was more than most could do. During family gatherings the boy was given bits of paper and a pencil and wrote his name for admiring audiences.

His father was a big, brutal man who did not know what humor was and who always seemed angry, or on the verge of violence. He beat Fred and the other children at any provocation.

At age fifteen Fred slipped out of the house one night and never went back.

He found work here and there, doing chores for food or maybe a shirt—he was always hungry and ill-clothed. Most of the work he found was farming, plowing, digging, putting up fences. . . .

When he was nearly thirty-five he married Louise. He had very little, but she brought him a dowry and with it they purchased a small farm in Arkansas near the McAdams and the Beckets.

Fred was not the best neighbor; he had many shortcomings, one of which was borrowing. He borrowed and forgot to return. His neighbors stayed out of his way, except for Dud Hurley, when he bought his farm nearby. Dud got along with everyone.

Angus Porter proved to be a quiet, hardworking man. Along with putting up the log house and shed, he plowed part of Dud's land and put in corn, beans, sweet potatoes, and other vegetables.

He also built a forge in the shed, set up his anvil, and as his first job, repaired Fred's wagon.

Angus was a taciturn man, not unfriendly but never very talkative. Jeff thought he tended to look on the dark side of things. But perhaps, as Dud surmised, he had too frequently played in bad luck. There were people like that. Bad luck seemed to dog them— Fred had had some of it. As Dud said, if a man always expects the worst to happen, it just might. Dud went out of his way to make the Porters feel welcome.

As summer ended another family appeared, with a wagon and two mangy-looking horses. They made camp near the palisade, first asking if they might stay.

Their name was Tilley and they had come from Missouri, looking for land. They wanted a place to start over. Lucas Tilley— "folks calls me Luke"—talked vaguely about troubles in Missouri that had driven them out. They had rented land, or something of the sort, and were unable to make the agreed payments. It sounded as if he had been sharecropping, but Jeff did not ask direct questions. Luke seemed an open-faced sort, poor as a frog, but eager.

Tilley's wife, Hester, was a buxom young woman who had a smile for everyone. She apparently had only one dress to her name and they probably had been living out of the wagon for months. It was a hard life when a young woman had to use a water bucket for a mirror.

Tilley put up a battered canvas tarpaulin and built a circle of stones outside it for cooking and heat. He turned the horses into a field to chomp grass.

Dud looked them over and said to Jeff, "They seem at home and content."

"Is he a farmer?"

"I talked to him and I don't think he's anything. He doesn't own a plow. Doesn't seem to have a trade."

Jeff sighed. "Will we have to feed them this winter?"

"We might."

They discussed the Tilleys with Fred and Angus. Fred suggested telling them to move on. "We don't need folks who won't work."

Dud objected. "We don't know Tilley won't work! Let's offer him work in the fields. He can help you, Jeff, and he can work some of my land come spring. That way we can raise more."

"It's worth a try," Jeff agreed.

Fred shook his dark head. "He won't do it."

But Luke was happy to try. He had walked behind a plow before, he told them.

And he proved to be a very good shot. He had a rifle, an old punkin-slinger that had belonged to his pa, and when he went hunting with Jeff he brought down the first deer.

As winter approached they hauled more logs from the forest and put up a small one-room house for the Tilleys. Luke was grateful as a puppy. He and Hester had been sure they'd have to live through the snows in their canvas hut. Now they had a log roof and a fireplace!

When the house was finished Hester went to each of them with tears in her eyes, to thank them.

After the first rains Jeff and Dud piled a wagon high with corn, sweet potatoes, and beans and made the trip to Pommer once more.

Dud had been trading continually with travelers and had a gunnysack full of small items, along with a few guns and knives. He went into business along the streets as Jeff took the produce to Titus and then loaded the wagon with their supplies.

When he had concluded his trading, Dud entered the store and sat by the belly stove with Jeff and Titus, listening to the news and gossip. A man named John Tyler was now president, Harrison having died after a few weeks in office. The newspapers said that Tyler was practically a Democrat and he and the Whig congress were at loggerheads. There had been some kind of rebellion in Rhode Island and the governor, Thomas Dorr, had been thrown in prison. Daniel Webster had settled a boundary dispute between Maine and Canada. And the Comanch had raided only twenty miles from Pommer and burned out another family.

"You had any Indian troubles lately?" Titus asked.

"Not for about a year," Jeff said. "I guess they don't like our palisade."

"It was smart, puttin' that up." Titus nodded.

He had two more pepperboxes for sale, with bullet moulds and metal powderhorns. "I sort of was savin' them for y'all," Titus said, taking them out of a drawer. "Iffen you don't want them, I can sell 'em tomorra."

Dud wanted one and Jeff bought the other.

Titus said, "They's some talk the Sam Colt company is makin' a new revolver, better'n the Patterson and the Dragoon. It ought to be available in a few years."

"Order me one," Jeff said.

"I got a dozen on order now."

"Will they be as good as the Allen pistols?"

Titus shrugged lean shoulders. "They say it'll be better. Them pepperboxes shoot good and fast, but you can't aim 'em as well as you might.''

That was true, Jeff reflected, and their range was short. . . . He wished they'd make a rifle that would give a man six shots.

As they gabbed, Dud mentioned they had two new families on Eden Creek.

"Eden Creek!" Titus exclaimed. "Y'all renamed 'er?" It was the first time he'd heard the name.

"Had to," Dud said. "The women wouldn't have Dead Hog Creek. And you can't blame 'em.''

Titus laughed. "Guess not. So your little settlement is growing. Well, we got more'n a dozen new families here in Pommer this last year alone. I think the press of folks in the states is pushin' 'em outward, shovin' out the edges. The damn country is bustin' its seams.''

Dud agreed. "Seems that way.''

They started homeward in the middle of the afternoon. About an hour out of town they saw two Indians moving along in the trees a few hundred yards distant. Dud was driving the wagon and Jeff came up next to him on the bay. He pulled the Hawken across his thighs and Dud laid the pepperbox in his lap.

"They're lookin' us over," Jeff said softly. "You see any more of 'em?''

"No—but that don't mean they're not there.''

"If they come close, they'll try to shoot the mules. That'll stop us in our tracks." He fingered the rifle, watching them. "If they turn to'ard us I'll give 'em a shot.''

The Indians appeared to be young ones, mostly naked, each with a single feather in his black hair. Jeff could see no firearms.

Dud nodded. "All right." He kept his eyes on them. When one of the Indians swung his horse toward them, Dud reined in instantly. Jeff stood in the stirrups, aimed carefully and fired.

The shot caused the brave's horse to rear. The animal turned, limping, and Dud yelled in glee. "You hit 'im! You hit 'im!''

Jeff jumped down, reloading quickly. He rested the rifle barrel on the wagon's side and aimed high. The hostiles were within range if he guessed right. When he fired he heard the ball hit a tree very close to them. Both Indians turned at once and disappeared.

"They didn't like that a little bit!" Dud chortled.

Jeff reloaded and mounted the bay again.

They saw no more of the Indians and arrived home just before dusk.

Chapter Eight

Two days later, as the sky was turning gray and wind was scuffing the creek, three men on sturdy hammerheads showed up. They were well armed, dressed in rough clothes, unshaven, and looked as if they'd been in the wilds for some time.

The leader, a man who said his name was John Delfry, looked them over carefully, smiling all the while. "We come from over east, looking to hunt."

Dud said, "You come here to hunt?"

"We figger to sell meat in town. How long y'all been settin' here? That's a mighty tight little fort y'all got."

"We've been here a year or two."

Delfry's two companions gazed hungrily at the women. Rachel stood in her doorway for a few moments, until she noticed their glances. Leah stared back boldly and Hester smiled at them until she saw Leah's frown. The two men looked gaunt and uncivilized—it was the best word Dud could think of for them. Delfry mentioned their names as Tom and Willie.

Delfry asked permission to camp by the creek for the night, and Jeff nodded. He could hardly refuse. Dud visited them when they had made camp, but quickly returned. They had nothing to trade, and though Delfry smiled a lot, the others were surly.

Their guard schedule had become habit. The guard sat in the tower as a rule and was relieved every two hours during the night. Occasionally the guard walked in the fire step, round and round. It was lonely and often cold duty but necessary, because an Indian could ride his horse close to the palisade, stand on the horse's back, and climb over easily. If enough hostiles followed, they could all be slaughtered in their beds.

When Jeff went to relieve Simon at four in the morning, he found the other asleep.

Jeff shook him awake. If he'd had a canteen he'd have poured water over the sleeper. Simon woke, growling, and climbed down the ladder grumpily.

In the morning, at first light, Jeff, in the tower, saw that Delfry and his two snarly companions had departed in the night.

And then he discovered the gate was unlocked and his bay was missing.

He was furious. He would have attacked Simon had not Dud and Angus held him back. "That damned Simon was asleep when they stole my horse!"

Simon protested he'd been dozing only a minute—but no one believed him. Jeff shook free and went into the house. He examined the loads in both pepperboxes, shoved them into his belt, looked at the Hawken, and started out.

Rachel was astonished. "Where are you going?"

"After them."

She followed him to the corral. "They're three men! You're only one! Get the others to go with you!"

He shook his head. "I'm the one lost the horse." He saddled a big black mule.

She knew it was no good yelling at him. She stood and watched him ride out and turn south. Feeling cold inside, Rachel took the baby and hurried to Leah's door.

"Jeff has gone after those three men—they stole his horse last night."

Leah swore under her breath and pulled Rachel inside. Dud was out in the fields somewhere with Luke Tilley. She sat Rachel down. "It's no good you worrying yourself to death."

"But they're three to one!"

"Jeff's no fool, honey. Dud says he's the smartest man his age he ever saw. He's not going to get himself shot up by some fool mistake. You'll see." She shoved sticks into the fire. "I'll make some coffee."

The tracks of the four horses were easy to follow. The men had walked away from the palisade, then, half a mile distant, had galloped for a few miles, moving straight south. They ignored the creek and went through the pine forest, possibly six or seven miles thick, and continued south.

Jeff lost the trail once and spent an hour hunting it, discovering finally that the three had turned east abruptly on hard ground. They probably knew they might be followed.

By late afternoon he figured they were an hour, no more than two, ahead of him. If they stopped for the night he ought to come

upon them. But if they halted they would probably set an ambush
. . . just in case.

He was a long way from the creek now, in an area of low wooded
hills where a soft breeze brought the smells of earth; the sky was
coming close, with dark gray clouds moving across saffron mists,
curdling and sullen. He prayed it would not rain till after he had
met them. . . .

The three were riding steadily, never stopping. Putting himself
in their place, he might think he was far enough away by now to
pause and fix a meal and maybe to nap.

In early evening he came to a wide, weedy field and halted within
the shelter of the trees, gazing at the open space. Tracks led straight
across the field and into more woods. Jeff leaned on the pommel;
he would bet anything the men were sitting there with rifles ready,
watching the backtrail. It was a perfect spot for an ambush.

The field was maybe half a mile across, and he could see no way
around.

Stepping down, he let the mule crop grass while he stretched out
to wait for full dark. He dozed and woke to look at a murky sky
that held no moon. The field was a sea of darkness; he could barely
see his hand before his face.

Mounting the mule, he started across slowly, paralleling the
tracks, the rifle across his thighs. It took forever to cross the wide
field and when he reached the trees at last, he paused to listen . . .
and heard nothing but an owl off to his right.

Dismounting, he left the mule and the rifle and walked slowly
through the trees, a pistol in each hand.

A few minutes later, he halted—was someone moving ahead?
He strained to hear—was it horses? He went forward silently and
almost ran into a picketed horse.

There were four animals, one his bay, and beyond them the coals
of a fire.

Where was the guard?

Jeff knelt behind a tree, searching the area with his eyes. Was it
possible they had considered themselves so secure they had not
posted a guard? The dull red coals of the fire provided almost no
light at all. He could barely make out the lumpy forms in the deep
shadows of the little clearing.

Then someone struck a match to light a cheroot.

Jeff saw the man's face quite clearly. It was the one who'd called
himself John Delfry. He was sitting with his back to a tree on the
far side of the fire.

When the match went out, Jeff could see only a pinpoint of light from the end of a cigar. It glowed redder when Delfry puffed it.

Should he wait for sunup? They might be duller then. . . .

One of the horses stomped, jingling a bridle and snorting.

Delfry stood at once, dropping the cigar into the coals, drawing a pistol. He moved cautiously to the horses, only a deeper shadow in the night. He waited there several minutes, then came back to the fire, evidently satisfied.

Jeff was about to move when a voice said, "What's wrong, Johnny?"

"Nothing. Thought I heard something."

Jeff saw that one of the lumpy forms by the fire had moved and was sitting up, scratching his head. He had them all placed now. Jeff slid out from behind the tree . . . and the sitting man caught the movement and yelled. He tossed a handful of dry leaves on the coals and they blazed up, making the clearing bright as day for a moment.

Delfry fired and Jeff felt the bullet rap into the tree near his head. He pulled the pepperbox's trigger, again and again. Delfry crumpled, firing into the ground. The man by the fire rolled away and a pistol spat at him as Jeff ducked low and emptied the pepperbox.

The third man near the fire had tossed off the blankets and was scrambling to get up. Jeff ran at him and clipped him with the pistol barrel. The man dropped with a moan and lay still.

It was suddenly silent. Powder smoke drifted away through the trees. Looking around warily, Jeff saw no movement. He pushed a handful of sticks onto the fire and it blazed up yellowly. Delfry had been centered. He lay on his back, chest bloody, arms outstretched. The second man had been hit twice, once in the forehead. He was very dead, crumpled in the brush.

Jeff methodically reloaded the two pepperboxes, disarmed the unconscious man, and gathered up the other weapons. He shoved the pistols into a sack and smashed the locks of the three rifles; they were too awkward to carry.

Then he tied the sack on behind the cantle, mounted the bay, and led the mule and the other horses back the way he had come.

When the third man came to he could do as he pleased, afoot and unarmed.

It was too bad that two men had to die over a stolen horse, but they had brought it on themselves, Jeff thought. He felt no remorse. A horse thief deserved nothing.

Miles away, he set the three horses free. Maybe he had the right to take them, since the three were horse thieves, but he did not want them.

When he returned, he found Rachel asleep on the bed with the baby in the cradle beside her. She woke groggily as he opened the door and came to sit on the side of the bed. She clutched him and began to cry.

Chapter Nine

Dudley was annoyed with him, too. "You shouldn't have done that alone, Jeff."

"It came out all right. . . ."

"But it might not have. There's such a thing as chance. A bullet will go through you as easily as the next man. And you've got a family now. . . ."

"All right—I hear you." He showed Dud the sack of pistols he'd collected. "More trade goods."

Dud was practical. "What about their rifles?"

"I smashed them. Too much iron to carry."

One of the pistols was a Patterson revolver made by Sam Colt. Jeff handled it, thinking he might keep it, but it didn't impress him as much as the Allen pepperboxes, though the idea of a cylinder turning instead of the barrels seemed sound.

Dud had started work on the boat he intended to build during the winter. He still talked about a bridge across the creek, but to Jeff the task seemed almost impossible to accomplish. He himself could not figure how one even started such a project. And he had a good idea that Dud knew no more. Every bridge he'd seen, over twenty feet long, had piles driven into the bottom of the stream. How did they drive those posts? It seemed likely to him that if they were not driven deep into the bottom, the first flood would wash them out.

When he mentioned it Dud said, "Maybe the weight of the bridge will keep the piles there. . . ."

"You want to spend a summer building a bridge to find out?"

"Well . . . maybe we can ask somebody."

A pontoon bridge was the next possible idea, but it would mean an enormous amount of work. At least ten boats would have to be built and fastened together, one alongside the next, and a roadway built across them. It would probably not be affected by floods—

48

unless the fastenings came undone—and maybe it was the most practical for them.

How much did they want to get across to the other side?

Dud was positive that the fact of the bridge would bring travelers, who might be willing to trade this and that. Jeff said it would also bring the kind of people who stole horses.

Dud replied, "That's life. You have to expect the bad now and then, with the good." He shook his finger. "But people are mostly good."

Jeffrey Becket did not think that way.

But of course Dud was a kind of philosopher.

Dud was also disposed to forget and forgive Simon for sleeping in the tower on watch. Jeff wanted to hold court and try him, convict him, and mete out a punishment. He had jeopardized all their lives.

But he was overruled.

It was a mild winter. The wind was the worst, pushing into the house through tiny cracks, beating them as they went outside, crooning darkly at night as they lay in bed.

When it was cold enough to freeze, Jeff tossed water from a bucket onto the side of the house. It froze there and stopped the wind from blowing through the cracks.

The snow came, spilling from dark skies, hard flakes rattling against the windows, lying on the fields and roofs heavily.

Then the weather changed and the snow was gone, almost overnight, and rains fed the creek. The water became a raging monster for a fortnight, then it too moderated.

When the wind and the cold permitted, Jeff and young Tilley went hunting for meat and brought in deer, which they divided among all. Dud had traded for fishhooks in town and was successful fishing through holes chopped in the ice of the creek.

Dud also finished the boat and turned it upside down near his door, waiting for spring.

It was dark inside the palisade, even when the sun was shining. The houses and the log wall were too close; the wall seemed to press in upon them and the house was in shadow much of the time.

Dud said, over and over again, "The palisade has served its purpose. It's got to go."

They had a discussion about it. Fred said, "It's kept the redhides from attacking us."

Dud asked, "How do you know?"

"Well they haven't, have they?" Fred glared at them. Once he had spoken against the palisade, now he was for it.

"We don't need it any longer," Dud said. "There're six men here now and we've got plenty of guns."

Fred growled. "You're not thinkin' of taking down the tower?"

"Of course not." Dud shook his head, looking at Jeff as if to say, "don't mention Simon sleeping in it."

Jeff almost did anyway.

Dud went on quickly, "There's another reason for taking down the palisade. We promised our wives separate houses and it's coming up on three years now that each of us has been living in less room than my horse used to have in his stall back in Arkansas."

"If we take down the palisade," Jeff said, "we can use the logs to build two more houses."

"Who gets the house we're living in now?" Fred asked.

"Draw lots for it?"

"Wait a damn minute!" Fred snapped. "We ain't decided about the palisade. I say leave it up another year."

Dud disagreed. "Take it down this spring."

They looked at Jeff. He sighed deeply, thinking of Rachel and the baby. Would they be as safe without the log wall?

Dud asked, "Jeff?"

Jeff nodded. "All right. Take it down this spring."

"You going to be sorry for that," Fred said, darkly.

Dud was cheerful. "Shall we draw lots for the house?"

"Might as well. . . ."

Dud rattled three coins in his hand. He gave each of them one. "Each man lays a coin down on the table. Odd man gets the house. All right?" He looked at them and they nodded. Fred examined his coin.

Dud said, "Lay it down, now."

Each of them laid his coin down. They were all the same.

"Do it again," Dud said. He picked up his coin.

Fred rubbed his on his pants.

Dud said, "Now." He laid his coin down with the others.

Dud's was the odd coin.

"Damn, you git the house," Fred said in an annoyed tone. "You allus was a lucky fool, Dudley."

"Well, I know *you*, Fred."

Jeff laughed and Fred looked puzzled for a moment, then he shook his head and walked out.

Jeff and Rachel decided they wanted a two-room house, to begin with. When little Roy grew up a bit they would add a room, or build a loft. Loft rooms were desirable because heat rose; they were often the warmest in the house.

The snow came again, light flurries that carpeted the fields and slowly disappeared under the weak sun, except in shadowy patches. Then it rained off and on for a week. The creek surged full, depositing gray foam along its banks and tossing driftwood aside on the curves.

Suddenly it was spring again. Everything was green except for a porridge of mud that slowly dried. The sun grew more and more like its old self and not the watery imitation they'd seen now and then during the last months.

But the grass was up and, on one of his hunting trips with Luke Tilley, Jeff cut Indian sign. A party of unshod horses had passed their way, only a mile from the houses, six or eight riders.

Comanches.

They hurried back to the houses. Fred, Angus Porter, and Simon were in the fields and Jeff called them in. But no hostile showed himself that day.

"They give us a look and passed by," Fred said. The others hoped he was right.

Little Roy seldom cried, except when he was hungry and no one seemed to be doing anything about it. Rachel put his crib near the fireplace because he loved to watch the dancing flames, chuckling happily when the wood popped and sputtered.

The ice in the creek broke up, and Dud and Jeff carried chunks of it to cram into the icehouse. That done, they planned a trip into Pommer to buy staples.

They wheeled a wagon out and Jeff went over it carefully while Dud examined its harness. Then they cleaned, oiled, and loaded the pistols and rifles and fashioned dozens of cartridges, packing them in pouches to be hung on belts alongside the cap pouches.

Titus had showed them metal cartridges that a few firms in the East were manufacturing, but they were much more expensive than handmade ones, and had to be fired from redesigned guns. Titus assured them that brass cartridges were in the future. One day all would be metal, probably brass, and of course much quicker to load because they would do away with the little copper caps. Caps were devilish to shove onto a nipple when a man was in a terrible hurry. A lot of men had died, Titus said, when they forgot the cap altogether in their rush.

But that day was not near. Titus thought it might be twenty years away, and even then many would keep to the old cap and ball because of the cost, or because they were used to it.

They were handed lists from everyone and then made the three-hour trip into town without incident. Dud drove the wagon while Jeff, on the bay, circled ahead or dropped back, looking for trouble but finding none. If the Comanch were out, they were somewhere else.

Titus had heard news of a few families to the west of town who'd had a brush with hostiles and lost some animals. But the news he was full of was the electric telegraph. He showed them a newspaper printed in Baltimore. A man named Professor Morse had invented a kind of machine that could send combinations of dots and dashes through a wire that was stretched between two cities, Baltimore and Washington. These combinations, according to the paper, had been formed into an alphabet so messages could be sent instantly from one city to the other!

"It's the goddamn finger of God!" Titus declared. "It don't seem possible a man could do that!"

Dud frowned over the paper. "It says here, a circuit of eighty miles. Messages went both ways."

Jeff asked, "How can they be sure it really happened?"

Dud looked at him in surprise. "Because they answered questions."

"Pretty hard to believe. . . ."

Titus said, "If it really works, people won't be writing letters no more." He sat down on a barrel. "They'll just send what they want over the wire. Hell, I could order my goods that way. I wouldn't have to write for anything."

"Yeah, but it means they'll have to string wire everyplace," Dud said, reading the paper. "It'll mean one hell of a lot of wire. I wonder how long it takes them to tap out a message. . . ."

"How could it go instantly?" Jeff asked, snapping his fingers. "Instantly is damned quick."

"Instantly is what it says here," Dud replied. "And lightning is electricity, isn't it? *That* goes pretty fast, as I remember. So I guess these dots and dashes go like lightning."

"I think you're right!" Titus said admiringly. "I never thought of it that way."

There was other news too—talk of Texas becoming a state in the Union. The gossip said that Southerners wanted it to come in as a slave state.

Titus asked, "Y'all ever know anybody who had slaves?"

"There were some in Arkansas," Dud said. "People with large farms and so on. But we never knew any of them."

"Slaves cost a heap," Titus said, nodding. "And you got to feed and house 'em . . . buy 'em clothes. I don't see how it would pay."

"It isn't right, anyhow," Dud said. "Slavery shouldn't be allowed. I can't see but the whole thing is going to cause trouble."

"It already is," Titus said.

They started back as soon as they loaded the wagon and it was a peaceful journey. Jeff rode beside the wagon for miles while Dud talked about the telegraph, which fascinated him. Electricity had mysteries that men were still fumbling to investigate—ever since old Ben Franklin had nearly killed himself with his kite and iron key.

Electricity has power, Dud thought, and one day men would find that it could do a lot more than send messages over a wire.

"Power!" Jeff said. "Could it move a wagon?"

Dud laughed. "Well, I wouldn't go that far."

Jeff thought all of it was farfetched. Newspaper stories were not always correct. Maybe the entire telegraph thing was a hoax. How did one make electricity anyway? Dud didn't know. Maybe they didn't manufacture it, it just happened. It was all mysterious: did they have to wait for a storm? And if they did, how did they capture lightning?

Rachel didn't believe it at all when he told her.

Chapter Ten

Iт was an early Sunday morning when the Comanches came in like whirlwinds, screaming their war whoops like mad things. Jeff rolled out of bed instantly as a shot was fired from the tower—then another.

He pushed his way into pants, grabbed his rifle, shoved the pepperboxes into his belt and rushed out, hearing Rachel yell. He paused to call back, "Bolt the door!"

Dud shouted at him as he climbed the near ladder to the fire step and looked over. He could see ten or fifteen Indians, all converging on Angus Porter's house.

They were tearing down his corral and one brave was attempting to climb in a window. Jeff swung the Hawken up and fired. The man dropped out of sight, a red smear on his back. Pulling the pepperboxes, Jeff fired into the yammering hostiles. In the tower, Tilley was firing at them and Dud appeared, pale as a sheet of foolscap, but clenching his jaw. He thrust a pistol over the parapet and began firing—and the Indians suddenly scattered, leaving three on the ground.

Jeff reloaded, watching them depart, galloping in all directions. He glanced around. They had long ago decided on each man's place in time of danger, and he was glad to see Fred Caine and Simon at their appointed posts, at the other end of the palisade. All sides of the palisade had to be watched in case the redskins made a diversion and came over the wall somewhere else.

A few minutes after the firing ceased, Angus Porter opened the door of his house and looked out. Jeff waved to him and Dud yelled, "They've gone." Angus nodded.

The two mules in Angus's corral had been killed, but no other real damage had been done. The corral poles could be put up again in a jiffy. The Indians had not harmed the stout log house.

They dragged the three bodies out to the field and left them. Far off, in the trees, they could see the hostiles watching.

Luke Tilley came down from the tower to say he hadn't seen the

Indians until they were almost at the house. They had come out of the misty dawn, silent until they reached the house.

"You figger they'll come again?" Tilley asked.

"Nobody can tell about Indians," Jeff said. "Did any of 'em have guns?"

No one had seen any. They had attacked the door with hatchets and poles, and made only small dents. Fred thought maybe they'd had enough. They weren't stupid, were they?

"They aren't stupid," Jeff said, "but they're sneaky. I think they'll come at us again, if only for revenge."

"When?" young Tilley asked.

"God knows. Maybe tonight, maybe in a month." Jeff shrugged. "When they get ready."

It was decided to have the Porters and the Tilleys spend the night inside the palisade, with their animals. And all went well; there were no alarms when Jeff climbed up into the tower after midnight, relieving Dud.

There was little wind and a pale half moon stared down on them, ice-white and cold. Jeff peered into the shadows, looking for movement, and saw none.

He set himself to quarter the land, moving along the tower, searching each section with his eyes . . . and an hour passed.

When he came again to the area around the Tilley house, he paused—but only for a second. There was a glow behind the house that had not been there before! And he knew instantly what it was. The redhides were trying to set it afire!

He sent a rifle shot into the sky and slid down the rope.

Angus and Fred were the first out of the houses, with Simon on their heels. Jeff yelled to them, ran for the gate, and slipped out, a pistol in each hand.

As he sped to the Tilley house he could hear hoofbeats, and when he rounded the corner of the house saw the redhides retreating. He emptied one pistol at them, but saw no result.

They had built a fire against the log wall, and it was just blazing as Jeff reached it. In a moment he had kicked the fire apart and, using some of the unburned wood, knocked the rest of the burning sticks and brush away.

Big, heavy logs could not be set afire easily, and these were only blackened a bit, with no damage. He was kicking dirt over the embers when the others arrived, Luke Tilley among them, swearing under his breath.

Fred said, "Damn good thing they didn't have no coal oil."

Luke was voluble in his thanks to Jeff. In the middle of their discussion, however, there was a scream from inside the palisade.

They ran back through the gate. Two Indians were hacking at Fred's door and another Indian was coming over the wall. Jeff fired at the two and a fusillade smashed the Indian on the wall. He fell back outside.

But two more were inside and an arrow out of the dark sliced Jeff's shoulder. Luke fired as Jeff went to one knee, and a redhide tumbled off the roof.

Angus found the other under the fire step and shot him when the brave threw a hatchet. Then from the parapet Dud reported that the Indians had gone.

Luke Tilley had been hit by an arrow, but his broad, thick leather belt had saved him. He had a few deep scratches which Hester bound up.

Jeff doffed his shirt inside the house, feeling his shoulder stiffening. The wound was fairly deep but clean. An inch lower and it would have been trouble. Rachel, biting her lower lip, bound it, and Jeff put the shirt back on.

Angus and Simon dragged the dead Indians out to the field and left them. Their friends would come and get them as before. It was to be hoped, Dud said, that they would get tired of that procedure.

There was no other Indian attack that year. Apparently they were considered too tough a nut to crack. The Comanch had not fared well against them. A half dozen had been killed and no telling how many wounded.

Later, in the fall, two more families came to settle near them and claim land. Their names were Bowman and Mills. They made it through the winter living in tent shelters, and in the spring both began to cut timber for houses.

As spring came round, Jeff, Dud, and the others began to dismantle the palisade. They piled the logs neatly to use in building the two new houses, and the women went out to gather stones again for the chimneys.

During the first month of summer Jeff and Dudley began preparing to make another run to Pommer. They pocketed lists from everyone; Dud had sacks of items to trade, and everyone was eager for news.

When they were ready to leave, Simon showed up with his horse, asking to go along. He had a rifle, and wore his father's pepperbox in his belt.

Dud shrugged and looked at Jeff.

Simon said, "Henry Mills will take my place in the tower."

Jeff nodded. There was really no way he could refuse Simon. He smiled and made the best of it. "Very well, come along."

The trail to Pommer was no longer a shadowy track that one might lose if one wasn't observant. It was now a well-traveled path winding through the trees and the new gold leaves of early summer. Their wagons and others had deepened the ruts, so the rains did not wash them out.

The travelers met no one until they were in sight of the town's rooftops. Pommer had changed in the months since they'd seen it. They passed a newly erected board on a stake. Someone had lettered in black paint: POMMER POP 874.

The main street was as wide and rutted, and not at all straight; a surveyor would wring his hands. There were wagons and a few buggies parked everywhere along the street, as well as dozens of horses standing at hitchracks.

Dud said, "I think we came in on market day."

The dry goods store and restaurants were the same, but there was a new hardware store and six saloons instead of four. Even Jerry Titus's mercantile store looked different. When Jeff went inside he saw that it had been enlarged. A wall had been pushed out for more space.

Titus came from behind a counter to grab his hand. "Jeff Becket! Glad to see you! Where's Dudley?"

"Outside, trading."

"How'd you winter?"

"Not bad." Jeff looked around. "Things look prosperous."

"Had to hire me a clerk." Titus sighed. "Too damn much going on. The town is sprawlin' out. Don't know where the hell folks is comin' from." He looked over his glasses. "Innans didn't get y'all?"

"They tried to. What's the news?"

"Well, we going to have an election next year." Titus indicated a chair. "Sit down, Jeff. Somebody named Polk is runnin'. D'you care who's president?"

"Not much."

"I got some newspapers from the East. Sell you one 'fore you go. Not many Indian problems lately." He took the lists Jeff handed him. "I'll see these get boxed for you. You going back today?"

"We figure to."

It was Simon Caine's first trip to Pommer since that first day years ago, and he did not remember anything about the town. The settlement had only one cross-street, which petered out into fields. The buildings were ramshackle and unpainted for the most part, some with board awnings over the walks, some with no walks at all.

He guided his horse along the length of the town and back, looking at everything, listening to the sounds, all unfamiliar to him. Music spilled out from the saloons, and as he paused to listen to one he noticed the girl standing in an upstairs window. She smiled at him boldly, and crooked her finger.

Simon stared at her; she's wearing very little, he thought, and his face reddened. He nudged the horse quickly and went on by. Jesus! A painted girl wanted him to come upstairs! She had to be a whore girl—he had heard about them. But he had never been to bed with a female . . . and he had an enormous curiosity about all of it.

He rode to the end of the street again, thinking about the girl in the window. How long would Jeff and Dud stay in town? He could see Dud talking and laughing with a knot of men on the street. Jeff must be in the store.

He had a few dollars in his pocket. What would a whore girl cost? He had no idea. He rode back and dismounted in front of the saloon. Wrapping the reins around the hitchrack, he went inside and leaned on the long bar.

The room was dim and smelled of beer and tobacco. Simon stared into the backbar mirror with several others who were chatting. There were items tacked to the wall: an Indian tomahawk, arrows, a round painted shield, a cavalry guidon. There was also a painting of a naked woman with shiny black hair who seemed to be looking back over her shoulder at him.

Simon asked for beer and drank it slowly. Oil lanterns hung from the ceiling, only two of them lit now. In the far corner was a piano where a small man tinkled it with no enthusiasm. There were card tables scattered here and there and a few men hunched over them, slapping cards down.

And there were two painted girls. One came to him with a big smile. ''Howdy. Y'all new in town?''

Simon nodded, trying not to stare at her. He was surprised when she rubbed against him. He could see down the front of her dress— farther than he'd ever seen before! He forgot to sip his beer . . . and then somehow he was walking with her, going up the steps to the second floor and into a tiny little room.

Then she took hold of him where no one had ever grabbed him before.

She smiled and let go, and asked him for money.

Chapter Eleven

JEFF and Dud sat by the big stove with Jerry Titus and cracked walnuts. Dudley wrote down the names of suppliers as Titus ticked them off. Dud could write to them direct for wholesale prices when his trading post was established. He wanted such things as pins, needles, thread, fulminates and powder, salt, sugar, tobacco. . . . He would trade for anything that came his way.

But when he and Titus got into a long discussion of store-minding, Jeff stood up and wandered out. He leaned on the wagon and lighted a cheroot, looking at the town. Where had Simon got to?

He glanced at the sun. In another hour they ought to be on their way. Maybe he should mosey into the deadfalls and find Simon.

Dud came from the store and looked around for Jeff. Where had he and Simon gone? Their horses were here. Well, maybe Jeff had gone to find Simon. He turned to reenter the store. And a smooth-faced young man stopped him.

"Would you be interested in milk goats, sir?"

"Milk goats?"

"You bet. Finest goats in town. Give 'em to you cheap. It happens I need the money."

Dud looked the other over. He was poorly dressed, in a sack coat and worn pants—but then who in a town like Pommer dressed like a dandy? "Where are these goats?"

The man pointed. "Right down at the end of the street, sir. Come on, I'll show you."

"All right." Dud made up his mind quickly. They could certainly use milk goats at home. This was a providential meeting.

They walked along the street quickly. The other said, "My name's Johnny Smith."

"Dud Hurley. We're in town for supplies. I live down on Eden Creek."

Johnny nodded as if he'd heard of it. He led Dud around behind a barn and pointed to a line of pens and coops. "There they are."

Dud smiled at half a dozen young goats in a wire pen. They looked to be in excellent condition, well fed. His eye was caught by the coops.

"Are those chickens for sale too?"

"You bet!" Johnny said eagerly. "You want chickens?"

"I'd rather have chickens than goats."

Johnny Smith considered. "All right. I'll gi' you the bunch." He counted. "Twelve chickens—you can have 'em for a dollar apiece."

"Twelve? All's I got is ten."

Johnny sighed. "All right, ten dollars then."

"How about pens for hauling them?"

"Take them all. They go with the chickens."

"All right. Write me a bill of sale."

Johnny had a paper in his pocket made out for goats. He crossed out goats and wrote chickens and handed it over.

Dud gave him the ten dollars. "I'll have to go back for the wagon."

"That's all right. You just pick them up when you get back. I'll be in the house." Johnny pocketed the money and left.

Dud examined the coops. He could probably save space by hauling them in one coop instead of two. It took him half an hour to effect the move, amid much cackling and cawing. The chickens did not want to cooperate and were noisy about it.

As he got the last hen into the coop, an older man came around the barn with a shotgun. "What the hell you doing?"

Dud was surprised. "I just bought these chickens."

The shotgun moved to center on him. "The hell you did!"

"I got a bill of sale!" Dud held it out.

The man ignored it. He was about sixty, Dud thought, skinny, with a lined face and no-nonsense eyes. The shotgun never wavered in his hands. "This-here's my land and them is my chickens. I never sold you nothing."

"But Johnny Smith—"

"I don't know no Johnny Smith. My name's McCann."

"He said he'd be in the house. . . ."

"The house is locked up. I been away till a minute ago, heard the chickens squawkin'. You been whiffled, mister. That paper ain't worth shit."

Dud sighed deeply. Johnny Smith had diddled him for good. He had been so damned eager to buy chickens he'd accepted the man's word! His shoulders sagged and the older man shook his head. "You was made a fool of."

"Guess I was," Dud said. And he was out ten dollars, too.

He found Jeff sitting on the wagon, waiting. "Where you been?"

"Buying chickens that weren't for sale." He told Jeff the story, leaving out nothing.

Jeff was annoyed. "Ten dollars?"

"Yes. I'm sorry, Jeff."

Jeff drew both pepperboxes and looked at the caps. He shoved them into his belt. "Come on. Let's find Mr. Smith."

"What—where you going to look?"

"Where you find those kind. Prob'ly in a saloon." He started along the street and Dud hurried to keep up.

Jeff paused at the door of the first deadfall. "You point out which one he is."

Dud nodded and they went in. There was no Johnny Smith in the room. He was not in the next one either.

But he was in the third, sitting at a far table at the end of the room with three others. Dud said, "That's him, in the rusty-brown coat."

"All right." Jeff walked to the table and pointed to Smith. "You. We want our money back."

Smith looked up innocently, "What money is that, friend?"

"The money you took for chickens that weren't yours," Dud said.

A man sitting to Smith's right, big and red-faced, growled at Jeff. "Y'all lookin' for trouble?"

"Yes I am," Jeff said. He indicated Smith. "Put ten dollars on the table."

"You got the wrong man. . . ."

Red-face stood up suddenly and reached for a pistol. Reaching out, Jeff yanked him across the table with one hand and hit him with the other. He fell onto the table, which collapsed, and Smith jumped back, overturning his chair. He scrambled up and started for the back door. Jeff fired into the door ahead of him and Smith halted, looking around. Jeff motioned with the pepperbox and Smith came back slowly.

"Ten dollars," Jeff said, one eye on Red-face, who was getting to his knees.

Smith counted the money into Dud's hand. Dud pocketed it and Jeff picked up Red-face's pistol. He laid it on the bar and he and Dud left amid silence.

At the wagon Dud began to laugh. He leaned on the wagon and laughed till tears ran down his cheeks.

"What the hell you laughin' at?"

"You're a ring-tailed terror, Jeff Becket."

"We got what was ours, didn't we?"

"Yes, and scared that poor man half to death."

"Too bad about him," Jeff growled. "Where the hell is Simon?"

Simon pushed into his jeans and pulled on his boots. He slid the shirt over his head. So that was what it was all about? Not much to it. The girl—she said her name was Rose—said, "Hurry up." She went out.

She had sure changed since she met him in the saloon. She had been all kitteny then, and as soon as she had his money she practically yawned in his face.

He went down the stairs and glanced into the saloon. Rose was smiling and bantering with another man, rubbing his thigh boldly. Simon sighed and went out to the street. He didn't feel any different than he had an hour ago. It had been only a little fun—because Rose hadn't cooperated at all. What men did was apparently of little interest to her. All she wanted was the money.

He had considered taking his money back—but she would probably scream and raise hell. Then someone might come after him with a gun. . . .

He mounted the horse and rode to the wagon. Jeff and Dud had loaded it and were waiting for him.

"Here he is," Dud said, "You ready to go, Simon?"

Simon nodded. He wasn't a virgin anymore—Rose had mentioned that. He wondered if it showed.

They took the now rutted road south under a soda-cracker sky. Jeff glanced back now and then to see the smoke of the town fading. He'd bought a brooch for Rachel, a pretty thing that had caught his eye. She always appreciated presents when they were for her alone— something she could wear. They softened what Dud called the "hard" life. Dud had said many times that he was surprised women were willing to go with them and put up with all the hardships.

Dud thinks about things that never occur to me, Jeff mused.

They were perhaps seven miles from the town on a flat stretch of prairie when Jeff noticed the horsemen. There were four of them, walking their horses toward the wagon. He was not terribly surprised to see that one of them was Johnny Smith and another was Red-face.

But Dud was astonished. "It's Smith!"

"Yeh. He's come to get the ten dollars back."

Simon asked, "What's this about?"

Dud explained quickly as Jeff laid the Hawken across his thighs. He said to Dud, "Get the shotgun out. Make sure it's capped and loaded. . . ."

"This ain't my fight," Simon said.

Red-face, dressed in a blue shirt and jeans, was riding beside Smith and scowling at Jeff. Johnny Smith had a hat on, a brown bowler. The other two men were of a size, one with a striped shirt and army kepi, the other in a red shirt and jeans. They were grinning like urchins.

When the wagon halted they spread out, barely within hailing distance. Smith called, "Leave the wagon and go back t'ward town or we shoot the mules."

Jeff said softly, "You take the two on the left. Leave me Smith and the other."

Simon backed his horse and said again, "This ain't my fight. . . ."

Dud glanced at him. "Your pa's got vittles in the wagon."

"I don't care."

Jeff paid no attention. Suddenly he stood in the stirrups, aimed, and fired at Red-face. Then he dropped the rifle in the grass and spurred the bay, pulling the pepperboxes. As he charged Jeff heard the boom of the shotgun. He fired at Smith, then watched the man try to turn his mount, slip sideways, and fall. The horse dragged him a dozen feet and halted.

Red-face was sprawled in the weeds, not moving.

Jeff turned toward the other two and saw them fleeing. They were both low on their mounts' backs, galloping like the Devil himself was after them.

It was all over in seconds.

Dud jumped off the wagon, grinning. "I told you you were a hellion, Jeff Becket!"

Jeff swung down and began to reload the pistols. Simon sat his horse on the road a hundred feet away, shoulders hunched, staring at them.

Dud said, "Don't jump all over him, Jeff. . . ."

"He was asleep in the tower, too."

Dud sighed deeply. "He doesn't have our advantages. He comes from poor stock."

"You're too goddamn forgiving, Dud."

"Yes, it's a sin, I know. But it takes all kinds to make a world."

Jeff grunted, mounted the bay, and rode out to look at the two downed men. Red-face had been hit once, through the ear. Jeff was mildly surprised that he'd aimed high. Johnny Smith had been hit twice in the chest. He untangled Smith's foot from a stirrup, gathered up the weapons, and put them in the wagon when Dud drove closer.

"What about the horses?"

"I guess they're ours," Dud said. "Right of combat. They were going to kill our mules."

"That's right."

"So let's keep the horses until someone shows up with a valid bill of sale."

Jeff smiled and went to collect them. Dudley had a very sensible way of looking at things. He pulled off the saddles and piled them in the wagon and tied the horses on behind. He said nothing at all to Simon when he came in.

"We'll have to leave the bodies as is."

Dud clucked his tongue. "It's a shame two men had to die over ten dollars." He nodded. "We have no shovel. Yes, have to leave them as they are, I expect."

What had to be, had to be.

Chapter Twelve

THEY reached Eden Creek in several hours, without incident. Someone waved from the tower when they came in sight and Rachel and Leah met them at the gate.

Both women said the same thing at nearly the same time: "What'd you bring me?" They both laughed.

Jeff stepped down and slid an arm about Rachel. "Bring you something? I brought you me. Isn't that enough?"

"It is—if you brought me something else too."

Leah asked, "Where'd you get the horses?"

They told the entire story as they unloaded the wagon. Dud told most of it, leaving out any mention of Simon.

Rachel noticed the lack and over supper asked Jeff about it. He told her what had happened with Simon. "He can't be trusted any farther than you'd throw a cow."

He gave her the brooch at bedtime. She found it on her pillow and whooped in delight, running to a mirror to pin it on her night-dress.

They built two separate houses that summer, one for the Beckets and one for the Caines. Dud cut doors through to make one house out of the three rooms, and decided to use one section for his trading post.

He axed logs to make counters and shelves and piled up the goods he'd been collecting and saving: lead, fishhooks, powder, and the like. He painted a sign to hang over the door: EDEN TRADING POST. His dream was coming true at last.

A dozen or more travelers came by, straggling in by ones and twos mostly. Then a wagon train, nine strong, came from Pommer, and the people camped for the night near the creek. They were headed for Arizona, they told Dud, where they had relatives. They brought newspapers and news. A man named McCormick had invented a mower and reaper that would make farm work easier. And someone named Howe had invented a sewing machine! There was a picture of it in one newspaper, which the women pored over. Imagine! A machine that could sew!

The most disturbing news was about slavery. People were beginning to take sides in the East. The politicians were making speeches and compromises, but many said slavery was an evil that would not go away. It would be with them forever. Others said slavery would be the salvation of the nation.

However, the issue did not affect them on Eden Creek. No one knew anyone who owned slaves—or could afford them.

After the nine-wagon train had gone, there were no travelers till nearly fall. Then another group of five wagons appeared with men driving a small herd of cattle.

Dud traded them vegetables, powder, and tools and secured three milk cows before they went on. He sold one cow to Jeff so the baby could have milk.

Angus Porter prospered too that summer and fall with his blacksmith shop. He proved to be a tinker as well, and was able to mend almost anything made of metal. The sound of his hammer seemed continuous. It was a homey sound, very comforting in its way.

Luke Tilley, Fred, and Simon spent their days in the fields. They had put in some wheat along with other crops. The new families were also planting their own plots; the area was becoming very agricultural, Dud said.

In late fall Dud and Jeff loaded two wagons for Pommer, both piled high with corn and sweet potatoes. Simon came and asked to go along, but Jeff would not allow it.

"He's not riding with us."

Dud could not get him to change his mind.

It proved to be a fateful trip for Jeff. It was the time he bought his first beef cattle. He paid three dollars a head for eleven cows. He drove them home and turned them into the field behind the houses.

While Dud and Jeff were away at Pommer, Leah had opened the trading post when travelers came by. She and Rachel had done a bit of business on their own. They had traded vegetables and a side of venison for some chickens.

Dud was delighted.

"Now we'll have eggs," Rachel said, kissing her husband.

"A milk cow, and now chickens," Jeff said. "It's getting very civilized here. Next thing you know we'll have a school."

"I've thought of it," Rachel admitted.

They built a coop for the chickens and a pen to keep them in bounds. At night the animals were locked in the coop as a protection from predators. With the palisade gone everything was much more vulnerable.

Dud had spent all his hard money and had traded with Titus. He was willing to consider trading most anything that was useful, unless it was something that could not be resold or kept for any length of time.

He was a smart, sharp trader despite his easygoing exterior. But all that aside, the thing that endeared him to everyone was the knowledge that Dud Hurley was incapable of dishonesty. His word was his bond . . . and no one doubted it.

Leah had been the youngest of four children and the only one unmarried when she'd met Dud. The Elkins family lived five miles down the road and were well settled. Leah's father was a Methodist preacher who farmed on the side. However, Leah never became a churchly type. Maybe she lived too close to it. As a girl she had disliked too much regimentation and organization; she was something of an insurgent and agitator, speaking her mind even when she was a young girl.

It was her independence that first attracted Dud. He was never in any doubt from the beginning where he stood with her. She told him. She did not know how to simper and be coy. She also did not pretend, as many women did, to be helpless.

Dud married her as soon as it was possible. He knew he would never find another like her.

When winter came that year it was a hard one, and stayed longer than usual. The creek froze solid and the snow was very deep. Jeff had to haul feed for his cattle. He built them a shelter of sorts, a roof, and cribs so they did not wander away.

He and Tilley went hunting every week when the weather permitted, and brought back meat. Dud chopped holes in the creek ice and fished successfully, and they traded fish for venison.

Their roofs did not leak, there was plenty of firewood ricked up, and inside they were snug and warm. Little Roy played with homemade toys while Rachel knitted. Jeff and Dud frowned over the chess board for hours, and Jeff fretted when the wind howled, lashing the window with snow.

It was still winter when, in bed one night, Rachel confided that she was pregnant again. She thought the baby might be due in July.

* * *

In the spring Dud went out in his new boat and sounded the creek. He found the bottom to be shallowest about a hundred yards from his trading post door.

"It's not over seven feet," he told Jeff. "And that's in the center of the stream."

They knew that in the summer the creek would be more sluggish and only about fourteen feet wide. During the spring runoff it was more like twenty-two or -three for a short period. Dud thought the bridge should be at least twenty-five feet long.

They axed down two pine trees in the forest that were longer than what they needed, lopped off all the limbs, and hauled them to the bridge site. However, the men had no way to get the trees to span the creek. They were much too heavy to muscle across using the boat.

"We'll have to wait for winter," Jeff said. "Then we can slide them on the ice."

It was the only way.

Chapter Thirteen

I<small>T</small> was a mild winter, more rain than snow, though the creek froze over for a few weeks. They had just enough time to haul the two big logs across the ice to make a bridge. The men were able to peg the logs together, and when the spring runoff came Dud had his wish. A man could cross on foot, but it was impossible for animals or wheeled vehicles. So they added more logs and gave the bridge a solid platform.

Dud was elated when he drove the first wagon across and back. They had a bridge at last!

In the spring Jeff had four new calves, increasing his little herd to fifteen. But before there could be more he had to acquire a bull.

Another family, named Yellen, came to settle near the creek, and Dud suggested they begin to think about laying out streets—at least one main street.

"It won't do for folks to just build houses anywhere they want," he said. "We must have some organization."

Even Fred Caine agreed to the idea. But of course his house, Jeff's, and Dud's were all in a line, more or less. So the main street was staked off in front of their homes. It would run the length of the town-to-be that they'd staked out years before.

One of the new families, the Bowmans, objected. John Bowman had planned to build his new home where the street was staked. He had even hauled foundation logs and pegged them in place. But when faced with Jeff and the others, he quickly changed his mind.

Later in the year they learned from a traveler that Texas was now a state of the Union. Dud acquired a newspaper with the details; it said there had been much talk of dividing the territory into a number of states, but that had not happened. Texas came into the Union a slave state, the largest of all, with the little town of Austin as its capital.

They learned, however, that the Texas question was not settled. Mexico claimed the Nueces River as the international boundary,

not the Rio Grande as the Texans claimed. The two sides were up
in arms about it. The newspaper speculated that a war with Mexico
was brewing. This time the United States, not the weak Republic
of Texas, would lead the way.

There was also a ruckus rising about Oregon Territory. The Brit-
ish claimed it, even though the Lewis and Clark Expedition had
explored it decades ago when Jefferson was president. The Hudson
Bay Company wanted Oregon kept as a wilderness area for the fur
trade. But a man named Dr. Whitman was taking settlers there to
form a colony of Americans.

The newspaper mentioned the possibility of another war with
Britain over Oregon.

"Sure a hell of a lot happening in the world," Jeff mused.

Dud agreed. "Ever since Polk was elected, the country's been
spreading out. But Oregon's a hell of a long way from the States."

"The country'll never spread that far," Jeff said.

Their wheat crop was not good. Fred, Angus, and Jeff walked
over the fields examining the stalks, chewing the kernels. Stem rust
and chinch bugs had destroyed much of it. Angus thought the soil
was too sandy for wheat, though the corn was doing fine.

They harvested what they could, but it was barely enough for
their own use. They would have to depend on the corn, some yams,
and other vegetables to sell in town.

Fred had a bumper crop of corn, which he piled high into a
wagon, announcing a trip into Pommer. The women hurried to give
him their lists, and Rachel handed him a letter for her folks in
Arkansas. It was past time she wrote them, she said. They didn't
even know about little Roy.

Fred drove the wagon into town, with Simon riding alongside on
a roan, thinking about Rose.

While his father dickered with Titus in the store, Simon rode on
to the deadfall where he'd met her. But she was not in the saloon
when he entered. Maybe it was early for her. He stood at the bar
and sipped a beer. The room was dim and smoky as usual, smelling
of tobacco and lamp oil. A few card players were sitting at a rear
table near the piano, and the bartender was leaning over the bar at
the far end, talking earnestly with two men.

As he finished the beer Rose came down the back stairs. Behind
her, a farmerish-looking man shrugged into a gray coat. The man
whispered something to her that made her smile, then he went past
Simon and out to the street.

Another man walked into the saloon at that moment and started

for the bar. Simon moved to meet Rose, who saw him at once and
came toward him with a wide smile.

But the newcomer intercepted her and turned her about, holding
her by the elbow. Rose was surprised and tried to pull away, looking
over her shoulder at Simon.

Simon growled, "Hey . . . there . . ."

The stranger paused, scowling at Simon. He was older and bigger, with a grizzled face and rough clothes. His expression said he
was not a man to fool with. "Yeah—what you want, kid?"

Simon said, "You pushed in front of me!" He saw Rose yank
her arm away—and in the next instant the man doubled his fist and
knocked Simon to the floor.

It hurt. Simon felt a white rage. He clawed at the pistol in his
belt and, lying on his back, fired four times as fast as he could pull
the trigger. He saw the bullets pop dust on the man's shirtfront.
The other was flung back and left sprawled in a bloody heap, having
knocked over a table and chair.

Powder smoke drifted through the room as Simon stood up.
There was silence for several moments as everyone stared at him.

Rose had fled. The body on the floor did not move. Simon walked
to stand over the stranger; the man was dead all right. He shoved
the pistol into his belt, looked round at the other faces, and went
to the door. They were murmuring to each other as he pushed out
to the street.

He had killed a man!

But the sonofabitch had it coming.

Simon piled on the roan and rode back to Titus's store. Jumping
down, he hurried inside. His father was sitting by the cold stove
with Titus. Simon said, "I got to go back, Pa."

Fred looked around at him in surprise. "You go back when I
do."

"No—I got to go now!" Simon ran out as his father yelled. He
mounted and spurred the roan, galloping out of town.

A mile or so along the road he reined in to walk the horse. His
anger had gone, replaced by cold sweat. The other man could have
killed him! He'd been armed. . . . Simon's hands trembled and he
hugged himself. Would the law come after him? There had been
half a dozen witnesses in the saloon. What if the dead man was a
friend of theirs? They'd all tell a different story.

Maybe he ought to leave and go somewhere—anywhere. Would
a shooting like that blow over, be forgotten? Maybe not.

He couldn't remember if there was a lawman in Pommer. He
had heard nothing about one. Maybe Dud would know.

He reloaded the pepperbox as the horse walked. Then he grinned suddenly. The pushy sonofabitch sure had been surprised for a second—as the bullets smashed his chest. He thought he could go in and do as he damned pleased, but he met somebody who wouldn't be pushed around. And now he was dead on the dusty floor.

Simon rubbed the sore place on his jaw where the man had hit him; it was very tender. It had been a glancing blow but a hard one. It would be in Simon's favor, wouldn't it, that the man had knocked him down? It ought to be. If the witnesses didn't lie.

No one came after him, and he reached the creek long before dark.

A man came striding into Titus's store, full of news about a shooting. Some kid had shot Jape Hickson over a saloon girl.

Titus asked, "When was this?"

"Just a few minutes ago."

"Who was the kid?"

The man didn't know. "He got on a horse and hightailed it."

Fred stared at the newcomer. "How'd it happen?"

"What I heard, they had a fight over a saloon girl. Jape knocked the kid down and the kid shot 'im." The man pounded his chest. "Right through the ticker."

Titus asked, "Did Jape have a gun?"

"Yep. Didn't use it though. Guess he didn't have a chance to."

Titus sighed. "Jape had a temper like a teased bull."

"Yeh, he did. . . ."

Fred looked at the storekeeper as the man left.

Titus met his eye. "You figger it was Simon?"

"Maybe. Is there any law in this town?"

Titus shook his bald head. "They been talkin' about gettin' a deputy from over at Chandler, but for now we're on the rounds. Chandler's about forty miles. Deputy comes over here 'bout once ever' two weeks."

Fred grunted. "I better git on back."

He loaded the supplies in the wagon and started out. Had Simon shot this Hickson? The boy did have a quick temper, and he had the pepperbox in his belt. Would he shoot a man over a saloon girl? Fred sighed. Hell, kids had no goddamn sense anymore.

He saw no one on the road and arrived home an hour before dusk. Simon was sitting on the top corral pole, waiting for him. He jumped down without a word and helped unhook the team.

Fred said, "All right—what happened?"

Simon shrugged. "I was in the saloon havin' a beer and this gent comes in and knocks me down."

Fred scowled at him. "Tell me all of it, dammit. What about the girl?"

"They was two . . . three girls in the saloon. I wasn't talkin' to any of them."

"Then why'd he knock you down?"

"Guess I was in his way . . . maybe he was feelin' his oats."

"So you shot 'im?"

Simon indicated the bruise on his jaw. "I was lyin' on my back— I thought he was gonna stomp me!"

"Was there any witnesses?"

"Sure. Half a dozen."

"And it wasn't a fight over a girl?"

"No it wasn't, Pa."

Fred went past him into the house. He thought he could believe maybe half of what Simon had told him. But since there was no law in Pommer, it might take a deputy a month or more to learn about the shooting. And maybe then the witnesses would be scattered. It could all come to nothing. Anyway, if a deputy came looking for Simon, they could run the boy off into the woods till the law got tired and left.

Fred delivered the supplies to the other houses and told them the news: The United States was at war with Mexico over the Texas question. An American army had invaded Mexico, in fact.

It was all very interesting, but so far away. . . .

He didn't mention the shooting.

That year Leah Hurley became pregnant for the first time. She and Dud were elated—and scared to death at the same time that she would lose it.

But she did not.

Rachel was growing larger with her second, and as July came closer she prepared as she had for Roy. She and Leah spent hours together, talking and sewing. Little Roy was walking, growing like a weed, getting into things. Many of the little shirts she'd made for him could still be used for the second child, he'd grown out of them so fast.

When Jeff and Dud went to town they learned about Simon's shooting from Titus. It was common gossip all over town that Simon had shot the man, Jape Hickson, because of a saloon girl named Rose. Several had seen it.

It happened, however, that Hickson had been a tough and a bully and was generally disliked. Most thought it was good riddance, his sudden demise. So no one mentioned it to the deputy when he made his rounds.

Titus said, "Nobody's goin' to make charges against Simon. They taken the body out in the sticks and buried him."

"Is the girl still in town?"

Titus shrugged. "I got no idea." He grinned. "You want to see her?"

"No. Course not." Dud worried his chin. "Fred never said a thing to us about this."

"Well, them Caines are curious folks," Titus said. "And Simon—he's going to come to a bad end, you mark my words." He rolled a thin cigar in his fingers. "You ast me about a bull, Jeff. Well, Charlie Larson got one for sale. Told me yesterday."

"Where can I see it?"

Titus gave him directions and Jeff rode out to the edge of town. The Larson place had a wide corral and a fenced field beyond the house. Larson turned out to be a rangy, middle-aged man with a heavy limp. Yes, he had a yearlin' bull for sale. He took Jeff to the field and pointed it out.

"He's gentle as a housecat," Larson said, "gettin' stronger every day."

It was a good-looking animal and they quickly agreed on a price. Larson was right: tied to the wagon tail, the bull dutifully followed the wagon all the way home and Jeff turned him into the field with the cows.

"Now we'll have a herd," Jeff told Rachel. "This is the beginning."

Rachel gave birth to a little girl the first week in August, with Leah attending her as before. Leah was rounding out also. By her count she was due in October.

Rachel named the baby Lili. She liked the sound of it. She had seen the name in a magazine, she said. Jeff was delighted with his daughter and held her for hours.

Before the rains Jerry Titus came out from town, accompanied by another man whom he introduced as a distant cousin, Nate Bowen. Nate, he said, lived in the East, a little town in New Jersey.

Titus had a letter for Rachel, an answer to the one she'd written her folks. She sat by the fireplace to read it while Jeff and Dud talked to the visitors outside.

Titus was amazed at their little settlement. "Hell! Y'all got the makin's of a city right here! You going to be bigger than Pommer one of these days.''

Dud laughed. ''Not for a while.''

''And you got a bridge across the crick. . . .''

''But we haven't got a jail.''

Titus looked down his nose, over his glasses. ''All we got one for is drunks. Wait till y'all gets a couple saloons.''

Jeff asked, ''What's the news from the East, Mr. Bowen?''

''Call me Nate.'' Bowen was a young-looking middle-aged man with the beginnings of a paunch. He was a storekeeper like Titus. He had sold out to a partner and thus had the money to travel. He wore jeans and a leather shirt with fringes on the sleeves and had an Allen pistol in his belt. He looked like a tourist who was ready for Indians.

The war with Mexico was going on, he told them. General Winfield Scott was marching on the Mexican capital the last time anyone had heard. ''He won ever' damn battle he fought.''

''What do folks say about slavery?'' Dud asked.

Bowen pulled at his chin. ''Well, those arguments are still going on too. The war has pushed 'em off the pages but there's a strong undercurrent in the North against slaveholding. The politicians are juggling the states, this one slave and that one free—I guess you know that Texas is in the slave column, whether anybody owns any slaves or not.''

''Yes, we heard.''

''They'll argue it for years,'' Bowen said, ''but slavery's here to stay. There's too much money invested in 'em. You got any idea what a good, strong, able-bodied slave costs?''

''Too much for us,'' Jeff said. ''Besides, it doesn't set right, one man owning another.''

''The whole thing will have to come down,'' Dud agreed. ''No matter what it costs.''

Bowen shook his head. ''It won't happen.''

Leah stood in the door, ''Stop arguing and come on in. Dud, you bring the cider?''

Chapter Fourteen

Leah Hurley's baby arrived only two weeks off her count, a fine boy. They named him Joshua. He had yellow hair like his father. Dud poured drinks all around, receiving the usual ribald congratulations of his neighbors. The celebration lasted late, and Rachel remarked next morning that it was good the Comanch hadn't heard the party, or they'd have come to it.

But there were no Indian troubles that year. Jeff cut sign several times, a mile or more away from the houses, as he and Tilley were hunting. But they saw no redhides and they lost no stock. The Indians were obviously watching them from a distance.

"We're too many rifles for 'em," Jeff said. "They'll go where there's easier pickings."

More travelers passed by, perhaps because of the accessible bridge, or maybe it was a sign of the times. People seemed restless, itching to move somewhere, almost anywhere, searching for land— or just looking for a different life.

Dud's trading post prospered. The war with Mexico was over, the papers said, though a peace treaty had not yet been signed. The eastern newspapers they received now and then told of the marvelous inventions coming into use: A Dr. Wells was using a gas to make tooth extractions painless; a company called Goodyear was making hard rubber goods, and knitting machines were being imported from Europe, along with friction matches; and a Frenchman named Daguerre was capturing images of people on paper!

Dud observed, "The world is at last getting civilized, even though we've fought an unjust war with Mexico."

"Unjust?"

"Of course." Dud shrugged. "It seems to me we took Texas away from Mexico because we were stronger, and when she objected we punished her by invading."

"The papers say we're going to pay Mexico. . . ."

"Yes, we should. But a lot of people died. You can't pay anyone for that."

Jeff listened, but didn't always agree. Dud was a philosopher, as everyone knew, and had some strange ideas.

"Husband . . ." Rachel said.

"Yes?"

"This little house is too small. There are four of us now. We need two more rooms—at the very least."

"Two more rooms!"

"Two more rooms," she said firmly. "With board floors in all of them."

"How about one room and a loft?"

"Oh—a loft!" She smiled. "Two rooms *and* a loft."

Jeff sighed. Put an idea in a woman's head . . . It was too late in the year to be adding on rooms. He found a bit of paper and began making plans.

Rachel had been thinking on it. "We can use this room as the kitchen, because of the fireplace. When we add the two rooms, one will be a bedroom and one a workroom. And when Roy grows up a bit he can sleep in the loft. Until he does, we can use it as a storeroom."

"Why do you need a workroom?"

"For my sewing. And when Lili grows up she can sleep there."

Jeff sighed again. As Dud often said, women were the civilizers. Put one down in a desert and she would make it bloom—so long as she had a man to boss.

There was plenty of room to enlarge the house. The corral would have to be moved but that was easy.

Luke Tilley had become the hunter for the little settlement. He did his stint at harrowing and planting but he loved to hunt, and he kept everyone supplied with meat, receiving vegetables and other staples in return. Dud traded him cloth, which Hester made into dresses for herself and shirts for Luke.

On one of his hunting trips, Luke stumbled onto a stony hill, a small area that was entirely composed of stones and shale in layers. When he mentioned it to Jeff, he went to look at once. The hill was about five miles from the houses, an easy trip for a wagon.

Wouldn't a stone house be better than a log one? No Indian would burn it—for sure.

Rachel clapped her hands as he told her, and so did Leah Hurley. They wanted stone houses! Jeff, Luke, and Dud set about hauling stones—great piles of them.

* * *

When they made their end-of-summer trip into Pommer, Jerry Titus showed them an eastern paper with a picture of a windmill. It was an arrangement that pumped water from under the ground. He was sending away for one, he said. It was a new patented device that had some kind of mechanics so a high wind wouldn't blow it to pieces.

"With this thing," Titus said, "you won't have to dig wells. Let the wind do the work."

"Order one for us," Jeff said. "It sounds like a sensible idea."

Titus also had a couple of newfangled oil-burning stoves for cooking. They were black, angular-looking things, rather strange. Jeff shook his head. Why would a woman want anything but a fireplace to cook?

Returning home, they hauled more stones till the rains halted work.

In the spring Jeff laid out the house area with stakes and built the foundation a foot or so above ground. He had thought to use shale for the floor, but it proved to be too brittle. He would have to return to puncheon.

Dud proved to be the best stonemason, perhaps because of his experience building chimneys and fireplaces. It took most of the summer to build the walls and timber the roofs. They built two houses, a smaller one for the Tilleys and three rooms for Jeff and Rachel. The windows were small and high up for defense, but there were more of them, and they were positioned to catch the morning and afternoon sun.

Rachel was delighted with her new home; she had three rooms! The roof was thick pine shakes, and the two doors were each made of heavy planks with metal hinges.

When their house was finished it was a rather handsome building, looking somewhat like a small fort. But Jeff built a wooden porch on the front with steps that made it look much more homey. It was definitely colder inside than the log house had been, but it proved to be no harder to heat. And there were no cracks in the walls to let in icy air.

Fred watched the progress of the two houses. He had been completely opposed to them in the beginning, as he was opposed to nearly everything new, but when they were finished he began hauling stones for his own.

Rachel declared herself well pleased—except she wanted only one more thing. . . .

"What?" Jeff asked. "A four-poster bed?"

"No. Glass for the windows."

Women were never satisfied, he reflected. He watched her sew curtains for the windows. When she got glass, she would probably want the windows to open and close. Next she would want pictures on the walls!

There was more and more traffic on the road to and from Pommer that summer, often as many as three wagons a month, and half a dozen horsemen. Most came to use the bridge over the creek. A family or two stayed and put up tents or shacks.

Dud kept a careful drawing plan of the town-to-be area, with each family's name and site. It had been agreed between them that every family could claim one hundred paces by fifty along the main street. But it was not so easy to tell the newcomers what kind of building to erect. So most of their dwellings were shacks. Many of the families were poor in everything but energy. Soon the little settlement had the look of a shantytown.

When Titus came out on one of his unexpected trips, he was surprised at what he say. Half the place was an eyesore.

"Y'all need a sawmill desperately. Do you got any crime yet? Stealing, I mean?"

"Not that we know about," Dud said.

"Well, you will have. Prob'ly petty stealing. We ran a family out of town last year for just that."

"You're right," Dud said. "We need a sawmill."

Titus stayed to gab and eat lunch with them in the new stone house. He admired it extravagantly and played with little Roy, looked in on Lili, asleep in her crib.

Before he departed he said, "I'm going to ask around about a sawmill. Y'all ought to put one down there by the trees, make the creek run it."

"We need somebody who knows how."

"I'll ask."

Dud and young Tilley went back to town with Titus. Dud needed crockery, oilcloth, spirits, and a few small items for the trading post. He could not keep crockery on the shelves. The women bought it up as fast as he uncrated it.

The two came back the same day and had a brush with Indians an hour out of town. Five Comanches came over a hill, screaming and yammering. Dud pulled up and Luke jumped down, one of Dud's pepperboxes in his hand. He fired the six shots as Dud used the rifle, seeing one brave fall. He grabbed the other pepperbox and got off two more shots before the redskins were out of range.

"Reload, reload!" Dud shouted, grabbing a powder flask. His

heart was hammering and his hands were shaking. Luke was calmer, reloading quickly. "One of 'em had a rifle, Dud."

"Damn. We were making so much noise I didn't notice it."

"Think I hit one," Luke said. "You hit one too—I seen him fall."

They were sniped at with a rifle as they continued along the road. Luke fired back but it was impossible to tell if he hit anything. The Indians did not charge them again. But when they got home there were several bullet holes in the wagon. Luke showed them to Jeff.

"They gettin' rifles somewhere."

"From the folks they raid."

"They can't hit nothing," Luke said, fingering the holes in the wagon. "They aiming at the mules and hit the tailgate."

"That's because they jerk the trigger instead of squeezin' it. Just hope they never learn."

"I drink to that."

Chapter Fifteen

WHEN he was not actively harrowing or plowing Jeff spent much of his time in the saddle. He kept his little herd close to home and always watched for redhides.

He had an agreement with Luke Tilley: Luke would work his land for shares, since Luke had no seed nor money to buy seed. He had staked out some acres for himself, across the creek, and would work them when he could.

He and Hester were much better off in a year's time—now they had a stone house and plenty to eat and were putting down roots. Luke had asked Dud to teach him to read and was making excellent progress. Coming to Eden Creek and settling was the best thing he and Hester had ever done.

Luke was a round-faced young man with long brown hair. Hester whacked it off with a butcher knife when it got too unruly. He got along with everyone, especially Jeff, whom he admired. Although Jeff was a little younger, he was always the leader. Luke was content to follow.

He was an orphan and had been reared in an orphanage in Illinois, where he had been poorly treated and half starved. When he left there at the age of fourteen he had scavenged on city streets to stay alive. Then he apprenticed himself to a wagon maker for a short time—and had been beaten for every tiny mistake.

After a particularly savage beating Luke had crawled out and made his way west to Missouri, doing odd jobs for food and a niche to sleep in. He had never had an hour's schooling and never learned a trade, but Jeff had never seen anyone more eager to learn. Once shown, Luke was determined to do a job right.

He was a fine shot with a rifle and was a good companion on a hunt; he did not talk constantly or ask fool questions. And no one worked harder doing whatever it was he had set himself to do.

* * *

As Jeff's herd increased naturally, he also bought a few head here and there, including more bulls, and soon had a hundred in the fields. He employed Angus Porter's boy, Jason, to keep them within bounds, since building fences was out of the question.

Jason was going on thirteen and had a fine sorrel pony. The boy seemed part of his horse, an angular, skinny lad who would probably grow up to look very much like his father.

Jason too was sitting at Dud's knee, learning his letters and numbers, with a bit of help from his mother, who had a few books and who could read very well. It was a pleasant enough chore for Dud when he had the time, but, as he told Jeff, "We really ought to find ourselves a school teacher."

"And then if we do you'll want a school building."

"Certainly."

Jeff sighed. "Why do we need all that book learning out here?"

"Because it's good for the soul." Dud smiled, brushing tawny hair back from his forehead. "And it's broadening. There's more to the world than the view across Eden Creek."

"Schooling is costly."

"Yes, I suppose so. But do you want Roy and little Lili to grow up knowing nothing?"

Jeff shook his head and turned. "You're as bad as Rachel! Go away. I'm not married to you."

Dud laughed. "I'll go away—but the idea won't. One day we're going to have a school here."

Jeff looked around. "What we need is a sawmill, not a school. Log cabins use up three or four times as much wood as a board house."

"But they're sturdy."

"And hard to add on to, and drafty."

"But much better than sod houses. We make do—though I could use more room in the store already."

The growing traffic between Pommer and Eden Creek, and beyond, was good for Dudley's store, as a matter of business. And it might be very good for something else, Jeff told Rachel as they sat over supper one night after the children were in bed.

"Something else?"

"I mean, me and Dud and Fred and the others are hauling to Pommer and back a dozen times a year or more."

"Of course. We have to have the staples, things we can't get here."

He nodded. "That's exactly what I mean. I've been thinking about starting a freight line."

She stared at him in astonishment. "A freight line!"

"Why not? With three or four wagons and mules I can haul from here to Pommer, and maybe even to Hartigan or Chandler."

"You'll be gone a lot—and you'll have to pay drivers."

"Yes, but each haul ought to pay the expenses. If it doesn't, I'll quit. And when I get it started I don't have to go along on every haul."

"What about Indians?"

"If a driver don't have guns, I'll issue him some, and never send one man alone. But we haven't had much Indian trouble lately."

"They came at Dud and Luke not long ago."

"Yes, but they don't like our fast-shooting guns."

"You've thought about this. What about money?"

"We've got some saved. I think it'll work."

Jeff talked to Dud about the freight line idea and Dud was enthusiastic. "It'll solve a big problem for all of us. Leah's got her hands full, what with young Josh, and she doesn't care to tend the store anyhow. So I wouldn't have to run to town every month. And it'll keep you busy and out of trouble, and maybe make some hard money."

"That's what I figger."

When Fred Caine heard about the idea, he thought it foolish. "Hell, they won't be enough in it to make it pay."

Jeff said, "I'd haul farther than just to Pommer."

"Folks in Pommer ain't got nothing to be hauled!"

"We'll see."

When he talked to Dud again Jeff said, "He had me worried. I was afraid Fred would like the idea."

"Not much danger of that." Dud dug his pipe into a tobacco pouch. "I've got a bit of hard money put aside, Jeff. I'd like to invest in your line. You're going to have to pay wages and buy equipment."

"Well, I figger to start easy, two more wagons and mules, some guns. But I appreciate it. How much you want to put up?"

"I don't know. Why don't you buy what you need and figure what the line is worth and I'll put in a third. We can arrive at a profit scale later—if it turns out there *is* profit to be made."

"All right." They shook on it.

Dud said, "I won't be able to be active, but I can do paperwork. We'll need to keep accurate records."

"Yeah . . . I'm not much for paperwork."

Jeff made the trip to town, taking along Luke in case his rifle was needed. He wanted to discuss the idea with Jerry Titus. He found Titus full of news: A cholera epidemic was devastating the Comanche nation!

"I heard it from a army lieutenant. He brung his column through here only a few days ago. Says a good half of the Comanch is affected. They dyin' like flies."

"Jesus!"

"They probably won't be doin' no raidin' for a while. Maybe not ever again."

"He sure about that, is he?"

"Hell, yeh. Says he seen it."

Titus's other news was in the form of a rumor. It was said that gold had been discovered in some river in California. No one knew anything more.

"Hell, folks is discoverin' gold all the time," Titus said. "It'll prob'ly fizzle out."

"Too damn far away anyhow," Jeff said.

They sat down around the cold stove to discuss the freight line, and Titus was for it, as enthusiastically as Dud had been. "Wish somebody had done that a long time ago."

He knew who had wagons for sale and who would part with mules. He had also just received a shipment of pepperboxes and laid them out on a counter, six of them.

"These is Bolen Life and Property Preservers. They a bit bigger than yours. These is thirty-six caliber with six barrels, made by the Allen Company of Worcester. Lookit them! Six-inch barrels. Ain't they beauties?"

Jeff handled them lovingly. "They are! Can I take all six of 'em?"

Titus grinned. "I hid 'em just for you. And I also got some kits with bullet pouches, oiled patches guaranteed the same thickness for accuracy, wormers, picks, bronze moulds, and sprue cutters, and here's a little kettle to melt lead, with a ladle and lead bar."

"Sold," Jeff said. "Put 'em in a box." He loaded one of the big pistols and put it in his belt in place of the smaller.

He went to see the man who had wagons for sale. In his years of partnership trading with Dud and his dickering with Titus, he had amassed nearly four hundred dollars. This fortune he now dipped into to buy two light wagons and four mules.

Luke drove one wagon and Jeff drove the other back home. It finally hit him: He was starting in the freighting business, and he knew nothing at all about it.

* * *

Both John Bowman and Henry Mills, recent settlers near Eden Creek, were sometime farmers. They farmed because it was all they knew and because they had to, to feed their families. Long ago they had come to grips with reality—neither had any schooling, or was fitted for anything but walking behind a plow. They were forced into the fields. So when Jeff came to them and suggested they become drivers with his new freight line, they were both delighted and agreed at once.

At the end of the harvest season Jeff filled three wagons with corn, beans, yams, and vegetables and headed for Pommer. Freighting, Jeff thought is worth a shot. It might work and it might not, as Fred Caine predicted. But he was no farmer and no cattleman either, not yet. If freighting proved a bad deal . . . maybe he ought to try digging gold in California.

It was a raw day, with a few torn bits of cloud moving slowly in the sky, their shadows blurring the corn-colored earth. Luke drove one wagon, Bowman and Mills the others; Jeff went ahead on the bay.

They arrived in Pommer without meeting anyone on the trail. Titus clapped his hands on seeing them. "Goddamn! You brought me corn! I ain't had any in a week. Pull them wagons around in back and I'll take all you got."

While the men unloaded, Titus said to Jeff, "They really is gold in California. People is flocking there, picking it up offen the ground!"

"Don't believe it," Jeff said. He had just been thinking about California.

"Yeah, it's all gossip," Titus agreed. "They's a little town there—what the hell is its name?—oh yeh, San Francisco. Three or four hunnerd people. They say the gold was found close by. . . ."

"It's prob'ly just a story."

Titus laughed. "You a damn hardhead, Jeff. You don't believe nothing unless you can see it or feel it. You mark my words, they's something there with all that smoke."

Jeff shrugged. "I don't see chasin' after moonbeams."

"Well, anyhow, you brought me corn. But now your wagons is empty. What's your plans?"

"Look around, I guess. Ask some questions."

"You want to go to Chandler? If y'all will stay the night I know three or four folks who'll fill up them wagons."

Jeff brightened. "How's the road?"

"Better'n the one to Eden Crick."

"Then we'll stay."

Jeff made a deal with the owner of the Hay, Grain, and Feed store, and he and the others slept in several of the empty stalls. In the morning Titus introduced Jeff to three merchants who had boxes and bales that should have gone to Chandler a month past. They were eager for Jeff to load up the goods.

Jeff named a price, figuring in salaries and maintenance; the merchants accepted without haggling. But as Luke and the others loaded the wagons, Titus took Jeff aside.

"You didn't ask enough. If they sent them things on to Chandler by themselves it'd cost 'em twice as much."

"I didn't figger to rob 'em."

Titus groaned. "You got to figger they's going to be days when you pay them drivers and they ain't got nothing to haul. Next time you think on it harder."

" 'Cept when I haul your stuff?"

"I want t'pay a fair price, dammit."

Jeff nodded. He had lots to learn, that was for sure.

The wagons were on the road long before midday. It was some forty miles to Chandler, west and a little south. The road wound over empty prairie and they saw no one. A wind came up in the afternoon and yellow dust filled the sky. They camped at dark and pulled into Chandler the next day near noon to deliver the loads.

Jeff scouted the little town and found freight waiting to go to Pommer. It was easier than he'd thought. If he had an office here . . .

When they arrived back in Pommer, Jeff and the drivers stayed overnight again. Titus had talked to people and had goods piled up waiting for him, boxes that had to go to Hartigan, as well as several men who would be passengers.

"Passengers?" Jeff said to Titus, aside in the store. "What the hell do I charge for them?"

"I been gabbin' to folks," Titus said. "You hit on something. There's goods by the ton to deliver. They sitting around, waiting for somebody to hook up the mules. As for passengers, you figger them same as bales of merchandise, I guess. They takes up space, don't they?"

"How do people deliver goods now?"

"Well, the buyer comes to get whatever it is, or the seller hires somebody to haul it—whatever it is. And sometimes it takes forever to do."

Jeff nodded. "All right, tell you what. You act as my agent here in Pommer. You line up the business and I'll deliver it and pay you ten percent. What you say?"

"Y'all got a deal." They shook hands.

The trip to Chandler had taught them a few things. It was evident the drivers were going to spend many nights on the road. And sleeping on the ground, especially in the rain, was not going to keep the help happy. Jeff bought a small trap wagon and had bunks built into it for sleeping and cabinets for provisions. The wagon was pulled by a single mule; he had to hire a man to drive it, but it would make a world of difference to the crew.

He took Luke Tilley aside. "You going to be wagon master from now on." Jeff had a paper that showed what was in the wagons and where it was to go. "You deliver these loads in Hartigan and try to get something to haul back here so you don't come back empty."

Luke was pleased. "Wagon master . . ." It sounded good.

"You're the boss of them wagons and the men."

"You ain't going with us?"

Jeff shook his head. "What I need to go for? You're the boss."

Luke grinned. He took the wagons to Hartigan, an eighty-mile trip. He delivered the goods and the passengers and found more freight bound for Pommer. He could have filled another wagon, he told Jeff when they returned.

The wagons would be away for a week, so Jeff rode to Eden Creek in the meantime. He spent several nights with his family, played chess with Dud, and rode back to Pommer in a misty rain. Winter was close upon them.

Titus had already arranged for freight to be taken back to Hartigan. "You got to buy more wagons, Jeff."

The storekeeper also had an idea. "Paint all the wagons one color, red or blue or something that folks will recognize. It'll be your trademark."

"Good idea," Jeff said. "We can do that this winter."

Luke had done even better in Hartigan; he had made a deal with a merchant there to act as agent for them. Jeff was very pleased. The kid with no schooling and no trade was taking hold.

Luke and his crew finished one more trip to Hartigan and back before the rains came to make the roads impassable. The condition of the roads was going to be a big factor; there would be months each year when business had to be suspended.

But all in all, as Jeff figured his costs, he had turned a profit. Dud went over the figures as rain pattered on the roofs at home, and could find no fault with them. So far the freight line was a success.

During the winter Jeff and the others painted all the wagons a rust red. Jeff had been partial to sky-blue, but the only paint merchant in Pommer had but a few cans of blue. However, he had a storeroom of red and gave Jeff a good buy.

He also painted his name on each wagon: BECKET FREIGHT COMPANY.

Chapter Sixteen

Dᴜʀɪɴɢ the winter Angus Porter went over each wagon carefully, replacing fittings and a few iron tires. The roads had been hard on the wagons.

Angus, like Dudley, was doing a good business from travelers. He replaced horseshoes and mule shoes, mended saddles and pack trees and pots, even repaired rifles and small arms, sharpened saws and knives. . . .

Fred Caine had finished his stone house and sold the old log house to Bert Yellen, another new settler. Fred had three rooms in his new home, the same as the Beckets'. But building the house had taken much out of him. That winter he spent much time sitting by the fire, sipping hot toddies.

On sunny days he came out and glowered at Jeff's red wagons, five of them sitting in a row behind the corrals. Jeff was bound to go bust, he told Dud. He was trying to do too much, too fast. Dud did not argue with him. Arguing with Fred was like shouting at the wind to stop.

Jeff turned his old log house into a stable that winter. He removed the board floor and built in stalls and cribs for fodder. He had bought one of the newfangled windmills from Titus and Angus installed it. The squeaking sound of its moving parts was soon as familiar as Angus's hammer.

It was a long, wet winter and the spring runoff brought trouble. The creek rose very high, and roiling waters swept away the bridge. The roadway was smashed to matchsticks and all of it was tossed up on a muddy curve a mile downstream.

Dud was disgusted. They would have to do it all over again. "But this time we'll build it higher."

The power of storm water was awesome. One of the long, stout logs was split more than half its length, good now for nothing but firewood. The other was intact and was dragged back to await winter's ice.

The numbers of travelers decreased that year. Most crossed at the ford, ten miles upstream, and never came near them. Dud did not lose money, but he did not make any either.

When spring came and the mud was dried, the red wagons rolled into Pommer again. Titus had loads ready, and Luke took all five wagons on to Hartigan. Jeff returned home with a pony for Roy.

The boy could hardly believe his eyes—a pony of his very own! He wanted to sleep in the stable beside his new possession, but Rachel would not allow it.

Roy quickly learned to care for the horse and to saddle it himself; it was difficult to get him off the animal. Jason Porter took him into the fields to help keep the cattle in bounds—until Rachel found out. She raised a terrible fuss, mentioning Indians and scalps. Jason assured her he had never seen an Indian anywhere near, but she was unconvinced.

When Jeff was told, he sided with Roy. It was impossible to guard a child against every ill; the boy had to grow up to face danger, not to flee from it or hide from it. Besides, the Comanches were poorly because of the cholera. They were staying in their lodges. Let the boy ride in the fields.

But he took Roy aside. "You head for home as fast as your pony will run at the first sign of an Indian! You hear me?"

"Yeah, Pa."

"Keep your eyes open."

Roy nodded. "Can I have a gun?"

"When you're ten."

Jason was soon wanted at home to learn the blacksmith trade at his father's forge. So Jeff hired Bert Yellen to ride with the cattle. The herd was increasing. Jeff drove a dozen cattle into Pommer but got very little for them. It was hardly worth it, he said to Titus.

"Stick with the freight line," Titus advised "What you want with a lot of cattle anyway?"

The way to make money, Titus said, was to build a road to California, and charge tolls. Everybody and his cousin Jedediah was on his way to the gold fields, according to the papers. They were streaming across country in wagons and carts, even on foot, and sailing around the Horn of South America. Nothing could stop them. Hell, gold must be a foot deep out there!

"Lookit this!" Titus said, holding up a thin book. "They printing guidebooks. This's called 'The Emigrant's Guide to California: The Digger's Hand-Book.' It's got routes and instructions how to dig the gold and what t'do with it, living expenses, maps, and so on."

Jeff looked at the book as Titus continued. "It's all a flimflam. You mark my words, not one in a thousand'll make his beans."

Jeff said, "There's pictures of gold." He showed the illustration to the other.

"That's a drawing, not a photograph!"

"Hmmm." Jeff put the book down.

There was also news about slavery. Southerners were saying a man had a right to move anywhere he wanted and take his possessions with him. It sounded like a just argument.

Only they mentioned that slaves were possessions also.

"*That's* the thing going to cause trouble," Titus said darkly. "It's the one thing that could split this here country wide open!"

Many newspaper writers thought so, too. If a thing was legal in one part of the land, why was it not legal in another? It was a tangle, a snarl that would not soon be unraveled, they warned. Would it eventually come to a great division of the nation?

Jeff bought two more wagons and sent them, loaded, to Chandler. When Luke returned from Hartigan, he packed up and went right back. He was getting to know every tree and rock along the way by its first name, he said.

He was also certain he could profitably haul to Bowers, fifty miles farther on.

Mindful that someone else could start his own freight line, Jeff said, "Then do it . . . if you can go loaded both ways."

The nearest town south of the creek was Norton, reached only by a trace. That fall Jeff sent John Bowman there with two wagons, one driven by a man from Pommer, Zeke Bates.

The road was poor as hell, Bowman said when he returned, but passable. He had charged a little extra over their regular rates because of the conditions. Before the weather halted them, Jeff sent Bowman to Chandler in charge of four wagons.

It was a good year.

Late in the fall Jeff bought a mud wagon and had it painted red. It would haul passengers and some small items back and forth from Chandler on a regular schedule, beginning in the spring.

Pommer had almost doubled in size in two years, and just after Christmas a deputy sheriff was assigned to the town. So now there was law. A circuit judge would include Pommer in his rounds.

Civilization was creeping upon them.

Since the matter of the Jape Hickson shooting never had been raised again, it was as if he had never been. Simon Caine came to Pommer usually once a month, but he did not frequent that particular saloon. In any event Rose, the saloon girl, had packed her carpetbag and gone long since.

When winter came again, Fred Caine was ailing. Dud went to see him frequently—because no one else did. He said to Jeff that the man looked pale and weak, nothing like his old self. There were times, Dud said, that Fred would not recognize him.

"He drinks his hot toddies all day long and is drunk by nightfall."

"Maybe that's the best thing for him."

"And Louise can do nothing about it."

Simon also had no idea what could be done.

Dud thought Fred was not going to last. "I'll be surprised if he sees the spring."

"What's wrong with him?"

"I don't know. But he's certainly sliding downhill in a hurry."

Jeff scratched his chin. "And there's no doctor within a hundred miles."

Dud sighed. "I suspect it's too late for a doctor." He gazed out across the creek. "We're going to have to make another decision."

"What do you mean?"

"Where will we put the town cemetery? Over there across the stream?"

"I guess so. . . ."

Two weeks later, Fred died in his sleep.

Simon came to tell them and Dud went at once to the house, finding Louise in tears, unable to do anything but wring her hands. Simon stood by stonily, and Dud came away shaking his head.

He and Jeff walked across the creek ice to the far side. The week before they had hauled logs from the forest and laid them on the ice to await the spring thaw. Then they would build a new roadway. Now they had to decide on a piece of ground to stake; they would call it the cemetery.

They agreed on a slope of gentle hill and paced off a section several hundred yards square. Dud took Simon there later and watched him set to work with a pick and shovel.

The ground was hard, and it took Simon three days to finish the grave. And when it was done they brought the body to the site and lowered it carefully. A cool wind blew from the north, rustling the grass as Dud read passages from the Bible. . . .

Fred's death put a damper on everyone for a week or so. He had not been generally loved, but he had been one of them, and the oldest. His advice was seldom if ever sought because it tended to be predictable. Fred had been consistent in that he had always been against anything new or different. But he had been one of them.

Louise stayed in bed for days, with Rachel, Leah, and Hester looking in on her—Simon was useless in that regard. She finally got up to totter around, moaning that she did not know what would become of her. . . .

Simon seemed hardly touched by his father's passing.

In spring the freight line moved again, rolling to Pommer with Luke Tilley and John Bowman as whips. Jeff rode along on a sorrel. The bay was getting on and he'd turned it out to a well-earned pasture.

In Pommer, Titus told them his cousin, Nate Bowen, had gone out to California to scoop up some of the gold that cluttered the earth. Nate was unmarried and had attached himself to a party of emigrants heading west across the country. He promised to write as soon as he got there.

There was news: the hero of the Mexican War, Zack Taylor, was now president. His men called him "Old Rough and Ready," according to the newspapers.

Titus shook his head. "It's a terrible mistake, electing a general. What the hell does he know about running a whole country?"

Jeff sat by the cold belly stove and unfolded a newspaper. "It says here that they're goin' to make California a state."

Titus grunted. "Well, we took Texas and New Mexico away from the Mexicans. Why not grab California? Hell, I wouldn't be surprised if they attack all of Mexico."

"What we want with all that land?"

"That's what I say. California's a million miles away across the goddamn Rockies. What we going to do with all that desert in between?"

Jeff chuckled. "Let the Indians have it."

"And that's another thing! The goddamn country between here'n California is full of Indians and buffalo! It ain't any use to anybody and never will be. Why the hell them politicians want to make a state out of California? Sometime I think they ain't a grain of sense in Congress. Not a goddamn grain!"

On Titus's recommendation Jeff hired a man named Amos Mitchell to drive the mud wagon to haul passengers. They worked out a schedule between them; the wagon would run between Pommer and Chandler only. It was an easy route on flat ground, a trip that usually took fifteen hours. It would be better with a way station, but that refinement was for the future.

Jeff had some signs painted. The wagon would pick up passengers in front of the general store and stop at the store in Chandler.

It was not a success.

After the first month Jeff totted up the figures. The passenger run was barely breaking even, not showing a profit. There simply was not enough passenger traffic between the two towns to justify the service. The mud wagon, after a month, needed extensive repairs. Any vehicle without springs, on rutted roads, tended to shake itself apart.

He sold the wagon and transferred Amos to drive one of the trap wagons.

On his last trip to Bowers, north of Hartigan, Luke Tilley had reported trouble. Several toughs had approached the wagon trail from two sides, yelling at Luke to halt. But Luke and two other drivers had drawn pepperboxes and fired, dropping one of the three would-be robbers. The others had galloped off when Henry Mills stood and emptied the shotgun at them.

"You can bet they'll be layin' for us, Jeff," Luke said. "They can do us a power of harm."

"I'll go back with you next trip. We'll see."

The next trip was nine days away. Luke loaded four wagons in Pommer and started north with Henry Mills driving one, Zeke Bates another, and Amos Mitchell in the trap. Jeff scouted ahead of them on the sorrel, the old Hawken across his thighs. Titus had told him that no one had seen an Indian in the area for months. Maybe the Indian trouble was giving way to the highwayman problem. Of the two he might prefer the Indians.

They delivered goods in Hartigan and left Henry and one wagon there, heading out toward Bowers in the early morning. They reached the town without incident about nightfall of the next day. Luke made the deliveries in the morning and picked up crates and various freight bound for the south.

Jeff wandered through several saloons, asking questions. He knew most of the bartenders and learned that a tough named Troy had been badly shot up by Luke's men and was not expected to last. And Troy's friends had been making threats against the Becket Line. A barman knew them only as Jock and Andy. He told Jeff, "They mean as catamounts. You watch your back."

The men were apparently not in town, but when the wagons moved out on the road back to Hartigan, two figures appeared on a ridge far to their right. So they had been watched. Jeff saw the riders at once and pointed them out.

He rode toward the two horsemen then reined in, lifted the Hawken, and fired. Both riders turned away, disappearing behind the ridge.

Reloading the rifle, Jeff paralleled the wagons. The two really had an advantage, depending on how smart they were. A wagon train pulled by mules or oxen was very vulnerable. One shot could halt them; he would have to try to keep the outlaws at long range.

An hour slipped by, then two shots came from the right. One hit a wagon, the other plowed dirt forty feet away. Jeff fired instantly at the smoke. Then he turned back to the road and spurred the sorrel, galloping to his left. The two men had separated—he was positive. One shot had hit a wagon and the other had missed by about forty feet. Probably one man had fired both rifles as fast as he could handle them.

Suddenly Jeff saw a burly, black-haired man on a gray horse, who was leaning far over the animal's mane on a dead run toward the wagons, a pistol in each hand. He glimpsed Jeff and swerved in surprise as Jeff fired at him, four quick shots.

The highwayman dropped one pistol, fired into the ground, and slid off the saddle into the brush. The gray ran off into the trees.

Dismounting, Jeff pushed at the other with his boot toe. There was blood all over the man's shirt front. He had been hit twice, once through the neck and once in the side; he was very dead.

Jeff sighed and took a long breath. He stared down at the highwayman and reloaded the pepperbox, shoving it in his belt. What a foolish way to die.

Picking up both pistols, he mounted and rode to the wagons and dropped the guns in the nearest vehicle. Luke said, "You got one?"

Jeff nodded. He left the road and ranged far to the right, but saw no one. Maybe the second man was less adventurous. He followed the wagons, looking at every rock and tree.

They made camp that evening far from timber and posted guards, but the night passed serenely. However, at first light a shot slammed into one of the wagons from long range. Jeff raced toward the spot on the sorrel but found no one. It had been a parting shot. The last tough evidently had decided not to push his luck.

Chapter Seventeen

THE slavery question had apparently been settled.

Dud Hurley was very interested in it—all politics interested him. He read everything the newspapers had to say and questioned travelers. Henry Clay, called the Great Pacificator, with wonderful eloquence urged the necessity of mutual compromise and forbearance, and was seconded by, of all people, Daniel Webster.

Clay's compromise, or Omnibus Bill, was finally adopted by Congress; only the Free Soil Party spoke against it. It seemed to settle the question for all time.

Dud said, "They ought to elect a man like Henry Clay to be president—instead of these puddingheads like Fillmore."

General Taylor had died soon after taking office and Millard Fillmore, Vice President, had stepped up to the high office.

When Jeff talked politics with Titus, the grocer agreed with Dud. He said, "We ought to have men like Clay or Calhoun or Webster as presidents, but they're too strong-minded for the party hacks."

"Where'd this man Fillmore come from?"

Titus made a face. "The papers say he was a congressman and held some office or other in New York when he ran with Taylor."

"Well, I'm glad the slavery thing is done with."

"It ain't done with," Titus said, growling. "You mark my words, that Fugitive Slave Law is gonna make trouble."

And Titus was right. When owners attempted to arrest their runaway slaves in the North, riots broke out and rescues were made, and several northern states passed laws to protect the runaways and prevent their being sent back.

Dud shook his head. "They have to settle this thing. It's never going to go away. They're tying it together with spit and string but it won't hold."

Jeff said, "What's the answer?"

"Get rid of slavery."

"How can you do that?"

"I don't know, but it has to be done. Some people think there ought to be two countries, north and south. One with slaves and one without."

Jeff said, "That won't work. I read in the papers that some say the slaves ought to be sent back to Africa."

"That's not right either. They're not cabbages or bales of cotton—they're people. To most of them Africa would be a strange land. It's a shame slaves were allowed here in the first place."

In the summer another family settled at Eden Creek, a man and his wife, Frank and Elinor Locke. They had a wagon with household effects; they put up a tent and Frank staked land and turned the soil with his plow.

Dud quickly discovered that Elinor Locke had been a teacher. He was delighted and set about organizing classes. They would pay her in barter for teaching the children—or anyone who wanted to learn. Dud even pushed the men into discussing plans for a single-room schoolhouse.

"We can use it for town meetings in the evenings."

"We ain't a town," someone said.

"We will be," Dud assured him.

Elinor had a few books, Dud had a few more, and they could always send away for what they needed. It took forever for anything to arrive from the East, but eventually it did.

She had five students, all very young. Jason Porter was the oldest, at fourteen, and not much interested, but his father insisted. Roy was seven now and eager to learn. He already knew how to read and figure, and looked forward to riding with his father on the freighting trips.

The winter before they had replaced the bridge, and several families settled across the creek. That was the year that Isaac Closs and his wife came to settle. Isaac was a big, burly man with huge arms and curly dark hair. He had come to talk to them, looking like a big friendly bear.

"Want to build me a sawmill. Y'all got any objections?"

"A sawmill!" Dud said. "Welcome, welcome!"

"Figger I can harness this here creek. Mr. Titus over in Pommer said—"

Jeff shook the man's hand. "Jerry Titus is a friend of ours. We need you, Mr. Closs."

Dud asked, "Have you got the equipment to put up a mill?"

"It's all in the wagon."

"Then what can we do to help you?"

"Tell me where I can squat." Closs pointed. "Like to go down there by the trees. . . ."

"That's where you go then," Dud said.

Simon Caine worked the fields, plowing, sowing and reaping. Then he hauled crops into Pommer as his father had, but he never seemed to get ahead. Fred Caine had left almost nothing behind, a few dollars and not much else. Simon was going on twenty-five with no prospects but the plow.

Jeff Becket, on the other hand, was pulling in money from his freighting line and from his crops.

It wasn't fair . . . and there was not a thing Simon could do about it. There was no way *he* could start a freight line. And he had no money to hire anyone to help with the plowing.

When Simon did receive hard money, usually from Titus in Pommer from the sale of corn or other crops, he kept it to himself. It was his money, not his mother's. He saw to it she was taken care of, but he told her nothing of what he did or thought. They were strangers living in the same house.

He told her nothing because he spent a good deal of his money on saloon girls. He knew every whore girl in Pommer and he even bought some of them presents. When he came into the saloon, they were all smiles.

But he went home alone. Jeff Becket had a wife to go home to.

Simon enjoyed a certain notoriety in town because of the shooting of Jape Hickson, who had been a bully. Simon always wore a pistol and he had already proved he would not hesitate to use it. There was a deputy sheriff assigned to Pommer now, a man named Paul Trask. Trask had heard the story, but the shooting had taken place a long time before he'd arrived. Only a damn fool went looking for trouble, and he had his hands full on weekends as it was, without poking around for more. There were few forms of entertainment in a little two-bit burg like Pommer, and drinking was one of them. The jail cell was always full on Mondays, when Trask emptied it. Simon drank very little when he came to town, so he barely had a nodding acquaintance with the deputy.

Simon was sitting in the Alamo Saloon late one afternoon, sipping a beer, waiting for one of the girls, when he saw Jerry Titus cross the street to the barbershop.

It started him thinking. Titus had two clerks in the store now, to help out. He had enlarged the store twice and lived upstairs over it. There was no bank in town. What did he do with his money?

He must have a hell of a lot of money socked away by now. Where did he keep it?

Probably in the store. Where else? He must have a safe. He knew Titus had a small office where he did his accounts and paperwork, but he'd never been in it. The safe must be in there.

But if Titus had a safe, it was certainly locked at night. How did one get into a locked safe? Simon had no idea . . . except to force Titus to open it at gunpoint. And that would mean he'd have to get the hell out of the area fast—or kill Titus in the robbery.

Simon sighed deeply, watching the girl, Hetty, come down the stairs. Titus's safe might as well be on the moon. He waved to the girl and she smiled and walked to his table.

Indians were not active anywhere in this part of the country, Titus told Jeff. "Not accordin' to the army. They was a patrol through here last week. It ain't Indians, it's whites."

"What d'you mean?"

"Army lootinant said they's a man named Marty Webb—you ever hear of him?"

"No."

"Well, neither did I. Anyways, he's got a gang together and they raidin' folks that lives out by theirselves, like y'all do."

"Is the army doing anything about it?"

"They patrollin'. Guess that's all they can do. If I's you, I'd put some guards on your wagon trains."

It was good advice. Jeff tacked up a handwritten poster in front of the store asking for shotgun guards, offering to pay a dollar a day, "You furnish your own shotgun and pistols."

There were a dozen applicants. He and Titus weeded them out and Jeff hired one man for each wagon. The drivers were armed as well, so that four wagons meant eight well-armed men, enough to cause a raiding party trouble.

But the summer passed in peace.

The wagons were hauling to Norton, seventy miles south of Eden Creek, and each wagon boss, arriving there, was asked to haul farther on to Winship, some thirty miles south of Norton.

Jeff went along on the first trip. The road was fair and well marked and the trip was successful. Winship proved to be a larger town than Norton. The merchants clamored for such items as crockery and women's frills. Twenty wagons filled with those articles would not be enough, they told Jeff.

He was also hauling an occasional passenger—when there was room. Each was asked to come armed and ready to lend his weapon to repel bandits. Jeff discussed the idea of buying another mud wagon or even a Concord to establish the stage line again. He discussed it with Titus and with Dud; both advised against it—for the time being. Dud was deep in paperwork and falling behind. Rachel helped out, but it was obvious that a full-time accountant was needed.

Jeff put up a poster at Titus's store: ACCOUNTANT WANTED. The poster gathered dust for more than a week before young Sam Harris asked Titus about the job. Titus sent him to Eden Creek.

Sam was slim and blondish, with an open, round face and ready smile. He had been through the eighth grade in Ohio, was excellent at arithmetic, and was certain he could handle the job. He was twenty-two, unmarried, and had come west, drawn by the national restlessness. His money had about run out, however, and he needed to go to work.

Dud showed him the books, such as they were, and outlined his system, which Sam saw in a moment was very primitive. Dud was not an accountant by any stretch of the imagination.

Sam spent several hours with the books and papers, then went to see Jeff. "You're not making the best use of what you have. You should rent an office in Pommer and run the business from there. Trying to run it from here is not sensible or profitable. You need an office, a freight yard with repair sheds and corrals. . . ."

Jeff was annoyed at this newcomer's ready assessment. "You spent a couple of hours looking at the books and now you figger to change ever'thing?"

"Not so much change it, Mr. Becket, as make it more efficient."

"Call me Jeff. What's wrong with our efficiency?"

"Mostly it's scattered. The first thing: You've got no place where people can do business with you."

"Jerry Titus is our agent in—"

"That's not enough. Mr. Titus does fine, for what he does. But he's got his own business to run. So far you're depending on repeat business, and doing well that way, I must say. But you could probably double the business in a year and—"

"That's all guesswork."

"Of course it is. I don't know the future any better than anyone else. But I can see prospects. Also, I've seen freight companies in the East."

Jeff sighed. "You want to spend a lot of money."

"Yes, I admit it. But it'll come back to you. I would get an office, a freight yard with a crew to keep wagons in repair, and a baggage room. Right now you've got three wagons waiting on your blacksmith in Eden Creek. Those wagons aren't bringing in a penny while they sit there."

"If the blacksmith was in Pommer could he do any better?"

Sam grinned. "Yes he could. Because I'd be on his tail and he'd be doing nothing but work on the wagons. As it is, your blacksmith is doing work for a dozen others."

Jeff rolled a cheroot in his fingers. Young Sam had a lot of answers, didn't he? But pretty good ones, he had to admit. They were standing near the corrals, behind the barn. He walked away and paused to light the cigar, looking back at the boy. Sam leaned on the top rail, waiting. So far the freight line was paying. He could afford to do as Sam suggested—and he had a suspicion the boy was right. He made up his mind.

He walked back and stood in front of Sam. "All right, I'm listening. What else do you want?"

Sam nodded. "With all due respect, Jeff, you can't be everywhere at once. And I have a feeling you're not worth a damn in an office. But you're worth a dozen men outside it. So what I want is for you to appoint me general manager. I'll run the freight line from an office in Pommer and you be the troubleshooter. You go where you're needed and I'll report to you as often as you like."

Jeff smiled. "How do I know you won't up and skeddadle when things get snarled?"

"Because I won't. If I ever have to leave on my own, I'll give you plenty of notice."

"That's good enough. All right. We'll ride to Pommer in the morning. From now on, you're general manager."

Chapter Eighteen

RACHEL was astonished. "You made that boy general manager?"

"As of this afternoon, yes."

She stared at him as if he had gone mad. "How old is he?

"He said he was twenty-two."

"Jeff, for goodness' sake! Does he have any experience?"

He smiled at her. "I doubt it. But he's damn well going to acquire it in a hurry. I'm buying his brains and guts."

"But he's so young!"

"He's older than I was when I had brains enough to marry you."

She laughed and kissed him. "But he's not *you*."

"I don't expect him to be. He's got good ideas and he'll take the paperwork from Dud. We're going to Pommer in the morning and he'll run things from there. I'll try to be back tomorrow afternoon."

"Have you told Dudley about this?"

"No, I'm going to see him now. But I predict he'll approve."

She shook her head. "You know Dud would never go against you."

"He has a right to his opinions. I listen to 'em."

Jeff was right. Dud did approve of the decision. "Pommer's a central point, and there's stores and materials there. Sam Harris is correct. You need an office where people can come to do business. You've gotten along so far with a lot of luck. But you've outgrown it. Now you need to get down to cases."

"We'll start changing things tomorrow."

"Good." Dud clapped him on the back. "I want my one-third interest to be in good hands. Of course after we get to be a town here, you can move the offices."

Jeff nodded. "That's awhile in the future yet."

"Sam boxed up all the books and papers. He says you're both going to Pommer. Are you going to be able to let him run things?"

"He's general manager."

"That's not what I asked you."

Jeff chuckled. "I'll let him run the whole shebang—until I think he's wrong. Then we'll talk."

"Privately."

"Yes. If he convinces me he's right, I'll back off."

"I hope so. Give the boy a chance."

"I intend to."

They left at sunup. Sam drove a light wagon with the boxes of records in the back; Jeff rode the sorrel with the Hawken in the boot.

They met no one and were in Pommer long before midday.

Sam wanted to find a place on the edge of town. "We'll need room to spread out," he said. "This company is going to grow."

There was a barn on the main road with some sagging fences around it. There had been a house near it, but only the sketchy foundation remained. Sam reined in, looking it over. "Who owns that?"

"Titus will know."

"That old barn?" Titus said. "Billy Bonnet built it five years ago. Had a house but it burned down. Y'all innerested in it?"

Sam said, "It could be just what we're looking for."

"Then you go see Miz Bonnet. She lives with her daughter now. Billy up and died." He gave them directions.

Mrs. Bonnet was interested in selling. She had no use for the land. She was in her seventies, she told them. Billy had had a small herd of dairy cows when he was alive and sold the milk in town.

Jeff and Sam talked with her, then rode to the property and looked it over again. It was all level land, with plenty of room for another building or two and shops. Jeff examined the barn critically. It needed only minor repairs.

"This will do fine," Sam said. He walked over the ground, pointing. "We'll use the barn as is and build here on the street, some offices, a baggage room, and a waiting room."

"A waiting room?"

"Yes. We'll use it for storage until we need it as a waiting room. We'll be in the stage business before long, Jeff. Another year or so. We should plan for it."

Jeff nodded, smiling.

"We'll put the repair sheds along here and the corrals there behind the barn. We can tear out the stalls in the barn and use it to store fodder—and we'll need a well."

"So you're satisfied with this?"

"You bet." Sam grinned. "You want me to talk to Miz Bonnet?"

"No. You go see Titus. He'll know where you can find a carpenter. I'll talk to Miz Bonnet."

Jerry Titus did. He recommended a man named George Stackpole. "He's the one enlarged this-here store, and he put up half the buildings in town. You know what you want?"

"Yes. Where'll I find Stackpole?"

"Don't you figger you ought to wait, see if Jeff's goin' to buy that land?"

"He'll buy it."

Titus grinned. "I think we's goin' to get along, young feller."

George Stackpole turned out to be a middle-aged man with reddish hair and a weathered face. He lived in a small, neat house with big, clumsy furniture. His wife sat in a corner, sewing busily, and said nothing at all. The room smelled of cooked food as Sam sat down at a table with the carpenter.

Stackpole said, "You got any plans, Mr. Harris?"

"Call me Sam. No, I haven't. But I don't want anything fancy." He drew lines on a piece of paper. "I want three offices, one large enough for four or five clerks and some cabinets. I want a good-sized baggage room, a small waiting room, and a porch, all in one building."

"Y'all don't haul no passengers now, do you?"

"No, not many, but we will one day. We won't need a heating stove in the waiting room for a while, but fix it so we can put one in."

"All right. Wood sidings and tar-paper roofs?"

"Yes." They discussed room sizes and the placement of doors and windows, and Stackpole marked them on the sketch. "Jeff Becket goin' to pay for this?"

"Is his credit good?"

"Like solid gold. He's a friend of Jerry Titus. Jerry is a nosy gossip but his word's good. Is there anything on that land now?"

"Only the barn, which you can repair. There's some old fences. I'll have them torn down." Sam got up and went to the door. "Hire what men you need. I'll see you in the morning."

Sam returned to the store to find Jeff had just arrived and was gabbing with Titus. He had completed the sale. They now owned five acres of land and an old barn.

* * *

Jerry Titus had a copy of a book which he said was sweeping the country. "Ever'body's readin' it! I asked for five copies and they sent me one. The damn book is sellin' like a Holy Bible signed by St. Peter hisself."

"What book is that?" Jeff asked.

"It's called *Uncle Tom's Cabin*."

"It doesn't sound very interesting."

"It's about how slaves live or something. I ain't read it yet."

Jeff laughed. "Why would folks care to read about how slaves live?"

"You damn fool, Jeff—it's agin slavery! That's the whole thing of it. Nobody gives a damn how slaves live—it's what happens to 'em."

"It it a true story?"

Titus shrugged. "I dunno. I'll read the book and tell you."

"Any other news?"

"Well, there's goin' to be a World's Fair in New York in a place called the Crystal Palace. Pretty fancy name, huh?"

"A World's Fair! I'd like to see that. . . ."

"The paper says . . . let's see, here it is. 'The fair's going to be about products and industries, like steam presses, power looms, sewing machines, steam shovels, and farm machinery.' "

"What's a steam press?"

"I ain't got any idea. But they got one. It must do something or they wouldn't invent it. Hell, they inventing so many damn things nowadays a man can't keep up with it."

Jeff frowned. "How would you fix a shovel to work by steam?"

"Jesus! They don't mean a little shovel you push with your foot." Titus pushed the paper in front of Jeff. "Here's a picture of one—it's a great big damn thing. Dig up half a ton at a time."

Jeff stared at the drawing. It was a big, curious-looking thing all right. He gave the paper back. They must have invented just about everything by now. What would it be like to attend a World's Fair? Rachel would love it. But it was half a world away; by the time they made the journey the fair would be over.

He left Sam in town and rode back to Eden Creek in the late afternoon. Roy saw him coming and rode out to meet him on the high-stepping pony.

"Hey Pa, you promised me a gun."

"That's right, I did."

"I'm ten now."

"All right. We'll pick one out at Dud's store."

Dud had a large collection of rifles and pistols, traded for from travelers and others. The rifles were standing in a row along one wall. Dud looked at Roy and selected a shortened rifle.

"This's a Starr that's been converted from flint. It's just about your size."

Roy handled the weapon, looking pleased. It was almost as tall as he. Dud also had a power horn and cap pouch to go with it. "You know how to load that gun, youngster?"

"Yessir, I know."

"Then it's yours."

Roy was delighted. He was eager to shoot the gun at once, so Jeff took him down along the creek, past the sawmill that big Isaac Closs was building. They halted where there was a high bank on the far side of the creek, a good hundred feet away.

They stepped down and Jeff said, "Load the rifle."

Roy did it deftly, looking as if he'd been doing it for years. He put a cap on the nipple and looked up at his father.

Jeff said, "The first rule is—you always want to know where your shot's going. That gun will shoot a mile, so you want to make sure you don't hit somebody's milk cow."

Roy nodded.

"You know how to use the sights?"

"Yessir, I know."

"All right." Jeff pointed. "You see that white rock embedded in the bank across the creek? Let's see you hit it."

Roy lifted the rifle, pulled the hammer back, and sighted. When he fired a chip flew off the rock. He grinned at his father.

Jeff grunted and mounted the sorrel. "I guess you know what I was goin' to show you."

"Well, Jason and I been practicin' with his rifle."

"Get on your horse. Let's go have supper."

It was a nuisance to have to ride all the way to Pommer for a girl. Simon swore every time he made the trip. He had to manufacture excuses or simply disappear for a day. Just making the ride took up at least six hours and each time he returned he told himself it wasn't really worth it. He was also sure that some of the hangers-on in the saloons were making fun of him behind his back.

Jerry Titus always gave him odd looks when he appeared, but said nothing. Titus knew what he was about. Sooner or later the storekeeper learned everything that happened in the town.

Simon never followed the road on the trip back to Eden, and one day he came across Hester Tilley gathering berries a long way from the house. Her husband, Luke, was out somewhere with one of Jeff Becket's wagon trains. She must be lonely. . . .

Simon got down and began talking to her. Yes, she was lonely, she said. Luke was away so much. But it was always nice when he came home. And they were getting on well now that he was working for Jeff. The job was like a godsend. Luke always brought her things—she had more clothes now than she'd ever had in her life.

She was a pretty thing, he thought. A little more plump than the saloon girls perhaps, but much younger. Hetty must be almost forty. Someone had told him that whore girls tended to drift farther west the older they got. The competition in the East was fierce.

Simon pushed Hester down in the grass. She was surprised at first, then alarmed—and fought him. But he overpowered her and swept her skirts up, ignoring her cries.

He was through with her quickly—much more quickly than with Hetty or one of the others. Of course they encouraged him and said things no respectable woman would utter—Hester only cried and whimpered, and when he was finished would not look at him.

"Don't tell nobody," Simon growled at her. "I don't want to hurt you."

She was sitting in the grass, head down, when he rode away.

Chapter Nineteen

GEORGE Stackpole proved to be a steady, hard worker. He first hired a man with a big brown mule and a heavy chained log to level the five acres around the barn. After clearing it of debris and fences he worked a half day with the log and a pan of water as a level.

George ordered board lumber, tar paper, nails, and windows. Titus had the tar paper and nails, but the rest came from Hartigan and took a week.

When the lumber arrived, George organized a crew, four men in all, counting himself. By then he had excellent plans drawn, approved by Sam Harris, and in another week had the office building framed. It faced the street and stood in an L shape with the offices to the rear.

Sam was on the property each morning early, watching every nail being driven, conferring with George, planning as they built. The building looked different as a reality, not a drawing on a flat bit of paper. Sam decided he needed two more doors as the rooms took shape, and he also decided not to false-front the building.

Luke Tilley had interviewed a blacksmith who lived in Bowers. After a letter from Sam, the man agreed to come to Pommer with his family and equipment; it took two wagons to carry his things. The blacksmith laid out his shop on paper for George, and two other shops were constructed in a line with it, facing the yard.

The carpenters were repairing the inside of the barn with two painters working outside when Jeff showed up from Eden Creek. He was astonished at the progress. A sign painter had delivered his work, a large board that would be placed over the baggage room: BECKET FREIGHT COMPANY.

Jeff shook with Sam. "I think I hired the right man."

Sam grinned. "We'll be in full operation here in less than a week."

They walked around the lot, with Jeff poking into everything. Sam also had other plans, he said. "Soon I want to build some way stations. One between here and Chandler and one between here and Hartigan.''

"You mean to change mules?"

"Yes. We'll have fresh mules in the corrals. But another reason: We can do away with the trap wagons when we get all the stations up. It'll save us salaries and we can sell the traps. The men can sleep in the stations.''

"But we have to pay somebody to run the way stations."

Sam nodded. "At the moment we have three traps running. When we expand we'll have more—and more maintenance. With all the stations up and operating we'll save on maintenance and mules. I'd like to hire men with wives to run the stations, so that when we start hauling passengers the women can operate restaurants for the travelers.''

"I see you've been thinking about this."

"Night and day."

"Do you want my approval?"

Sam grinned again. "Not necessarily. I'm the general manager.''

Jeff laughed. "What else do you have on your mind?"

"One other thing. I've written to the postmaster at Bowers, asking for a contract to deliver mail sacks from there to Hartigan, Pommer, Eden Creek, and Chandler. I'm waiting for a reply.''

"How do they deliver it now?"

"They send the mail sacks by anyone who happens to be going that way. Not very businesslike.''

"Jerry Titus has a mail basket in his store."

"Yes, I know. It's what started me thinking about it. Anyone can come in and rummage through the letters. I want to change that. If we get the contract, people will come here to the baggage office and ask the clerk for their mail. The clerk will be the only one to handle it. I think people will appreciate that.''

"Who's the baggage man?"

Sam smiled. "At the moment, me."

Jeff, as usual, stopped to gab with Jerry Titus, who was excited at the progress Sam Harris was making. "That boy is a wonder! He'll set the goddamn world afire, you mark my words!''

"Well, I hope not."

"You know what I mean . . . he's a go-getter! He'll put this town on the map!''

"Have you read that book yet?"

"*Uncle Tom's Cabin?* You bet. Hard to put down. The paper

says it sold half a million copies! Can you 'magine that? Stirred up a hornet's nest, too. It's got folks mutterin' about slavery . . . and Henry Clay, Calhoun, and Webster dead.''

"Others'll take their places.''

"Yeah, they toutin' a feller named Jefferson Davis as a comer. By the way, I got a new gun for you.''

"What is it?''

Titus went into his office and came back with a cardboard box. "Had it hid away. It's the new Colt revolver. They call it the Navy.'' He opened the box and handed it over. "Ain't that a gun, Jeff!''

"Jesus! What a beauty!'' Jeff handled it lovingly. It was brass-mounted with an octagon barrel; the cylinder had a ship scene etched on it. It was a six-shot pistol with an attached rammer. It felt like no other gun he had ever held in his hand.

Titus said, "It's thirty-six caliber, shoot two hunnerd yards as good as a rifle. I got a dozen on order. Don't that hannel good though?''

"It's perfect. Old Sam Colt did himself proud. This's for me?''

"It's yours.'' Titus showed him how the wedge came out to remove the cylinder. "If you got another one loaded, you can just quick-change cylinders. Then all you got to do is replace the caps and you're in business again. It's the latest thing in guns.''

Jeff took the wedge out and replaced it.

Titus pointed. "The best thing is every Navy pistol is inter-changeable. That cylinder will fit every Navy made. Ain't that amazing?''

"It sure for certain is. You got molds and caps . . . ?''

"Of course.''

Jeff loaded and capped the Navy, feeling like a boy with a new toy. His two pepperboxes were in holsters on the sorrel horse, but this one he would carry with him, in his belt. This one was some-thing special.

They went back and sat near the belly stove. Titus said, "Bad news. That feller, Marty Webb, remember I mentioned him? Well, he shot up and robbed a bunch twenty, thirty miles over west last week. Hope he ain't comin' this way.''

"How many he got with him?''

"Nobody said.''

"He won't raid into a town, will he?''

Titus made a face. "I wouldn't think so, but how can you figger Indians and outlaws?''

* * *

Nate Bowen returned from the gold fields in California. He was thinner; his face was lined and he moved like an old man, saying he was tired to death. He took a room in the only hotel and slept for a day and a half.

When he went back to Titus's store after a good meal he was beginning to feel like his old self, he told them. He was glad to get back. The gold fields were a sham. Not one man in a hundred made enough to keep him in beans. Most were broke, scrabbling to stay alive, and prices were out of sight. "It cost a dollar just to mail a goddamn letter!"

"Ain't there no gold there at all?"

"Oh, there's gold. But poor folks like me, we have to pan it or sluice it and they's no work that's harder. There's no law in most towns and the vigilantes run the camps. They ain't but one thing a man can depend on."

"What's that?" Titus asked.

"That pretty soon he's goin' to be hungry again."

"So you got out."

Nate nodded. "I come back acrost the plains, worse off than when I went. But I was lucky on the way. I got with a group that knowed the way to go. There's some folks, they told me, got caught in dry sections where they's no water for a hunnerd miles. Lots of 'em didn't make it across and some cut off their mule's ears to drink the blood."

"Jesus!" Titus said. "I told you, that land ain't worth a damn. Never will be."

"Well, anyways, the Rush is over," Nate went on. "Most of the streams're played out and folks are turnin' to farming. If I'd had any money I'd have bought some land. Damn good-lookin' land in California."

"Well, are you glad you did it?"

"Hell, no. I'd have been better off stayin' here. It was hard getting there and worse coming home. All's I want now is a nice easy job so's I can rest for about a year."

Titus said, "You good at figgerin', if I remember."

"I was an accountant."

"Well, you go and see Sam Harris. He might have something for you."

"Who's Sam Harris?"

"He's Jeff Becket's freight manager. He got an office down at the end of town. Y'all tell 'im I sent you."

"All right."

* * *

Sam looked him over and sat him down in the office. It smelled of new lumber, paint, and tobacco. There was a large map of the area on the wall and nothing else. Sam was a young man with a scrubbed face and an earnest manner.

"You're a friend of Jerry Titus?"

"He's my cousin."

"You know what we do here, Mr. Bowen. What can you do for us?"

"Well, I'm not worth a shake at drivin' mules, but I know figures. You got to keep accounts."

"Yes, we do." Sam gazed at the other. Nate Bowen looked down on his luck. But Jerry Titus was a good recommendation. He said, "I need a man to be in charge of handling freight—coming in and going out. The system we've got now is poor. It just grew out of nothing. It has to be made more efficient. Do you think you can handle that?"

"I think so. I worked in a freighting company years ago in the East."

"Oh yes?" Sam rose. "Come with me, if you will." He led the way into the baggage room. "Over there's a desk and some paper. Show me what you can do for us, Nate."

When Luke Tilley returned to Eden Creek he had three days at home before he had to go out again. He was disturbed to find Hester very subdued, as if something were weighing her down. He noticed it instantly. She was usually happy to see him but now, though she hugged and kissed him, there was something holding her back. Maybe she was pregnant; but when he mentioned it, she said no, she was not.

She was anything but her usual cheerful self, yet she denied there was anything wrong. He decided not to press her.

That night long after they'd gone to bed, he woke to find her weeping. He tried to comfort her, holding her tightly, and finally she slept. But in the morning she could not say why she had wept.

As the time came close when he had to leave, she was increasingly nervous and upset, not wanting him to go. She clung to him, begging him to stay.

"But I have to go. Jeff's dependin' on me."

He had to tear himself away, and he saw Jeff before he went on to Pommer. "Hester's takin' on about something."

"What's wrong?"

"I don't know. She won't tell me or talk about it, whatever it is. Maybe you could ast Rachel to look in on her now'n then."

"Is she pregnant?"

"That's the first thing I thought of, too, but she says no. She's usual happy. I never seen her this way."

"All right. I'll talk to Rachel."

"Thanks, Jeff."

When Luke arrived in Pommer, Sam sent him and five wagons to Hartigan.

Sam was trying to work out a schedule; regular routes instead of the hit-and-miss trips they were making. He was not at all sure they could stick to schedules, but if they were possible the freight line would be more businesslike, because then people could depend on their goods arriving and departing at specified times.

He received the mail contract he'd been angling for. It required him to pick up mail twice a week in Bowers. The contract did not specify how the mail was to be picked up, so now and then he had to send a horseman for it, rather than wait for a wagon train. But in general it was an easy contract to fulfill.

All the buildings and corrals in Pommer were finished and painted and in operation. Nate Bowen had devised a very good system for receiving, marking, and sending out baggage. It required a form to be filled out by the sender, part of which was attached to the baggage, part kept, and part given to the sender.

The system put Nate in charge of the baggage room and gave Sam more time for other duties, including drumming up business. He had flyers printed giving prices and times, and these were distributed by his drivers in the towns they visited. The wagons seldom returned empty.

Sam found they were hauling more and more passengers, many in the trap wagons, people who for one reason or another preferred not to travel by horseback. They boarded far north in Bowers and often rode to Winship in the south where there was a connecting stage line. Others came the other way, from Winship to Bowers or towns in between. It was necessary to put another trap wagon in service for that trade alone.

At the end of three months Sam reported to Jeff that the business was showing a steady profit, and that the amount spent on new buildings, land, and equipment would soon be behind them.

There was another unexpected consequence of the freighting business which Sam took quick advantage of. His drivers and guards constantly reported local news to him, from the towns they served. Sam had these items written out and posted on a bulletin board which people in Pommer could read at leisure.

The idea was very popular from the start. It was surprising how settlers wanted to know about their neighbors. It engendered much goodwill for the company.

One of these items concerned a man in Chandler named Robert McCoy. He wished to purchase one hundred head of beef cattle. When Jeff heard about it, he sent the man a note in care of Amos Mitchell.

On his return wagon trip, Amos reported McCoy would take one hundred head as a minimum and would pay four dollars each in Chandler.

"That's four hundred dollars!" Rachel exclaimed. "Can you drive cattle from here to there?"

Jeff shrugged. "I don't know why not."

She was sitting by the fireplace and stopped sewing. "Why does he want cattle?"

"I don't know. I'll find out when I see him." Jeff grinned at her. "Cows may pay off at that."

"It's an awful lot of money! Will you and Bert Yellen be able to drive them alone?"

"I'll take Roy along too, and probably someone else. Roy's big enough now to do a job of work."

"He practically sleeps with that rifle, you know."

Jeff chuckled. "So did I, with my first one, when I was his age."

After supper, when Roy and Lili were outside, he asked, "What about Hester? Is she all right?"

"No, she isn't." Rachel combed her dark hair with her fingers. "But I can't find out what's troubling her. She won't talk about it."

"Did she get bad news from home?"

"I asked her that and she shook her head. I don't think she has anyone to write to her. But something is definitely chewing at her. Leah's tried to talk to her too, but so far . . ." Rachel gave a little head shake. In a moment she said, "When are you going to start driving those cows?"

"In a day or two. We have some cutting out to do to get ready to drive."

"How far is it?"

"About fifty mile, give or take a few, across country. We might be gone a couple of weeks. We'll take along some pack mules and come back through Pommer."

Chapter Twenty

Roy was ecstatic when his father told him he was to go along on the cattle drive. He tried to be casual about it, as if he did that sort of thing every month, but Jeff smiled at the gleam in the boy's eyes. Roy hurried to the corral at once to begin brushing down his pony, talking to him in a low voice.

Jeff said to Bert, "We'll take only steers, no cows or calves, so's we can move along at a better clip."

"You want to road-brand them?"

"Why don't we build a chute and slash-brand them as they go through? It'll save us a lot of trouble."

"All right. We going through Pommer?"

"No, let's hit across country. There's water. We shouldn't have any problems. . . ."

Bert nodded. "We'll need another man."

"You figger?"

"Yeah, somebody to look after the horses in the drag."

"You got somebody in mind?"

"Feller named Jonah Sanford. I figger he'll do. You want to see him? I'll have him help me with the chute."

"Fine."

Bert had cut out a hundred and ten steers, and when the chute was finished he and Jonah poked them through one at a time, stopping each with a wood bar long enough for the slash brand to be slapped on.

Jonah was a recent settler at Eden Creek. He was fortyish, lean, and tired-looking. His wagon had broken down when he'd reached the creek and he'd put up a tent and built a fire. He was unmarried and glad to get the job.

It was a cool, brisk morning when they started out. The sky was mottled but the clouds were thin and faded into nothingness as the sun warmed the land. The little herd strung out in the first hour, moving slowly, grazing as it went.

Jeff put Bert Yellen in front and himself and Roy in the middle. Bert ranged ahead of the drive, making sure they came to good grass and water. Jeff and Roy kept the cattle from straying, which proved to be an easy job. The land was prairie and they navigated by the sun and stars. If we miss Chandler, Jeff thought, we'll come to the road, then all we have to do is follow it to the town.

They bedded the herd down at night and, after consulting the North Star, Jeff drew a line in the earth. It would be easy to go off in the wrong direction in the morning.

On the third day they met two ragged-looking men. Both rode horses that were equally ragged with patched saddles and one with a rope hackamore instead of a bridle. They appeared to be as far down on their luck as it was possible to be and still remain alive.

One asked, "Where you going with them cows?"

Jeff said, "To Chandler."

"Where's that?"

Jeff asked, "Y'all lost?"

The other looked at the sky. "Well, we's headin' south. Hell of a lot of trouble in Kansas, you know."

"Kansas! That's a far piece from here."

"An' thank the good Lord f'that. You got any grub to spare?"

Jeff called a halt and they built a fire. The two were named Hank and Trumpy; they were cousins and neither had eaten for nearly two days. They had tried to farm in Kansas, they said, but a gang of men had driven them out.

"They called us slavers," Hank said. "We from the South, Alabama by name, but hell, we never owned no slaves. Don't know nobody who does."

"The damn gover'ment tryin' to make a state out of Kansas," Trumpy added. He had part of a newspaper printed in St. Louis. He unfolded it and showed it to Jeff. "Lookit what them Northerners is sayin'."

Jeff read the article. It was about the "coming struggle in Kansas." The Honorable William H. Seward of New York had said in the United States Senate: "Come on, then, gentlemen of the slave states, since there is no escaping your challenge. I accept it on behalf of freedom. We will engage in competition for the virgin soil of Kansas, and God give the victory to the side that is stronger in numbers as it is in right."

Jeff shook his head. "Those're pretty powerful words."

"They're sayin' more than that in Kansas. Mighty bloody place. We's damn lucky to be shut of it."

The two men had lost everything they owned; their house and

barn had been burned down and the crops trampled. They'd barely made it away with their lives. Kansas was afire from one end to the other. They were grateful to eat and accept a packet of food to see them through the next days.

When the two had gone, Roy asked, "Why were they called slavers when they didn't own slaves?"

"Because they came from the South."

"But we come from the South, don't we? I mean, Texas is a slave state."

Jeff said, "It looks to be comin' to that. If you're from the South you're in favor of slavery, and if you're from the North, you're against it. It don't make sense, but that's the way it is."

Roy said, "I've seen pictures of them but I've never seen a Negro in my whole life. Are all slaves black?"

"In this country they are. Not in other places, like Asia . . ."

"Mrs. Locke says it's wrong to own slaves."

Jeff smiled. "Well, I think so too. Now go get on your horse. We got work to do."

Simon Cane rode slowly past the Tilley house. The door was closed and the windows curtained. But she was inside, maybe peeking out at him. . . .

Luke was away again with the wagon train; it was easy to keep track of him. He'd probably be away for a week or more. Simon wanted to slip inside and roll Hester on the bed, but no telling who might come along—or what she might do. She might scream bloody murder. And it was broad daylight, too. He kept moving.

She had liked it—hadn't she?—or she would have made a big fuss long before this. He wondered if she had told Luke—but probably not. Luke would have come after him with a gun if she had.

Simon made a wide circle about the house and rode back to his field. He hated working in the fields but he was forced to do so . . . or not eat. He had thought about Jerry Titus constantly since the day he'd seen him cross to the barbershop in Pommer.

But not only Titus. There were other merchants in the town, and all of them had to keep their own profits. Where did they store them? Somewhere on the premises, that was for sure. There was no bank closer than Hartigan in the north.

Where did Jeff Becket keep his money? And where did Dud hide his? He thought of these questions endlessly as he plowed and harrowed. There ought to be someone who could supply the answers. Did he know anyone who had once been a merchant? He didn't think so.

His father had worked at farming all his life and had died without a damned thing to show for it except some acres of land. But anyone could stake land. Simon didn't want to end up the same way. But he was dirt poor, with no prospects. Jeff Becket might give him a job if he asked for it—but he'd be damned if he'd give Jeff that satisfaction. No, he'd starve before he asked Jeff for anything.

They arrived in Chandler without losing a single head of the little herd. Jeff rode into town and found Robert McCoy at the newspaper office, making out an ad.

McCoy was a lean, older man with a white goatee and glasses. He had a courtly manner and was delighted, he said, to meet Jeff at last. He had heard much about him and his freight line.

"I've leased corrals at the edge of town," he said. "You can drive the cows in there and I'll take possession."

McCoy had an arrangement with the cavalry to supply them with beef. He would be driving the herd another hundred miles or so to the west.

Jeff returned to the herd and guided them into the corrals, where McCoy was waiting. Roy and Jonah led the animals through open chutes to the corrals, while Jeff on one side and McCoy on the other made tallies.

The job was soon completed and each man had exactly the same figure: one hundred and ten.

"Good-looking steers," McCoy commented. "You drove them easy."

Jeff went into town again with McCoy to the other's office, where he counted out four hundred and forty dollars in greenbacks.

"Nice doing business with you, Mr. Becket."

"My friends call me Jeff."

McCoy smiled. "Mine call me Bob." He supplied cigars and a match. "Next year I'll want more cows."

"Just let me know. You'll have them."

Chapter Twenty-one

Dud Hurley spent the summer enlarging the store. The tiny room in the three-room log house had been crowded from the start. He'd put up shelves on every available bit of wall, built a loft and cabinets, and had to squeeze himself into the room.

Big Isaac Closs had the sawmill running now, and Dud was able to buy board lumber which made rebuilding easier. He removed one wall of the house and extended it, making a large L. It tripled the size of the store.

He put a tar-paper roof on the extension and Henry Mills brought him a new black-belly stove from Titus's store in Pommer, along with a handful of eastern newspapers, some only two weeks old.

The trouble in Kansas had blossomed; now they were calling it "bleeding Kansas" and the fight between the Free-staters and the Slave-staters was being called a civil war. Also, a new political party was forming and the founders had adopted the name "Republicans." Their southern opponents labeled them "black Republicans."

"This slavery thing is getting out of hand," Dud said to Jeff. "The politicians can't seem to settle it. They never should have let it go on this far."

"I thought they had it settled once or twice. . . ."

"Not really. Those were only temporary compromises. But as soon as the situations changed both sides were right back at each other's throats again. There's only one way to put an end to it—and they resist it to the death! They've got to get rid of slavery altogether."

"Will they do it?"

Dud shook his head sadly. "If the past is any indication, no, it doesn't seem as if they want to."

"Well, maybe they'll go on making compromises forever."

Dud laughed, running a hand through his tawny hair. "Don't depend on it. There's too much hell been raised now for slavery to stop being a cause. There are always a lot of folks willing to march for one cause or another. And there're also a lot of folks eager to tell others what to think and how to live their lives. Slavery is a made-to-order cause for them."

Jeff said, "You're pretty pessimistic about the future."

"Yes I'm pessimistic about slavery. I really can't see the politicians allowing it to go as far as war. But then, I don't have a hell of a lot of faith in Congress."

"Now that Clay, Calhoun, and Webster are gone."

"Yes." Dud grunted, pushing a keg of mule shoes into a corner. "How's Sam Harris doing?"

"I've got no complaints so far. Of course he wants to haul farther and farther. . . ."

"He's a go-getter. Got his teeth into the business."

"He wants to build a way station here in Eden Creek. So I've got lumber on order. You got time for a game?"

Dud grinned. "I'll get the chessmen down. Shall we set a time limit?"

"Make it easy on yourself."

The wagon train was hit twenty miles north of Hartigan. John Bowman, in the lead wagon, had just entered a narrow, wooded valley when rifles opened up and their mules went down in the fusillade.

Bowman rolled off the seat and jumped to the ground under the halted wagon. The rifles had concentrated on the mules instead of the men. From his position he was unable to see what had happened to the three other wagons. He tugged out the Navy pistol and fired at muzzle flashes, seeing one man throw up his hands.

When the pistol was empty he pushed out the wedge and changed cylinders. He heard shouts, then saw a group of riders suddenly charge the wagons. Bowman scuttled out from under his shelter and rolled into the ditch alongside the road. He and the others were outnumbered—there were only seven of them. Jeff Becket had specified that each wagon was to carry two men, a driver and a rifleman, but Sam Harris insisted on schedules being kept. So, unable to hire a guard in Hartigan, Bowman had gone on without one. Not that one man would have made a difference. They had been very effectively ambushed.

He ran along the ditch and halted at the first turn. No one was following him. Panting, he shoved caps on the six nipples and slid the revolver into his belt. Was he the only one to get away?

He sat, catching his breath. He had run perhaps half a mile and now he could hear nothing at all from the ambush site. He debated slipping back along the ditch and decided to wait a bit longer.

But in an hour the breeze brought him a whiff of smoke. He stood, sniffing, and saw dark clouds rising. They had set the wagons afire! Whoever they were . . . Bowman swore aloud. Jeff would be mad as hell.

He moved back along the ditch slowly, pistol ready, but saw no one. He reached the wagons and discovered that they had been almost totally destroyed. All the goods they had been hauling had been ripped open and burned. Very little was left but fittings and parts of wagon wheels. All the mules were dead.

It was a disaster.

Two men of his crew were also dead. He did not find them at first; their bodies had been dragged off to one side. Both were fellows he'd hired in Pommer. Where were the other four? Maybe they had gotten away, too!

There was no sign of the attackers.

Bowman started back along the road to Hartigan, his heart heavy. This was the first real disaster the line had suffered, and it had come while he was in charge. He would have to send a crew back to clean up the wreckage and bury the bodies and the mules.

Five miles or so along the road, just as it was getting dark, he met another of the drivers, Joe Elsby. He too had managed to dive under his wagon, but his guard had been one of those shot. Elsby had crawled off into the weeds beyond the ditch and no one had come after him. He hadn't seen any of the others.

"They prob'ly scattered ever' which way, if they got away at all."

"Did you get a look at who was shootin' at us?"

"I seen a couple of them, but nobody I recognized." Joe was a skinny old-timer, hairy and loose-jointed. He had been in worse scrapes, he told Bowman, but he sure hated to have to walk all the way back to town.

They reached Hartigan late the next day. Bowman and Joe told their stories to the local law, and men were sent out to the ambush site.

That evening the other four men showed up, tired and bedraggled. They had scattered, as Elsby had guessed. None of them was hurt but they had all lost their war bags. Bowman put them and Joe into a hotel to wait for the next wagon train. He was as tired as they, but he got a horse from the livery and rode back to Pommer to report to Sam Harris.

* * *

From a vantage point Marty Webb watched the ambush, well pleased by the result. "Shoot the mules," he had told them, and they had done just that, halting the train, then turning their guns on the men. Most of the drivers had escaped, but they had nothing he wanted. "Let em go!" he yelled. Marty watched them disappear into the brush.

It had been easy. But the wagons had not been carrying much of value—to them. Most of it was iron goods, mule shoes, building supplies, nails, some tools. . . . His men looted the boxes and crates, arguing over small prizes. Then Marty had them set the rest afire, wagons and all.

He had lost one man. They carted the body to a dry creek and caved in a bank over him.

He led them south then toward Chandler. There was a bank at Chandler that had looked prosperous last time he'd seen it. He would ride into town and look it over again; maybe it could be cracked by a bold stroke. If not, there were girls to be had while he considered his next move.

Movement was important. Marty had learned that the hard way, by trial and error. The kind of men who rode with him were more restless than the average. They wanted to be almost constantly on the move, always ready for action of any sort. If he were to ask them to settle down for a month in fine weather, for instance, they would certainly all desert him.

They were content to let him do the planning; none could figure and plan, or think ahead, as well as he. The raid on the wagon train had been merely a diversion, thought up in a hurry, a way to keep them occupied. Marty had expected little from it. But the men had let off steam and were all in a merry mood afterward.

If the bank at Chandler proved to be too well protected he would simply move on to something else. Marty always made sure he had the odds on his side. His men were not afraid of danger, but no one wanted to die before his time—whenever that turned out to be. So he was reasonably careful of their lives.

Not for their sakes as much as his.

Sam Harris strapped on a revolver, took a shotgun, and rode to Hartigan with John Bowman. The Becket agent there, Rush Hopkins, also the general store owner, had seen to it at once that the two bodies had been decently buried, with a preacher to say words over the graves. Hopkins had also made sure the local newspaper printed the details, saying the Becket Line would be responsible for all losses.

And it was a respectable loss that Sam totaled up, sighing. But it had to be paid or the company would suffer in the long run. Goodwill was very important.

Sam questioned the survivors. "Did you see anyone you recognized?"

No one had.

"Did you hear anyone yell names?"

No one had.

The local law had no pictures of Marty Webb, but it was generally believed he had been the attacker. It was the kind of thing he did well. The deputy in charge had tracked the gang for a dozen miles before losing them.

Sam bought more wagons and mules, arranged to pay for the losses, and turned the wagons over to John Bowman. Sam rode back to Pommer pondering the company's dilemma. The line had lost hundreds of dollars. But there was really nothing they could do. To hire more shotgun guards would only make the entire operation a break-even or losing enterprise.

Amos Mitchell had gone south to Norton with three wagons. When he returned to Pommer Jeff Becket was with the train.

He and Sam sat in the office as Sam outlined what had happened and what he'd done about it.

"You did the right thing, down the line," Jeff said. "Too bad nobody recognized any of them. You think it was Marty Webb?"

"The deputy at Hartigan thinks so. He said there's no other gang operating in this neck of the woods."

"What does he know about Webb?"

"Not much, I guess. There's no picture."

As usual when he came to town, Jeff sat with Jerry Titus in the store. Jerry had heard all about the ambush, but he'd heard no gossip at all about Marty Webb.

"He's out there in the sticks somewhere, Jeff. Prob'ly lookin' for somebody to shoot. Owlhoots like him is hard to figure out or second-guess. You heard about old John Brown?"

"No. Who's he?"

"Calls hisself Osawatomie Brown. He's one of them Free-staters. He got a bunch together and murdered five'r six men on Pottawatomie Creek up in Kansas. He says he going to kill slavery."

"By murderin' folks?"

"Well, hell, he ain't right in the goddamn head. By all that's holy, you mark my words, that sonofabitch belongs in Congress!"

When Amos was ready to go on to Hartigan Jeff went along, and the three wagons arrived without incident. But the local deputy could tell him nothing he didn't already know.

There was no way the wagons could be better protected, outside of a troop of cavalry riding with each train. But since the Comanches had been quiet, townspeople seldom saw soldiers. It was too bad the wagons that had been hit hadn't been carrying a group of armed passengers. They might have put up a good fight.

Jeff stayed overnight and started back to Pommer the next morning. He thought, as he rode, there was one other thing they could use that would be of incalculable value to them: the telegraph. Wires were being strung between cities in the East; the telegraph was becoming almost common, according to the papers. It would save them all time if they had one single wire from Bowers to Winship, a mere two hundred and fifty miles.

When he asked Titus about it, the other only snorted. "Hellsfire, they ain't enough votes out here for them politicians to worry about. Did y'all ever *see* a congressman in your whole born days? You ast them to put up a wire for us folks and they won't even bother to laugh at you."

Chapter Twenty-two

HESTER Tilley was keeping to herself. She had once been outgoing but she had now become a recluse. Rachel and Leah were astounded at the change in the woman, and they discussed it endlessly. What in the world had happened so quickly to make such a difference in her?

Rachel asked Jeff if Luke was acting differently—perhaps the two had quarreled bitterly. But Luke had not changed at all, according to the men who worked with him. And when Luke returned home he was as baffled as everyone else. Hester was not the same girl he had married—and she would not tell him what was bothering her.

Leah said, "She's too young for the 'change.' It's got to be something else."

According to Luke neither he nor Hester had received any mail, so it couldn't be bad news from afar. "They ain't nobody to write to her anyways," he said to Jeff.

She was sleeping poorly and it began to show. Several times Luke woke in the night to find her awake, sitting in a chair. She protested on these occasions that nothing was wrong. . . .

Each time he came home she was edgy, but when he had to go she begged him tearfully to remain. "Don't leave me alone. . . ."

Luke mentioned this to Jeff, who discussed it with Rachel. "Did something happen to her while Luke was away?"

"I don't know."

"I think something did. Will you and Leah keep a closer eye on her?"

"Of course."

Jeff asked Sam to put Luke on the shortest runs so he could be home oftener, and with time, Hester seemed to improve. But she was still withdrawn and had moody periods. She was nothing like the girl who had come to Eden Creek. If, while she was in the company of Rachel and Leah, the conversation veered too close to an analysis of her problem, she was likely to get up suddenly and depart without a word. And then she would stay away for days.

Leah said, "We're never going to find out what's behind it. It's down too deep."

Then one day Roy came in from helping Bert Yellen with the herd and put his pony in the corral. Rachel was hanging clothes on a line, and when she had finished she walked to the corral where Roy was rubbing down his horse with corncobs. She leaned on a rail, talking to her son, when she noticed Simon Caine riding by the Tilley house. Simon was walking the horse slowly, watching the house.

Rachel was surprised to see him, and more surprised at his attitude. She mentioned it to Jeff later. "He looked like he thought she was going to come out. You don't suppose there's something between those two?"

He was astonished. "How could there be?"

"I don't know—but maybe that's it."

"But he didn't go to the door, you say. He just rode by?"

"She's a married woman. He wouldn't go to the door." She paused. "In daylight."

They stared at each other. Jeff fished for a cheroot and slowly lit it. How many times had he seen Simon in town with one of the whore girls? Had Simon forced himself on Hester? Wouldn't that explain Hester's actions? She would be too ashamed to tell anyone.

He said, "I think you've hit it."

"She's terribly unhappy. Maybe he raped her."

He nodded. "That's what I'm thinking. But what about proof? If we dig it out of Hester . . ."

"Yes. The shame of it may kill her."

He studied the glowing end of the cigar. "I'll go talk to Dud a bit."

Dud listened and shook his head sadly. "The supposition fits the known facts, but of course neither of them will admit it—for different reasons. And I agree you mustn't question Hester. Were you thinking of shooting Simon?"

Jeff smiled briefly. "Well, if *I* don't . . . and Luke ever finds out . . ."

"Yes, Luke will kill him all right." He sighed again. "And that might be the best way out of it . . . in the absence of law."

"We don't need law for this."

"Hotheads never do. What if you're completely wrong?"

Jeff was annoyed. "I'm not a hothead. If that sonofabitch raped her he deserves what he gets. Which side're you on?"

Dud made a face. "If, if, if. You *are* a hothead, Jeff. In your own way. You always were and you always will be." He waved his hand. "But that's not the question. The question is, what to do about Simon? You've got to find out the truth."

"If he did it, he can't stay here among us."

"I agree—if. But don't tell Luke what you suspect. The truth first. If Hester chooses to tell him one day, that's her affair. You stay out of it."

"Then I'll go see Simon."

"Yes. Do you think you can handle it discreetly?"

"What does discreetly mean?"

"It means without letting everyone this side of Kansas City know what you're about."

"What the hell do you think I am? One of those noisy newfangled steam engines?"

"Yes I do," Dud said.

Simon had become aware that people were discussing Hester Tilley. In such a tiny community every wart and ripple was talked about as if it were important news. Even his mother mentioned it one evening, saying that everyone thought something extraordinary had happened to Hester.

Their suspicions made him edgy. They were bound to find out, weren't they? Hester would probably break down and tell someone. Women gossiped about those things among themselves.

If Luke Tilley found out he would come after Simon with a gun. And Luke had a reputation as a fine hand with a firearm. He'd been hunting with Jeff Becket for years, keeping folks in venison.

Simon thought about it, and the more he worried it the more convinced he became that Hester would point the finger at him. Then maybe more of them than just Luke would come looking for him. They might come with a rope.

He would be damned smart to slide out one night. And head for—where would he go? Somewhere else. Anywhere else.

He packed a war bag, rolled his blankets, wrote a note to his mother saying he was heading north. Then he saddled his horse, went across the bridge, and pointed south.

The next morning Jeff came to talk to Simon and found his mother reading the note. She handed it to him with surprise in her voice. "He's up and gone, Jeff. He don't say why."

He read it and shook his head. "And he don't say when he'll be back."

He swore inwardly. He had missed Simon by a few hours, and

where the other had gone was anyone's guess. He certainly had not gone north. Louise could recall only that Simon had several times mentioned going to Kansas City, if only to see what a really big town was like. But, she said, that had been a long time ago. Lately Simon had said nothing, aside from going now and then to Pommer.

Dud thought Simon had two choices. "If I know him, he's broke. He never had any hard money that I know of. So he'll find a job or he'll steal."

"That's not much help," Jeff said sourly.

"Where would I go if I were Simon?" Dud shrugged. "I find it impossible to put myself into his boots. You're going to have to do that without me."

"His leaving means he's guilty."

"It could. I suggest you ask Rachel to watch Hester closely. When she discovers Simon is gone, maybe the news will change her a bit. She may say something. . . ."

"Good idea." He made the suggestion to Rachel then rode to Pommer and took Titus aside.

Titus had not seen Simon Caine. "He ain't been in town lately, Jeff. What y'all want with him?"

Since Titus was a notorious gossip, Jeff said vaguely. "We think he hurt somebody—but keep it under your hat. I don't want it to get back to him that I'm looking for him."

"Course not."

Jeff talked to Sam Harris and Sam hadn't seen or heard from Simon either.

"Ask all the men to keep a lookout."

"Is this serious?"

"It is to me." He noticed the papers on Sam's desk. "Are those plans?"

"They're for the way station at Eden Creek."

Jeff nodded, examining them.

Sam said, "We need a better bridge, too. I'm sending for an engineer from the East to come and supervise it. That log bridge is apt to go out at the first sprinkle."

Jeff could not argue with that. He was mildly surprised it had held up through the last runoff.

Titus sent him to see several men who had cattle for sale. He bought twenty head and Sam assigned a man to help drive them to Eden Creek. Jeff's herd now numbered about two hundred, according to Bert Yellen's last tally.

* * *

Work began on the Eden Creek way station about two weeks later. The new building was located near the bridge, and when Rachel saw it going up she approached Jeff.

Without any preliminaries she said straight out, "I want a new house."

"What?"

"I want a—"

"I heard you. A new house! What for?"

Rachel was patient. "Because, even though this is a fine house and all, it's too small. We're crowded in it. Besides, it's cold. I want a board house and now that Isaac Closs has his sawmill running . . ."

He looked at her suspiciously. "There's more to it that that, isn't there?"

"Well . . ."

"Tell me all of it."

She took a long breath. "Leah and I have been talking. If you build a new house, we can sell this one to the Hurleys. They're only three, and Dud can then use the entire house they're living in for his store."

"I see. Did Dud figure this out?"

"No. It was my idea . . . and Leah's. Dud doesn't know about it yet."

"And I suppose you have plans all drawn?"

"Well . . ." She smiled. "Yes, I have."

She got them out and laid the sketches before him. She wanted a five-room house!

"And I also want a veranda and a cellar."

"And I suppose you have a place picked out for it?"

"Well, no. I'll let you decide that."

He shook the papers. "Do you have any idea what this will cost?

"Yes, probably five hundred dollars. I want wallpaper inside too, and a pump in the kitchen."

"And a board floor."

"Certainly a board floor!"

He studied the sketches. "Can I have a room for an office?"

"Yes, you can put it here, off our bedroom." She drew in a rectangle.

He folded the drawings and put them in his pocket. "I'll talk to George Stackpole in the morning."

Stackpole was supervising the way station. She was wrong, he thought, about the cost. It would probably go as high as six hundred. But they had the money . . . and more. When they had built the stone house he, with Dud's expert help, had cemented a safe into one wall of their bedchamber. It had a recessed steel door with the best padlock Titus could provide. The safe now held over a thousand dollars in hard cash and greenbacks.

The safe in Sam Harris's office in Pommer held more than that. And Sam added to it every week, after wages and expenses were paid.

Yes, they could afford the house. And in this one Rachel would have real glass in the windows, and curtains. He would order them from the East at once.

The new way station went up quickly, built of boards and lumber from the sawmill. Grizzled George Stackpole supervised the work: a row of four cubicles, each with two built-in bunks, a tiny office, a large baggage room, and one room for the station manager and his wife. There was also a dining room and kitchen.

Jeff asked about the cubicles. "We're only a few hours from Pommer."

George said, "Sam's orders. I ast him the same question and he said there'll be times when the wagons or coach have to lay over for the night. He's allus lookin' ahead, Sam is. And it'll be cheaper to put them in now."

"All right. . . ."

As the station took shape Jeff went to talk to Angus Porter, finding the lean, angular man in his cramped shop, shoeing a roan horse. Jeff sat on a box and lighted a cheroot with a twig. "You need more room, Angus."

"Ain't that the goddamn truth."

"We're building a way station over there."

"I seen it."

"We're building a shop too, for a blacksmith. You can move your whole shebang there rent-free, do our work and yours too."

Angus paused, a rasp in his hand. He rubbed an arm across his brow and grinned. "A bigger shop—rent-free?"

"Twice as big as this."

"That's hard to turn down."

"Then don't. When you get free here, go over and talk to George Stackpole. Tell 'im what you want. He'll build it the way you say."

Angus nodded. "I'll see 'im this afternoon. You want me to sign anything?"

"What for? Ain't your word any good?" Jeff stood and they shook hands.

Chapter Twenty-three

ACROSS the log bridge Simon headed south and rode all night. He left his horse in the livery at Norton and sat in a saloon half the day. Where the hell would he go? He desperately needed money; the few dollars in his pocket wouldn't take him far.

He listened to the sounds of the coins as the bartenders dropped them into cash boxes as they served customers. One of those boxes would set him up for a month.

In early afternoon, with the sun past, he sat in a tilted-back chair on the boardwalk, facing the street, moodily staring at the stores opposite. A red Becket wagon train came along, mules plodding steadily. There were five wagons, each with two men aboard except for the small trap.

Simon pulled the hat down to cover his face. The lead driver was Henry Mills. But Henry did not glance his way.

Simon watched the wagons disappear to the north. More money in Jeff Becket's pocket. Everything Jeff touched seemed to turn to gold.

And Simon himself had nothing. Why hadn't his father thought of starting a freight line? Simon sighed deeply. Fred Caine had never thought of anything original in his entire life. Hell, he remembered his father saying that Jeff Becket would surely fail in his freighting venture.

Fred had been wrong every time.

Money. Where was he going to get money? He was sure one of those merchants would give him a job—but he didn't want it. The pay would be measly and the hours long. Besides, he had never worked for anyone. He had no experience at anything but walking behind a plow. He could barely read and write.

But he had a pistol, and plenty of bullets.

The revolver would open pockets for him. When dark came he led his horse from the livery and tied it down the street from the last saloon at the south end of town. Then he went into a restaurant, taking his time over supper.

Seating himself at a table that commanded a full view of the saloon door, he waited, watching for a victim. No one paid any attention to him as he ate. Men came and went from the saloon as the night wore on.

Then a better-dressed citizen walked from the saloon, gazed about blearily, and decided on a direction. Simon left some money on his table and walked out of the restaurant. The man staggered along the boardwalk and Simon followed.

When the man turned off to go between two buildings, Simon hurried and drew the revolver. He hit the other man alongside the ear and caught the bulky citizen as he collapsed. He lowered his victim to the ground and searched him quickly. It took only a moment to find a wallet, pull out the bills and coins, and depart. He walked to the horse and rode out of town.

In an hour he stopped and scratched a sulphur. He had twelve dollars and a few coins.

Not much, for the risk.

He continued on and arrived in Winship at dawn. It was a much larger town. He spent a dollar for a room in a hotel and slept round the clock. When he arose it was early morning again.

He went downstairs for breakfast where he saw the poster: WANTED: DEAD OR ALIVE. MARTY WEBB: $700 REWARD FOR INFORMATION LEADING TO ARREST AND CONVICTION. . . .

He ate breakfast thinking about Webb. *There* was a man who had gone into business for himself and was doing well, if the gossip was of any account. He wondered how many men Webb had in his gang.

Simon sipped coffee. He could start his own gang—if he could find someone to ride with him. It was one thing to rob a single drunken citizen, but to pull off a real haul he would need several men. He could hardly walk into a bank alone and expect to survive. He had read the newspapers; it took three or four to do it properly. And he would need that many or more to rob a Becket wagon train.

How he would love to tackle the train . . . then burn the entire thing! Every damned wagon!

His hands were shaking so hard he had to put down the fork. He glanced around quickly, but no one stared at him. He took several deep breaths to calm himself. That's what he really wanted—to hurt Jeff Becket!

When Hester heard that Simon Caine had disappeared, and probably would not be back, she perked up a little. When Luke returned home about a week later she was nearly her old self again.

Observing this, Rachel said to Jeff, "That *was* it, after all!"

"Well, don't let on."

"Of course not!"

The way station was finished and trimmed with the familiar Becket red. It was a very neat little group of buildings: an office, restaurant, and living quarters for the manager. A row of cubicles and workshops; and corrals on three sides of a square. Angus Porter occupied the largest shop area and erected a black-and-white sign, BLACKSMITH, over the door.

A month before, Jeff had told Titus they'd need a station manager, and he sent a man, Vince Ropers, to see Sam Harris. Sam listened to Ropers's credentials and sent him on to Jeff at Eden Creek with a recommendation to hire him on a trial basis.

Jeff looked the man over—he had come in a wagon with his wife, Mary, who professed to be a cook. She would supply meals to travelers, she told him.

Vince was twenty-six, he said, and eager to settle in Eden Creek. He was certain he could manage the way station, having done that sort of work before, and Jeff put him on. "In a month we'll talk again."

George Stackpole spent hours with Rachel as they worked out plans for the new house, showed them to Jeff, argued over rooms and space. But finally they were all satisfied. The lumber was hauled from the mill and piled on the site, which was just behind the old stone house but facing the opposite way, toward what was to be another street as staked out by Jeff and Dud.

The window glass was on order and was due in a week, George said, as were the red chimney bricks which would come from a yard just outside of Bowers.

It was agreed that Dudley and his family would move into the stone house when the Beckets moved out. Dud would then have the three rooms of the original log house for his store.

There were now eighteen families on Eden Creek, scattered along the town-to-be area, in company with a few bachelors, young and old. Dud had enlarged his merchandise stock. His store was no longer just a trading post. There were shelves full of airtights and kegs and barrels of meat and cheese, nuts and flour. . . . Nearly every wagon that came to Eden Creek from Pommer included one entire wagonload consigned to Dud.

There was also a constant flow of drifters and travelers, arriving at the creek to cross on the bridge, and most paused to visit the store. Dud was still willing to trade goods, though now he was much more selective.

He used one of the storerooms for stock, one as the store, and they lived in the other till the stone house was ready. Josh helped out in the store but Perly Dyer was in charge when Dud was away. Perly was twenty-three, unmarried, and bookish. When not working he could be found with his feet up, reading. He and Roy Becket read everything that had words on it . . . and pestered their elders for more.

Dud purchased newspapers whenever he could, even if they were a month old, and sold them in the store—after Roy and Perly had read them front to back.

Another newcomer to Eden Creek was Rufus Trotter. He was a scruffy-looking individual, bearded, stocky like a bear, and more shifty-eyed than most. He quickly put up a wood-framed canvas tent and lettered a crude sign: SALOON.

The deadfall had a dirt floor and a bar made of planks laid over barrels. Trotter did a brisk business toward sundown each day. He had a wagonful of bottles, rotgut whiskey for the most part, that had no ancestry. He told his customers he was contemplating a better edifice—when he could afford it.

The ground for the new Becket house was carefully leveled and a stone foundation cemented in. George Stackpole declared it would be best if the house were up off the ground a few feet. He also had his men dig a good-sized basement in the middle of the house area and line it with flat stones.

He had thick, heavy timbers hauled from the sawmill to use as underpinnings. Then he laid in a sub-floor and a smooth board floor atop that.

Rachel visited the house-abuilding every day, watching as it took shape. Despite the plans, she made sure the rooms were spacious by walking through them. She was determined not to feel squeezed-in and cramped as she had in the stone house. This would be their home for the rest of their days.

Leah knew exactly how she felt, but Leah was still eager to move into the stone house. She would cope, she said.

The plans called for two fireplaces, one in the kitchen and one in the parlor. Stackpole had had experience in building fireplaces, and he and Dud had a spirited exchange, arguing over the fine points. Dud could point to all the fireplaces in Eden Creek; they were all serving well and were his handiwork. He ended up building the two in the new house when Stackpole threw up his hands in defeat.

The basement finished, a wooden stairway was built to get into it. The steps rose to a hall door just beside the kitchen. Another steel safe was cemented into the basement wall.

The window glass was delivered two weeks late and Stackpole expertly installed it himself. It was the only window glass in Eden Creek. Elinor Locke brought her brood of school children to see and feel the glass. They had seen small items, but none had ever seen a glass window before.

Louise Caine died in late September. She had lived alone since Simon had left, and when she had not appeared for several days a neighbor went to knock on her door. No one answered and, the door being unlocked, the neighbor ventured inside. She found the body in bed.

Louise was buried beside her husband in the plot across the creek. Leah, Rachel, Roy, and Josh attended at the grave, with Dud reading from the Bible. Jeff was away in Pommer and had taken Lili along.

The Caine house had gradually deteriorated, with no one to look after it, and with Louise's death it was locked up. The yard and fields soon grew weedy. . . .

The neighbors wanted to take over the fields, "Why not? They just lyin' there."

"They belong to the Caine family," Dud said. "Maybe there's other relatives. We'll wait and see."

There was much grumbling, but no one cared to challenge Dud. Everyone knew Jeff Becket stood squarely behind Dud and no one wanted to tangle with Jeff. So the fields grew more weedy and the house took on a forlorn look, as if it were going to seed as well.

Rachel would not have a tar paper roof on the new house but Isaac was able to supply thick shakes, and the roof was completed before the first rains. They moved into the house with their old clumsy furniture. It looked even worse than it had before. She had been pleased with it in the log house, but now it was so out of place. . . .

"Can't we send for new furniture, Jeff?" She showed him pictures torn from newspapers and magazines, and he agreed to ask Titus to order from the East. He was glad she hadn't asked for a piano.

But she did want carpets. She also wanted silverware, but kept that to herself for a bit. Jeff had been very understanding of her desires. It might be well not to push too hard. Next year she'd ask for silverware, and maybe one of the newfangled copper bathtubs.

The coming national elections, according to the papers, would pit a man named James Buchanan, a bachelor, against John C. Fremont and Millard Fillmore.

"There's another potato-head, Buchanan," Titus said in disgust, putting down the paper. "We got one fool after another bein' elected president."

Jeff said, "You don't know who's going to be elected."

"No, but y'all can see none of 'em're worth the powder to blow 'em to kingdom come. You mark my words, this country is going to the goddamn dogs."

"You say that about every election."

"Well it's true, ain't it? What's happened to men like Tom Jefferson? Ain't they bein' born no longer? Now we got puddingheads like Fillmore and Buchanan."

"It doesn't make a damn bit of difference to us, does it? None of them know where Pommer is . . . do they?"

Titus sighed. "I guess not."

"And you can always vote against them."

"I do, I do." Titus looked at him over the glasses. "But it don't do no good, my one vote." He sighed again. "How's Roy these days? He ought to be able to drive one of your wagons by now."

"Yeah, he can drive a wagon. I'll give him a job if he asks for it."

"Luke tells me you got a teacher now, down at Eden Crick."

"Yeah. Woman named Miz Locke. She seems t'be doing the trick. You got one of them new cook stoves?"

Titus shook his bald head. "Had me a few, but they sold out. The women loves 'em. You want one?"

"Rachael heard about 'em. And when women hear about them things they got to try 'em. Order me one."

"The trouble with you, Jeff, is you're set in your ways. Them stoves is a hell of a lot better'n cooking in a fireplace. Don't you want to make life easier for your woman?"

"Of course I do, for crissakes! Didn't I just ast you to order me one?"

Titus grinned and scribbled a note.

Soon after Jeff returned to Eden Creek Sam Harris showed up to inspect the new way station. Mary Ropers had put up a sign, RES-TAURANT, and was feeding half a dozen customers each day. She made him a lunch of venison and potatoes with pudding for dessert. It was a better meal than he got in Pommer.

He visited with Jeff. His wagon crews had not been able to learn a thing about Simon Caine. "He prob'ly changed his name, Jeff."

"Yes, I guess so."

"Either that or he went someplace we don't haul to."

"Ummm. Well, tell 'em to keep their ears open."

Chapter Twenty-four

SOUTH Fork was a sleepy little town, especially during the week. It woke up a bit on Saturday, stretched and blinked a little, stayed up till eleven or midnight as a rule, singing and carrying on, and sank back into lethargy on Sunday.

It had been built on a gentle slope, and the main and only street started out straight but wavered and wandered, with some buildings jutting out and others pulled back like a badger in its hole. However, the street was broad and no one seemed to mind that wagons were parked along its center, sometimes for days at a time.

Simon arrived on Friday and put up at the five-room hotel called Snake Proof. All Rooms 50¢. Weekly Rates.

He went out to look the town over and was greatly disappointed. None of the merchants seemed to him to have as much as a dollar in their cash boxes. He saw not a single citizen who looked affluent enough to rob.

But as he sat in the Lone Star Saloon, a gambler walked in. The stranger was a tall man, lean as a whip, dressed in a black frock coat with a watch chain across a checkered vest. His black pants were tucked into shiny black boots and his face was brown and sharp as a weasel's. He ordered beer, sat at a table in the center of the narrow room, and began shuffling a pack of cards.

He looked around at the idlers. "Anyone care for a friendly game, gents?"

No one moved, but finally Simon got up and sat at the other's table. And as he sat down he laid his Navy revolver on the table in front of him.

The gambler eyed it. "No need for the artillery, sir."

Simon grunted.

"What's your pleasure, sir? Five-card draw all right?"

Simon nodded. "Lemme see the cards."

"Certainly." Smiling, the gambler passed them over. Simon

shuffled through the deck, not sure what he was looking for. They seemed all right. He handed them back.

They played steadily for the next hour. Simon won a few hands, but ultimately lost every cent he possessed. As far as he could tell he lost it fairly, though that fact did not improve his humor.

When he could not continue the gambler asked, "Are you flat, friend?"

Simon nodded sourly.

The other pushed a dollar across the table to him. "Never let it be said I took a man's last bean."

"Thanks." Simon took the dollar, got up, and left the saloon, annoyed with himself. He never should have played cards with a professional gambler. The man had probably cheated him and he hadn't known it. He had been foolish.

But the gambler was probably one of the few persons in town with money in his pocket. Simon walked back to the hotel thinking about holding up the man. Maybe the same as he had before, wait for him to come out of the saloon. . . .

He went to his room and flopped on the bunk, closing his eyes tiredly.

When he woke it was morning. He swore, sitting up, and running a hand through his tousled hair. Damn . . . he'd lost his chance. He splashed water on his face and went downstairs and across the street to a restaurant for breakfast. He ate eggs and bacon with coffee and returned to the hotel barely able to rub two coins together.

As he went up the stairs to his room he met the gambler coming down. The other paused. "Just the man I was hoping to meet . . ."

"Me?" Simon asked.

"Yes. May I speak with you a moment? Perhaps we can go to your room."

Simon shrugged. They went down the hall and he put the key in the lock.

As the door closed behind them the gambler said, "My name's Rowan Chace." He put his hand out.

Simon shook it briefly. "Simon Caine."

"Please to know you, Mr. Caine." He glanced at the hall door and spoke softly. "No offense, sir, but I have the impression you're down on your luck."

Simon grunted. "I might be." It did not please him to hear the man say those words. What business was it of his?

"Then I have a proposition for you."

Simon was surprised. "A proposition?"

"A matter of business, if you prefer. My trade is cards, as you know."

Simon blurted out, "Did you play fair with me?"

Chace smiled. "Certainly. I may say, intending no offense, that you are not an expert player—which is why I am here. I am sure you realize that one can win at cards against an inept player merely by experienced play, with no need of trickery or false dealing. I did not cheat you, Simon."

Simon let his breath out, feeling better all at once. He indicated the single chair. "Sit down." He sat on the bed, facing the other. "What's this business you mentioned?"

Chace sat. "I need a shill. When I go—"

"What's a shill?"

"A partner, in a way. I am well known in many establishments and sadly, in strange towns, there are those who will not gamble with a stranger of my profession. I suppose they assume I will cheat them, or they decide my experience is against them—as of course it is."

"You want me t'tell them you're honest?"

Chace laughed. "No, not at all. But I do want them to find it out for themselves. Let me explain. It has occurred to me that if I work—in secret—with someone like yourself who is obviously no card sharp, business will improve."

"You just said I'm not much of a card player."

"That is exactly right, and what I need."

Simon was mystified. "I don't understand."

"Let me say it this way. I will enter a saloon and sit at a table as I did when we first met. You will come to the table and sit in, I hope with others. But I will see to it that you will win."

"How?"

"By simply manipulating the cards. You will win forty or fifty dollars, and cash in, giving some excuse or other, and depart. You will go back to the hotel and wait for me. When I come in we will split the take."

Simon nodded slowly. The others would see that he, an obviously bumbling player, was winning from the professional, and that would put their fears to rest.

Chace said, "You will get up to give your place to another player. Do you understand it now?"

"Yes. But that means we can't be seen together."

"That's right. We will have to go into towns separately and meet as if by chance. You will not use my name until I introduce myself."

Simon nodded again. The element of secrecy was spice to the game. He grinned at the dark man. "All right, I'm in."

"Good." Chace pointed a finger. "I must impress upon you that secrecy is vital. If anyone suspected we were in collusion it could be very serious."

"Sure . . . I understand."

"Very well." Chace took a long thin cigar from an inside pocket. "When you come to sit in on a game and begin to win, this"—he lightly tapped the cigar on an imaginary tabletop—"will be the signal for you to cash in."

"All right."

"I had intended to stay in this little town only overnight, but let's use it to see how our plan works out. You come and sit in on a game late this afternoon."

Simon nodded briskly.

"Then tomorrow we will both leave, at different times, and go on to Linden. It's about thirty miles south and east on the stage line. We will both stay at the Drover's Hotel and meet there secretly."

"Drover's Hotel."

"Yes. I've been there before. There's a bar attached. I will be in the barroom. Do you have any money?"

Simon sighed. "No. . . ."

Chace took out a leather wallet and selected five dollars and handed them over. "This will enable you to sit in on the game later. Remember the signal for you to cash in."

"Yes."

"Any questions?"

"I'll just play the cards you deal me. . . ."

Chace smiled. "Just play them and win. Yes." He got up and went to the door, opening it a crack. He glanced back at Simon. "Later, in the saloon."

Jerry Titus sent a surveyor to Eden Creek. Johan Biggs had spent several weeks in Pommer, running lines. He seemed very efficient; those who had hired him were very pleased. He drove a light wagon that carried his tools and other equipment. It had canvas sides and top and on it was lettered: J. BIGGS   SURVEYOR.

He asked for Jeff Becket when he arrived. "Mr. Titus in Pommer suggested I see you, sir.

Jeff looked at the wagon. "You're a surveyor!"

"Yes. I'm told you have boundaries of property to determine."

"We certainly do." Biggs was a worn-looking man, perhaps

fifty, slightly stooped but apparently spry. He jumped off the wagon and followed Jeff into the house. He sat at the kitchen table as Jeff explained the circumstances of Eden Creek, making a rough drawing to show the various pace-staked areas.

Roy was sent to bring Dudley, and when he appeared he too was delighted to see Biggs. "We've been needing a surveyor for years. When can you start?"

"At once, sir." He looked at Roy. "Of course I will need an assistant. I usually hire one, and this young man will do fine, if he's a mind."

Roy nodded, eager for the job. Biggs said he could easily teach the lad everything he had to know, and it was settled. Dud went out with him to show him where he could pitch his tent.

When he returned to the house, Dud asked, "What will we do about the Caine land?"

"Let Biggs survey it. We'll keep the papers, and if Simon ever shows up we can decide then what to do."

"What if he never shows up?"

"Good riddance." Jeff smiled. "Then the land is yours and mine. Who has a better right?"

Dud made a face. "I suppose that's right. Where d'you suppose Simon's got to?"

"He prob'ly lit out, not knowing himself. He could be anywhere by now. I'd guess he heard something about Hester and figgered she'd tell us what happened."

"That's as good a guess as any."

Jeff smiled again. "And he knows what a good shot Luke is."

Elinor Locke was fortyish, a rather stout woman, graying slightly, with a quiet, easy manner, especially with children. She had a good grasp of ancient history and could impart a sense of its glory and color; she knew English well enough and could spell, but she was lacking when it came to arithmetic or anything pertaining to it.

Roy, taught at home to figure, easily surpassed her.

However, she was excellent when she taught Lili and the other girls the gracious arts. With Rachel and Leah she discussed Louis A. Goday's magazine called *The Lady Book*. It was filled with fashion drawings, essays on good manners, articles on prudery, and the place of women in society. And it was also an advocate of education for women.

Mrs. Locke sent away for recommended books written for boys and girls. She used them as reading exercises and allowed her pupils to take them home to read if they were interested. Roy consumed the books; he read everything available, including the Bible.

He borrowed all of Dud's books, one at a time, and asked for more. When he went to Pommer he even nagged Titus to find books for him to read.

Titus said, "That kid's curious about ever'thing! I never seen the like of it. If somebody'd write a story about the other side of the moon, he'd read it."

Jeff asked, "What's wrong with knowin' things?"

"Hellsfire! I think it's fine! I wisht I knew more'n I do. I wish them dumb politicians knew more'n they do."

Jeff laughed. Titus could pull politics into everything he said, sooner or later.

But books were only one facet of Roy's interests. He was sturdy, strong as coiled steel, and a dead shot with his Starr rifle—and with his father's Navy Colt, which he dearly loved.

He was eager to save money to buy his own things, and asked his father for a job driving a freight wagon. He had been put to work with Amos Mitchell, making the run between Pommer and Winship in the south—until Johan Biggs showed up to survey their lands.

Roy worked with Biggs through the summer and fall, saving every penny, and by Christmas bought his first brand new Navy from Titus. It was a squareback, and Angus Porter engraved his name on the brass backstrap.

Simon was already in the saloon, sipping a beer, when Chace entered and took a table, looking about for company. He motioned to Simon. "Care for a game, friend?"

Simon nodded and took a chair opposite and two others drifted by and sat, watching Chace shuffle the cards. Chace said, "I'm Rowan Chace, gents. Five-card draw fine with y'all?"

One of the men was Frank Scott, the other Bill Lachner. Simon gave his name and bought chips from the dealer with his five dollars.

Several men came to stand nearby, watching as the game progressed. Most eyes were on the gambler, who dealt and played smoothly, his expression never changing. Simon received two pair the first hand and lost to a straight. He threw his hands in until Chace dealt again and this time he received three kings. He won the pot, about twelve dollars.

Chace won a small pot. Then, when he dealt again, Simon received a spade flush and won seven dollars with it.

Two hours slid by, and when he saw Chace tap a cheroot on the table he cashed in his chips, saying he had to leave. He received forty-eight dollars and went at once to his hotel room. He itched to stay and talk to one or two of the painted girls, but the money in his pocket was not his and he did not want to jeopardize his new partnership. It was very promising.

Chace did not rap on the door for nearly three hours. Simon let him in and he sank down on the chair, sighing. It had not been his best night, he said. Scott had proved to be very dogged and even suspicious. Chace growled that he had only won seventy dollars in all that time and Scott had made several ugly remarks when he had cashed in.

"But the others knew that you had left a winner, so that made it easier."

Simon laid his money on the bed and Chace picked it up and gave him thirty-five dollars. "You leave first tomorrow. Wait for me a few miles out and we'll ride the rest of the way together. If I remember, there's only one hotel in Linden, but the town is larger than this one."

"Did it go all right tonight?"

Chace nodded. "You did just right, Simon. Do it that way in Linden and maybe we'll make some real money."

Chapter Twenty-five

IT was early afternoon before they left town. Chace did not roll out till noon and Simon met him several miles along the road to Linden, as they had agreed. Chace looked different in the cold light of day. His face was sallow and his eyes pale as peeled grapes. He rode hunched over and did not talk for hours.

They stopped toward evening and Simon made a fire to boil coffee. He gathered twigs and leaves and set the tinder to burning with a flash of powder from a snaphaunce firelighter.

"You go on into town from here," Chace said, sitting with his tin cup. "I'll follow in an hour or so. We'll meet in the barroom."

Simon nodded.

The town was only a short distance farther on. It was full dark when he mounted and left Chace by the little fire. The sky was black, with stars strewn in a remote brilliance against it. The prairie smelled of a distant fire. A soft breeze accompanied him to the first scattered shacks. He rode down the main street and stopped in front of the hotel. Linden was indeed a much larger place. The hotel was the Alberta and was next to the Palace Saloon.

He went into the hotel to the desk, asking for a room. The clerk turned the dog-eared register and Simon signed: Henry Crowe, the first name that popped into his head. Beside the register the flame of an oil lamp wavered and licked a sooty smudge up the side of its chimney.

He put his horse in the stable and went up to his room on the second floor to deposit the blanket roll and rifle.

He was sitting at a table in the saloon, poring over the local weekly, when Chace entered an hour or so later. Chace took another table with a stein of beer before him, and began to shuffle cards.

They stayed in Linden three days, playing in different saloons; at the end of that time they split two hundred dollars in winnings.

Chace was uneasy at staying so long, fearing that someone would notice Simon sitting in, winning, and leaving early each day. But no one complained. Simon did not hang around the saloon but went upstairs with one of the girls as soon as he left the game.

But on the third night, as they were preparing to leave town, he mentioned the girls to Chace and was astonished at the other's response.

Chace stared at him in anger. "I don't want you consorting with those women!"

"What—what business is it of yours!?"

"Those girls gossip constantly! If they find out what we're doing, one or both of us could get shot!"

Simon shrugged. "How they going to find out?"

"You'll get a few drinks in you, and you'll tell them."

"I will do no such damn thing!"

Chace glared at him. "I don't want to take the chance. You stop seeing those girls or go your own way."

Simon sighed. "All right. . . ." Jesus! This was something he'd never anticipated. How careful could a man be? He got his things together and went down to the stable.

The next town was Kennewick, a stage stop and crossroads. They put up at the only hotel, which was full of passengers waiting for the stagecoach to be repaired. They had been waiting two days and were restless. Chace had no trouble getting into a game, without Simon. He played for hours and met Simon much later in his room to say there would be no split.

"You did nothing, Simon. Isn't that right?"

"But I thought we were partners?"

"Not when I do *all* the work. We're only partners when you do your job at the card table."

"But I'm ready to do my job!" Simon said hotly.

Chace smiled coldly. "And when you're needed, you can do it."

Simon left the room convinced that the gambler was treating him as an inferior. Chace called the shots; he was the boss and Simon danced to his tune.

Did Simon want to play that kind of game? It was the easiest money he had ever made—but it was aggravating.

They stayed in the town five days and Simon did not sit in on any of the games. Chace never lacked for eager victims. When Simon watched the games it seemed to him that Chace was winning steadily, though not in spectacular fashion. He won the small pots and let others win big very occasionally.

None of the winnings came to Simon.

At the end of five days the stagecoach was ready to leave again. Chace played cards most of the afternoon and evening. When Simon went to Chace's room late, Chace protested he was exhausted.

"Let's talk in the morning, Simon. . . ."

Chace always slept late, so Simon did not go back to the room until nearly midday—to find the door unlocked and Chace gone. His carpetbag was gone too.

And his horse was not in the stable.

Surveyor Johan Biggs, found, as he had expected, that all the stakes were inaccurately placed. Pacing could never be more than a guess.

Jeff's land was larger after the survey than it had been staked. The town-to-be area was also much longer. The Caine land was found to be staked much wider than it should be. Evidently Fred Caine's steps had lengthened when he paced his own acres.

Roy enjoyed his work with the older man. Biggs was easy to get along with, though fussy in the extreme about accuracy. He was a precise man, everything in its place. Roy toed the mark and was sorry when the job ended.

Biggs presented his bill, was paid by Jeff and Dudley, packed up his gear, and departed.

Roy went back to driving one of his father's wagons, with Amos Mitchell as wagon master. But whenever he could Roy spent time talking with Sam Harris, listening to the problems Sam faced in running the line.

One of Sam's constant worries was maintenance. He tried to hire managers to run the way stations who were also mechanics and could repair the wagons when needed. The roads were so bad they tended to wear out equipment and mules. The answer of course was better roads. Good roads with tarred surfaces were being built in the East, but they cost money. No one in government, Sam said, was about to spend money for roads in the backwoods.

Sam went on: "If we had good tar-surfaced roads we could haul winter and summer. As it is we have to lay over during the deep snows and hard rains."

"Maybe one day . . ." Roy said.

Sam shook his head. "Changes come very slowly, very slowly. I doubt if there's even a department down there in Austin devoted to roads and bridges."

Roy saw his father occasionally. Jeff traveled the line on horseback, showing up unexpectedly to inspect this or that, listening to complaints and settling troublesome questions.

He could call every man by his name; he made a point of knowing everyone who worked for him. If he was near when a wagon train halted for its hourly stop, Jeff would be in among the men, laughing and jawing with them, slapping backs and telling jokes.

Sam Harris said, "That man's worth a regiment. The men know him and trust him. They know they can take any complaint to him and get it settled right away. They also know that nobody will be asked to do anything that Jeff can't or won't do."

"What is it about him?" Roy asked.

"I don't know, but I wish I had it. It'd make my life easier."

"One thing," Roy said. "He won't lie to you."

Sam nodded. "And I suspect we've had so few holdup attempts because people know Jeff will go after them if they do. You know he went after three men who stole his horse one time."

"Yes, I heard about it."

Roy made the trips to Bowers and far south to Winship, sleeping in way stations and now and then under the wagons. When a vehicle lost a wheel there was a delay. Once a month a wagon or two went farther west to Flatrock or to Lakso, and sometimes east to Hayes or Wayside.

At first the men treated him as the boss's son. But as they saw he did not expect special treatment, and was doing his job, they came to accept him. When one of the drivers provoked him into a fight, they came to respect him because Roy picked the other man up and tossed him into a ditch.

They also began to respect him for another reason. He was a dead shot with his Navy pistol. He was as good as Luke Tilley—maybe even better.

In the towns they hauled to there were gala days, for one occasion or another. People were so starved for entertainment it didn't take much to organize a holiday, and at every one there was a shooting contest. Roy always entered these, plunking down his entry-fee dollar.

The first contest he entered was in Norton. There were nineteen other contestants, all much older men. They were to shoot at targets fifty yards distant, and by the fourth round ten men were eliminated. Roy and nine others were left. Amos Mitchell came to stand by Roy, cautioning him to remain calm.

"Don't let them diddle you, boy. . . ."

"I'm fine, Amos."

Several in the crowd had remarks to make about the boy who thought he could outshoot the town's best, Tom Waler.

"Don't lissen to 'em," Amos said. "That's part of it."

Roy nodded.

Young Becket did not beat Walér when it was over, but the judges spent long moments deciding between them. One confessed afterward that it could easily have gone either way, but since Tom was a local man . . .

Roy came in second and received a prize of ten dollars. He went with Amos and the other Becket men to the nearest saloon and paid for the beer.

Roy won the next four contests he entered, months apart. Amos said, "That kid's got a eye like a goddamn eagle."

Chapter Twenty-six

RUFUS Trotter's saloon on the main street was an eyesore. It was the only tent amid board or log buildings, and the large, poorly lettered sign above it could be read for half a mile. Trotter had said when he built the thing that he would upgrade it, but he had not. The framed tent was soiled and battered and nothing inside was different from the day he had opened for business—except maybe the smell. It had increased.

Dud and Jeff conferred about it. As the two oldest settlers they had the right to tell Trotter to do something about the place.

"If *we* don't," Jeff said, "who does?"

"A very good question. I think we should make our word legal."

"Is there a way?"

"There is," Dud said reasonably, "if you're the mayor of Eden Creek."

Jeff laughed. "Mayor!"

"Why not? We're almost a town. Certainly a wide place in the road . . . now that we have a bridge."

Jeff shook his head. "I'm gone too often. I withdraw in your favor."

"A good argument," Dud said gravely. "Very well, I put it to the voters."

"I vote you in. You're hereby elected. Let's go see Rufus, unless you want to make a speech."

"Not at the moment."

"Good. I didn't want to hear it."

The saloon was deserted when they entered and Rufus, a bearded, bulky man with glittering pig eyes, was not happy to see them. He had laid out cards on the bar, playing solitaire.

"What you two want?"

Jeff asked, "How long you been here, Rufe?"

"Goin' on a year I guess, why?"

"Didn't you say then that this-here tent was temporary?"

"Maybe I did. . . ."

Dud asked, "How long is temporary, Rufe?"

The saloonkeeper gazed back at him. "Five years, more or less, I'd figger."

"Do you have plans for a permanent building?"

"Hell no, not yet."

Jeff said, "That's the wrong answer. Why don't you draw up plans and get some lumber from Isaac and put up a real building, say . . . inside of six months."

Rufus glowered at him. "Izzat an order, Jeff?"

"Well, you got two choices. You can do that—build you a real saloon—or you can pack up and go."

The other's eyes blazed. "What the goddamn hell business is it of yours to tell me what to do?"

"We're makin' it our business."

Rufus suddenly scrambled for something behind the bar. As he brought up a shotgun he looked into the muzzle of Jeff's Navy. He froze, both eyes red.

Jeff said, "Put it down easy."

Rufe complied, gritting his teeth. He laid both hands on the bar. "You two, git the hell out'n here!"

"A little more respect for the Mayor of Eden Creek," Jeff said, indicating Dud.

"We ain't got no mayor here! I never heard of sich a thing!"

"There's prob'ly a hell of a lot of things you never heard of. But you hear this one. Six months, Rufe. One way or the other."

They walked out in silence and went into Dud's store. Dud said, "Well, you make an enemy now and then. Can't help it, I guess. I wonder if he'll do it."

"Is he married?"

Dud shook his head. "At least he doesn't have a woman here. No children either."

"Make a note on your calendar. We'll go see him in six months."

A civil engineer from the East arrived with Henry Mills's wagon train. At the way station he inquired for Dudley Hurley and was given directions. He wore a store suit and black cravat and was a solemn-looking young man who introduced himself as Will Gordon. He laughed when Dud pointed to the creek.

"You want a bridge over that?"

"Yes. We've got a bridge, as you see. We want a better one."

They walked down to the creek. "How did you get those big logs to bridge it?"

"We hauled them across on the winter ice."

"Ahhh. Very good. How deep is the creek?"

"It varies, of course. Maybe eight, nine feet as a mean."

"Ummm. And it's twice as wide during the runoffs."

"Yes."

Gordon asked, "When do I start?"

"You started when you got off the wagon. Are your things at the station?"

"Yes."

It was arranged that he occupy a cubicle at the station, there being no other place. But Gordon declared himself used to hardship. He was just glad not to have to sleep on the ground.

In the following days he walked the creek bank and used Dud's boat to make soundings. He prepared plans, which he showed to Dud for approval. On gaining it, he began the actual work with a crew of hired men from Pommer.

James Buchanan was elected president of the nation, and Jerry Titus deplored the event. "He ain't even married!"

"Neither are you," someone said, to general laughter in the store, to which Titus replied, "But I ain't president."

That was not all the news, as Titus moaned to Jeff. He had a Baltimore paper. "Look at this—now they've done it!"

"Done what?"

"The goddamn Supreme Court decided that a slaveowner can take his slaves into any state of the Union—free or not—just like he can any other possession."

Jeff was astonished, "That's true?"

Titus shook the paper. "It's right here in black and white! They settled the case of some slave named Dred Scott. Scott said he ought to be free because he lived for two years in a free state. But the Court said he was not a citizen—lemme read this part." Titus put his head back to see through the bifocals. " 'The Court decided that a Negro, whether bond or free, who was a descendant of slave ancestors, was not an American citizen and therefore could not sue, even for his liberty, in the United States courts. It has furthermore been decided that Dred Scott had not gained his freedom by going into a free state, or into a Territory where Congress had prohibited slavery, since Congress had no power to do this'!"

Jeff said, "Does that mean a free state can't stop a slaveowner from bringing slaves into it and using those slaves there? Because if it does, that means *all* the states are slave states!"

Titus blew out his breath. "What the hell d'you think I'm sayin'?

That's exactly what this means!'' He spread the paper out on the counter and tapped it with a finger. ''This is gonna be terrible trouble, you mark my words. This is *big* trouble!''

Jeff nodded. The Court's decision apparently meant all the work that had gone before was now thrown out the window. He frowned, reading the other columns. People were saying that the law should not be obeyed. Others said the South should be cut off from the rest of the nation. And there was another financial panic that had started in Cincinnati. Eastern banks were failing.

Jeff shook his head. ''I don't see how they can figure to settle it with that kind of a decision. Dud's right. They have to get rid of slavery completely. It's the only answer.''

''The country's going to the bow-wows,'' Titus said with resignation. ''We can be damned glad we're out here in the sticks where they can't get at us.''

The eastern panic did not affect them except that it brought more ragged people streaming west, looking for ways to scrape a living from the land. Hard money was not easy to come by, and often Jeff's wagon masters had to accept barter and trade goods when they carried freight. Most of the time Sam was able to swap those goods or sell them in another town.

The panic also seemed to spawn petty thieves. Two holdup men appeared in front of John Bowman's wagons with drawn pistols, yelling at them to halt and pay up.

Bowman's shotgun guard toppled one from his horse and the other sped off in clouds of dust.

''A couple of wild young kids,'' Bowman reported to Sam. ''We dug a hole beside the road for the dead one. Nothing on him to tell 'is name. We tied his horse on behind.''

Roy was involved in a similar incident a half day from Norton. He was driving the wagon just behind Amos Mitchell when three mounted men appeared in the midst of some sand hills. It was getting on toward dusk and Roy knew that Amos was eager to reach the way station a few miles farther on.

He saw the three emerge from the brush and nudged the guard beside him, reining in. The guard stood and sent a shot toward the intruders. Amos's guard also fired. Roy slid out his Navy and fired four shots at the horsemen, who were scattering and firing back wildly.

When the smoke cleared, one of the holdup men was dead on the ground. Two horses were also dead. The others had gotten away, though Amos's guard was certain he had hit one.

Roy found his pulse racing, the blood pounding in his ears. His first gunfight! He had thought about it many times, wondering what he would do under actual fire. But when the time came he hadn't thought at all. He'd simply pulled the pistol and fired.

As he reloaded the Navy, Amos rode back to the wagon. "You all right, sonny?"

Roy nodded. "I'm fine. Who were they?"

"Don't know. Some pore goddamn owlhoots, I reckon. One's gone to meet Beelzebub. Prob'ly shakin' hands with him right now." Amos pulled out a sack and rolled a cigarette, watching Roy's hands. Hell, the kid wasn't shaking any more than his old man would.

They carried the body on to the way station. A couple of men dug a grave behind the stable and buried the body there, wrapped in an old blanket. Roy watched, hands deep in his pockets. Not even a headboard. That was the way some men ended up, without a single Christian word spoken over their graves. It was a stupid way to check out.

Simon sat in the saloon next to the hotel and sipped his beer. It was evident Chace didn't want him anymore and had slid out without bothering to say so.

Well, the hell with Chace. He didn't need *him*. He had learned a few things about playing cards. He could probably hold his own against farmers, as Chace called them. All he had to worry about was sore losers, men who would accuse him of cheating and back it up with gunplay.

He had seen the derringer that Chace carried in a clever little wrist arrangement, so that when he shot his sleeve—there was the pistol. All he had to do was grab it with the other hand, flip his wrist, and fire. It took only a second.

But Simon had no such trick holster. And he suspected that Chace spent hours and hours practicing with the little gun, just as he spent hours practicing with cards.

Simon had no desire to put in the time to be a card manipulator. He would take advantage of the odds in the way Chace had taught him. Careful play would win in the long run, as Chace had said over and over again.

Simon went to a gun shop and bought a small .31 Colt. It looked very much like a scaled-down version of his Navy. When he sat down to his first game alone, against three strangers, he slipped the small pistol into his lap.

The game lasted four hours, with several changes of players.

Simon modeled his actions on those of Chace; he was expression-less and machine-like. He lost heavily at first, then began to recoup. When the game broke up he was a little more than sixty dollars ahead.

He counted the money carefully in his hotel room. Easy money! It was better than working. He was jubilant. From now on this was his trade. He was a gambler.

Of course, not one like Chace. Anyone could tell Chace was a gambling man by the way he dressed; he advertised it. He would come into a saloon, sit down, and begin shuffling cards, looking about for someone to play with.

Simon decided to do the opposite. He would slide into a saloon and get into a game already in progress, protesting all the while that he was not very good at it. He would be one of the farmers Chace talked about with such disdain.

His second game lasted only two hours and netted him barely fifteen dollars. But his third game, the following night, was a di-saster! He lost nearly fifty dollars. It all went to a plump, pasty-faced little man with a scraggly brown goatee. He played his cards very close to his vest and peered at them through small round glasses perched on the end of his fat nose.

Simon left the game and went back to his hotel thoroughly frus-trated. He rode out of town the next morning.

He reached Big Springs the following evening. It was a small burg in the middle of nowhere, its being a stage stop the apparent reason for its existence. The only hotel, a small one, had a bar-room, and Simon spent several hours there, winning nine dollars.

The next afternoon he sat in on a game with a few men who had just come in on the stage. One was a stocky, thick-fingered man who looked as much like a hayseed as anyone Simon had ever seen. He had dull eyes and rambled on and on as he talked; he was the picture of a small-town porch-sitter. And yet he won nearly every large pot.

Simon watched him intently, with suspicion, as the other fum-bled with the cards he dealt. His big hands nearly hid them from view except as he spewed them out. His big fingers appeared to be so clumsy . . . and yet . . .

Simon had a flash of something—the corner of a card—and he growled at the man, "You're dealin' from the bottom of the deck!"

There was instant silence. The big hayseed glared at him. "You callin' me a cheat?"

Simon's hand closed over the small Colt in his lap. The pot in the middle of the table was piled up; there would be more than fifty dollars there. Simon gestured. "If you ain't, turn over your hand. Let's see what you got."

Instead, the hayseed went for a gun. Simon had a glimpse of steel. It came out of the other's waistband like a striking rattler.

Simon fired three times, as fast as he could thumb the hammer. The big man's derringer thumped on the table and he fell sideways off the chair, his belly spattered with blood.

The saloon was suddenly hushed as powder smoke rose and drifted away, then a babble of voices burst out. Someone jumped up and turned the hayseed over. "He dead as hell. . . ."

Another turned over the man's cards. Three aces and a pair of treys. "He was fixin' to win again."

One of the men at the table said to Simon, "What'd you see?"

Simon slid the pistol into his belt. "I seen him dealin' from the bottom." He made his voice very definite. Who was going to challenge him now? No one did. The others started talking about how the hayseed had won, over and over. Two men carried the body out to the street, half dragging it.

Simon got up and went to the bar, ordering beer. He was sipping it, still feeling the kick of the Colt in his hand, when the law arrived.

The law was a deputy sheriff, lean and gray-haired. He listened to the men around the table, looked closely at Simon, nodded and went out.

Simon took a long breath. Now he had killed two men.

Chapter Twenty-seven

DUDLEY checked off five months on the calendar. Rufus Trotter had done nothing at all toward building a new saloon. And he did not appear to be getting ready to depart.

Dud said to Jeff, "He's calling our bluff."

"We're not bluffing.'

"Well, he's sitting tight."

"He's got another month. How long would it take him to pack up and skedaddle?"

"A few days, I expect."

Jeff nodded. "I'll go by and speak to him."

Rufus was not glad to see him. He scowled when Jeff entered the tent. His big revolver lay on the bar at his elbow.

Jeff had selected a time when Rufe was alone. He walked to the bar and the other picked up the pistol.

Jeff's hand rested on the butt of his Navy. "If you pull that hammer back you're a dead man."

Rufe glared at him, but he hesitated.

Jeff said, "Put it down."

The other man took a breath, growled, and slammed the revolver on the bar. Jeff pushed it away.

"What're your plans, Rufe?"

"I ain't got no plans."

"I told you—six months."

"You got no goddamn right t'tell me what to do!"

"If you're going to stay here in Eden Creek you'll do what we tell you—or get the hell out!" Jeff leaned forward. "And just between us, I'd like to see you out."

"You're a goddamn bossy man, Jeff Becket!"

Jeff smiled. "You got one month, Rufe." He walked out.

Rufus Trotter was a man who carried grudges. He had run a deadfall in Missouri and had feuded with Howie Springer, over the man's wife. Although the Springers were separated Howie considered that the woman was his, and when Rufe made advances the two had words.

Rufe had thereupon stalked Howie with a rifle and had shot the other several times in an empty field.

There had been no witnesses. Everyone knew Rufe and Howie had bad blood between them but Rufe was not convicted of the murder. However, he was asked to move on. He had to sell out and go.

He did not want to do the same thing again.

A jackleg lawyer had told him that a jury could not convict him because there were no witnesses. No one could connect him to the crime, and so he went free even though everyone knew he was guilty. The law could be a friendly thing when it was in your favor.

He retrieved the rifle he had used on Springer and cleaned and oiled it. He selected Dudley for his first target. Jeff seemed to follow no pattern, going and coming at odd times. But Dud could be found in the store most days.

Just as Rufe could be found behind his bar. There was only one time when Rufe was free—the mornings. He seldom opened the bar till after midday. But Dud was in the store during the morning hours. It seemed to be an impossible situation. He could not go into the store and shoot Dud—either Dud's son or Perly Dyer would be there to see him.

Maybe he should leave it alone . . . except that it was eating at him. Those two, Dud and Jeff, were forcing him out, and they had no right! He had to get even. . . .

He found a sheltered spot beside a stable, where a board fence hid him from curious eyes. He had a clear view of the front of Dud's store, and as he watched, Dud came out of the store and stood talking with two men for several minutes.

Rufus grinned and ground his teeth together.

The range, he estimated, was slightly less than a hundred yards. There was no way he could pace it off; it had to be a guess. And he would only have one shot. As soon as he fired he'd have to get out fast. It might take them a while to figure out where the shot came from. By then he'd be back in the bar hiding the rifle.

The others would suspect him of course, but there would be no witnesses. After that was done he'd think about Jeff Becket.

Work on the bridge went forward quickly. Will Gordon proved to be an energetic young man who knew exactly what he wanted.

He selected a spot not far upstream from the old bridge and built piers on either side, then connected them and floored the span.

Dud walked to the site each evening to watch the progress. Now they would have a bridge that didn't sag in the middle when a heavy wagon went across.

When the bridge was almost finished, Jerry Titus came out from town to have a look. "Y'all civilizin' the country, Dud. When you goin' to build you a church?"

"Hadn't even thought about it."

They walked back to the store and Titus looked along the street. There was no boardwalk, but the surveyor's stakes were evident, with others hammered in to mark the street.

"You're gettin' to look like a town. 'Cept"—he pointed—"for that scraggly saloon."

Dud nodded. "Jeff and I've talked to him about it, matter of fact."

"Saloon keepers ain't allus pillars of the community, which I guess is an understatement. Did I tell you I'm thinkin' of getting married?"

Dud was astonished. He stopped and faced the other. "You—married!"

"I was married before . . . once."

"Who's the unlucky woman this time?"

"Widow named Sarah Sobery. She comes in the store alla time. Her children growed up and gone. Now she lives all alone."

"Well, I'll be damned. When're you going to do this thing?"

Titus grunted. "You make it sound like I'm goin' to a hangin'. Sarah is a good woman and I got a little spring left in my step."

Dud laughed. "All right, forgive me. Of course we wish you all the best."

"It won't happen for a month're more. She's goin' to arrange it at the church—you know we got a church in Pommer now."

"No, I didn't know."

"Bunch of Methodists, I think. They took over the buildin'. Used to be a millinery store. We going to send out announcements and such. Sarah wants ever'thing proper."

"We'll be there," Dud promised.

"You hear anything atall about Simon?" Titus asked.

"No, not a thing. He dropped out of sight."

"Well, good riddance, I say. What'ave you done about his land here?"

"Nothing. It's going to seed."

Titus nodded. "Claim it then. You mark my words, Simon won't be back. He's going to end up in a ditch somewhere and people wonderin' who the hell he is.''

Dud sighed. "I hope not. . . ."

Wagon master John Bowman brought a letter from Chandler addressed to Jeff Becket. Sam Harris sent it on to Eden Creek. It was from Robert McCoy, requesting another small herd of cattle. He would like two hundred head at the same price, delivered to Chandler as before.

"Eight hundred dollars!" Rachel said, thinking of silverware.

Jeff wrote back accepting the offer, saying he would begin the drive in a week. Jonah Sanford was available; he was working for Vince Ropers at the way station as a handyman and hostler. Vince would let him off for a week or two.

Bert Yellen rounded up two hundred steers and held them in a makeshift pen. Jeff sent word to Roy, asking if he wanted to go along.

Roy did. He was in Hartigan when he received the message. He went at once to Amos, explaining. There were several men available in town to take his place, so Amos assented. Roy rode back to Eden Creek, arriving the night before the drive was to start.

It was late in the summer, and when Roy walked into the house Rachel was startled at how he had grown in a few months, and how much he looked like his father. The boy had filled out that summer; he was as tall as Jeff, and nearly as broad. Beside him Lili was a willow, hardly casting a shadow.

As a small child Lili had evinced a desire and talent that no one in the family before her had ever shown. She begged scraps of paper and filled them with drawings of anything and everything that took her eye.

Elinor Locke encouraged her. "The child has a bent. Who knows, she may grow up to be somebody important!"

"But she's a girl. . . ." Rachel protested.

Locke curled her lip. "There have been famous women in the past. There will be more in the future. Being female doesn't mean that one is dull or stupid."

Both Rachel and Leah agreed with Elinor, though they knew the odds against a backwoods girl climbing from such beginnings.

But Lili was growing up a serious-minded, dark-haired young girl with her mother's eyes and expressive mouth. She did her lessons at Mrs. Locke's informal school, and pestered her father to bring her writing tablets, which she used to draw on. He ordered them finally by the dozen from Titus.

On one of his infrequent visits to Eden Creek Titus saw her drawings, and sent away for a watercolor set which he gave to Jeff to present to her. Lili was delighted. Now she could paint in color! She went through the tablets like a whirlwind and Rachel pinned up the paintings on the walls. There were flowers, horses, fields— everything she saw.

Dud requested some for the store, complimenting Lili extravagantly. They provided splashes of vivid color on the otherwise dull brown walls.

"They're quite good," Dud said to Jeff. "And she's only a child. She'll improve every day."

Jeff nodded and smiled, a proud parent. It was a harmless talent and gave her pleasure. He did wonder where she got it. Maybe from his mother's side . . .

Even driving twice as many cattle on the trail it was easier than the first time. The men knew the route, the water holes and places to avoid. They started on a misty morning, with Bert Yellen in the lead, Jeff and Roy in the center, and Jonah in the drag. It went smoothly.

Out on the formless prairie they met no one at all. The sky was an indigo blue, paler toward the horizons where, in the north, it merged with frothy layers of wan clouds. The herd grazed as it went, moving very slowly. The third day out it misted and drizzled, and toward evening a fog drifted over them, with spectral fingers eddying and forming haloes about the lamps as they camped.

They watered the herd in a huge shallow pool where wild magnolias grew in clumps, and as they got the cattle started again, Bert Yellen came back to report.

"Some gents watchin' us, Jeff. Over there to the right, along the ridge."

"How many?"

"I seen three."

Jeff nodded. "What you figger?"

Bert shrugged lean shoulders. "They maybe want to stampede us and pick up stragglers."

"All right. You stay here. I'll go see what they want."

Jeff pulled the Hawken from the boot, looked at the cap, and rode toward the distant ridge. Roy yelled to his father but Jeff motioned the boy back.

As he got close a shot spanged off a rock near him. He rested the butt of the rifle on his thigh and went on steadily. When he saw movement along the ridge he reined in and fired—without apparent result. He reloaded and spurred toward the ridge.

There was no one there when he reached it, only a higher swale, but off to the right several horsemen were riding away. He saw the blur of faces as they looked back at him.

Jeff paralleled the slow-moving herd for an hour but saw no one else.

There was no further incident, and they trailed the little herd into the rented pens at Chandler several days later. McCoy met them as they came in and Jeff got down to shake hands. The other looked exactly the same, elegantly dressed and courtly as ever.

McCoy had a man make a tally with Roy; they agreed on two hundred and seven steers. They had not lost a single one on the drive.

Jeff was mildly surprised. They had gained two cows. "We started with two hundred and five."

"Maybe I can't figger good," Bert said. "Two of 'em got by me."

"It happens," McCoy said.

Jeff and McCoy walked to the office, where the older man put out a bottle and two glasses then counted out the cash. "Always a pleasure to do business with you, Jeff."

"And you, sir."

He and McCoy went to supper at the hotel.

Henry Mills came into town the next day with three wagons, and Jeff and the others went back to Pommer with him in a light rain. Sam came out of the office to greet them; Henry and the drivers unhitched the mules and drove them into the corral as Jeff talked to Sam for a moment, then walked along the street to Titus's store.

Sarah Sobery was there, an umbrella clutched in her hands. She was a rather stout woman with reddish hair bound in a scarf and hard eyes.

Titus said, "Jeff, this-here's my betrothed, Miz Sobery."

"Pleased to meet you," she said, squinting at him.

Jeff took off his hat. "Howdy." She was bigger than he'd pictured, and looked tough as old boot leather.

She nodded to both of them, picked up her newspaper-wrapped parcels, and went out, pausing on the boardwalk to open the umbrella. Jonah Sanford, standing there, touched his hat and watched her walk away.

Titus said, "She going to help out in the store when we's married."

"That'll be nice," Jeff said.

"She got ideas about fixin' it up."

"The store?"

"Hell, yeh. What we talkin' about?"

Jeff sighed. Had Jerry really thought this through?

Chapter Twenty-eight

THE next town was only a short ride to the north, across a swift-running river. Simon rode over on a rickity bridge that squeaked and swayed and groaned at his passage, offering to dump him and the horse into the water.

The place was called Hendry; an agricultural center, according to a sign by the side of the main road, half hidden by Virginia creeper. He put his horse in the hotel stable and signed for a room. There was a notice in the hall with an arrow: BATHS. It pointed to the back, and Simon went out to find a small bathhouse with an iron tub. He lighted a fire to heat water and poured it into the tub, which had a wooden seat and back.

The bath was refreshing, though he had to put the same clothes back on. There was a barbershop next the hotel and he got a shave and his hair trimmed.

The largest saloon was nearly deserted when he entered it and ordered beer. He played solitaire at a table until men began drifting in as the sun went down. He got into a slow-moving game and it took several hours to win ten dollars.

Then a slick-looking man who reminded him of Chace sat in and the game perked up. The newcomer was obviously a gambler and the betting went up a notch. The stranger smiled all round, said his name was Pete, not offering a second name, and his hands as he dealt were a blur. He had long tapering fingers, and Simon wondered if he had a derringer in a trick holster on his wrist.

Simon quickly lost his winnings, and ten of his own. The chips piled up in front of the gambler. The two other players began to grumble, until one of them won a large pot.

Simon had seen Chace do the same thing. When a man began to grumble that his luck had turned bad and he was glowering at the gambler, Chace would deal him a winning hand.

Early in the game Pete had ordered coffee, which was served to him with a spoon in it. The silvery spoon was lying beside the cup and Simon stared at it. Chace had showed him how, with a shiny ring lying on the table, he could tell what cards he was dealing. Their reflection showed for an instant in the tiny surface of the ring.

Pete was doing the same thing with the spoon.

Simon's hand closed over the small Colt in his lap. He said, "Pick up the spoon, Pete."

The gambler looked at him in surprise. "What?"

"Get rid of the spoon." He felt the others staring at him. He said, "When he deals he can see the markings on the cards in the spoon."

The gambler's face hardened and dull red spots showed in his sallow cheeks. He glared at Simon, then made a sudden move, and a pistol appeared in his hand. Simon fired—once, twice, three times—and Pete's shoulders caved in and he slumped forward onto the table. The pistol thumped to the floor.

For a few seconds all talk ceased in the saloon as everyone craned his neck. Simon stood up and slid the pistol into his belt as the babble started again, louder than before. Another of the players turned the gambler's head. "Dead."

A man with a badge on his coat appeared at the table. "What happened here?"

Simon said, "He was readin' the cards with that spoon." He pointed to it.

"And winnin' steady, too," another remarked.

The lawman looked around. "Who was sittin' in?"

One said, "Me and Frank here, and them two." He indicated Simon and the body.

The lawman asked them if they agreed with Simon. Neither had noticed the spoon, but both said at once it was possible. Pete had been winning steadily, allowing them a pot now and then.

One said, "He got what was comin' to him."

Simon was not held. He had a drink at the bar and went back to the hotel. Had Pete been cheating? Maybe. There was no way he could be certain now. But neither could anyone else. He *thought* he saw a reflection in the spoon. . . .

The next day he sat in the saloon alone. No one offered to sit in on a game with him. He sat alone all evening. Even when the saloon filled up.

In the morning he rode out.

Rufus Trotter spent hours in his secret little niche, waiting for Dud Hurley to step out of the store.

Once Dud emerged with Jeff Becket and the two talked for several minutes, but Rufe held his fire. He did not dare challenge Jeff; and he did not dare chance a shot at him from any distance. Maybe at point-blank range, if he had the drop. He'd had it once, in the saloon, but he hadn't been able to make himself pull the hammer back—even though Jeff's pistol was in his belt. Because if his thumb had slipped—he'd be dead.

That was the trouble, facing a man like Jeff. You had to have the same cold nerve he had. Any nervousness or worry could be fatal. You couldn't think about who you faced—or you'd be dead. Jeff would never hesitate.

It made Rufe's hand tremble just thinking about what could happen. But shooting Dud was different. Dud was only a storekeeper.

Rufe listened to all kinds of talk in the saloon. And he was delighted to learn that Jeff had gone on one of his regular rounds and would probably be gone a week or two.

Two days later he had a shot at Dud. Hurley came out of the store and stood talking to someone, then he looked at the sky as the other rode away. Rufe aimed and fired—and saw Dud topple. He did not wait a second but ran back to the barroom and hid the rifle under the floor in his tiny living quarters.

Not long afterward he heard the sounds of yelling and stirring. The saloon was closed, and when he opened it for business an hour or two later, his first customers told him that Dud Hurley had been shot by someone.

"What! Who did it?" Rufe asked.

Nobody knew.

"Is he dead?" Rufe asked, trying to keep the eagerness out of his voice.

No, they said, he wasn't dead, but no one knew how bad he'd been hit. A few men had carried him home and put him in bed, where Leah had bandaged him.

Rufe listened to the gab, but no one mentioned the six-month ultimatum—so maybe no one knew about it. There was endless speculation as men drank and argued till late. But Rufe's name was never mentioned.

The shot had grazed Dudley's collarbone and gone on through, occasioning a very painful wound. Perly had come running out of the store on hearing the shot and had found Dud groaning on the ground. He and Josh had carried Dud into the store and tied on a crude bandage to stop the blood, then they and two others had carried Dud home.

Leah put a thick compress on the wound, soaking it with turpentine as Dud howled. Perly fed him whiskey till he could no longer feel the hurt, but it was not a bad wound.

Leah cried and swore by turns, making certain her husband was comfortable. Rachel hurried to the house on hearing the commotion, and they tried to find out from Dud who had shot him.

But the man's tongue was tangled and he could only sputter that he'd been facing the other way.

Leah said, "It was that damned Rufe Trotter."

Rachel tended to agree. Who else would shoot Dud?

Perly and Josh were surprised. "What's Rufe got to do with it?"

Leah said, "Dud and Jeff had words with him."

How that got out, they could not have said afterward. Maybe the door was open. But it was common knowledge in no time at all that Leah had accused Rufe of shooting Dud.

"That goddamn lyin' woman!" Rufe yelled.

But that night as he sat on the edge of the bed, unable to sleep, Rufe had strong second thoughts about his plan. The talk in the saloon was that whoever had shot Dud would answer to Jeff Becket. They had told again the story about how Jeff had gone after the three men who had stolen his horse and had killed all but one of them . . . and had set the other afoot unarmed.

Jeff, it was agreed, was a ring-tailed terror when he got mad. This shooting, they were positive, would put him into a rage. No one wanted to be around when it happened.

Even though there was no way anyone could prove he had shot Dud—Rufe was afraid of Jeff. He rubbed his hands together. What would Jeff do when Leah told him that Rufe Trotter had shot her husband? But how did she know? Had someone seen him? He thought he'd been so careful!

Feeling suddenly cold, Rufe grabbed his pants and pushed into them. He had best play it smart and get the hell out!

He shoved into his boots, pulled a shirt on over his head, and dug the rifle out of its hiding place. He had several hundred dollars in the cash box. He poured the money into a buckskin bag, shoved a revolver into his belt, dropped some cheese, bread, and two bottles into his saddlebags, and hurried out to the corral for his horse. He'd have to leave everything else, but it was his life if he hung around.

It was long after midnight when he saddled the animal. No one saw him walk the horse out of town and head east.

Chapter Twenty-nine

THREE days later, in Hartigan, Jeff heard about the shooting from Henry Mills, who had just come from Eden Creek. Dud was in good shape, Henry told him. "It was only a flesh wound."

"Who did it?"

"Ever'body thinks it was Rufe Trotter. He turned up missing the next day."

"Where'd he go?"

Henry shrugged.

Jeff was on the sorrel heading south twenty minutes later. He changed horses at the way station and again in Pommer and reached Eden Creek the following night.

He went at once to Trotter's tent saloon. It was closed. With his knife he slit the canvas and pushed his way inside. He struck a match and lighted a lantern. Rufus was nowhere about; the cash box was lying on the ground. The man's horse was not in the corral. Rufe had skipped out, all right.

As he left the tent Jeff knocked over the lantern, watching the flames leap to the dry canvas. In moments the tent was ablaze.

He mounted and rode to Dud's house. Leah met him at the door. "Jeff!" She stared at the burning tent behind him. "Did you do that?"

He went inside. "A lantern fell over. Where's Dud?"

Dud was sitting in the kitchen. "In here."

Leah said, "He burned down Rufe's saloon."

"He's impulsive," Dud said, grinning. "Sit down, Jeff. Leah, get him some coffee. We heard that Rufe's gone. Nobody knows where."

"Tell me what happened." Jeff took the cup from Leah.

Dud related again what he could. The shot had hit him unexpectedly. They had determined later where it had come from. All the circumstantial evidence pointed to Rufe Trotter, but no one had seen him fire the shot. And no one had seen him ride out.

Leah said, "He never did intend to build a proper saloon and he knew he had to leave anyway, so he tried to kill Dud."

"But he aimed a little high." Dud touched the bandage.

Jeff questioned everyone in the settlement. Had Rufe ever said anything to anyone about a place he might go from Eden Creek? A relative or friend to visit . . . ? In the course of several days he received varying answers. One said he'd heard Rufe say he had an uncle who lived outside of Kansas City. Another said that Rufe had once mentioned a cousin in New York City.

It was all rather indefinite.

Kansas City was too big a place, and there must be a dozen small towns around it. A man could spend years looking through that haystack for the needle. And Rufe was sure to change his name.

"He'll come to a bad end," Rachel said.

"Ummm. But I'd like to see to that myself."

The promised announcement arrived: Titus and Sarah Sobery would be married in two weeks at the little church in Pommer.

However, Titus was having second thoughts about it, but the plans had gone too far. He was squirming but could see no way to back out. He took Jeff aside. "She's a goddamn bossy woman, Jeff. She hid it perty good while we was courtin'. How can I get out'n this?"

"I doubt if you can. This side of dyin'."

"Speakin' of dying, I may wind up killin' her."

"How did her first husband die?"

"Jesus! I never thought o' that! I dunno."

"I'd find out if I was you."

Titus nodded soberly. "I'll ast around. Mayberry ought to know. He's the undertaker."

"Maybe you better let me do it. If it got around you were curious people might talk, and it'd get back to Miz Sobery."

"All right. Thanks, Jeff. How's Dud?"

"He's all right, back in the store. It was only a flesh wound. Hurt like hell but not much damage."

"Them's the best kind."

Mayberry had his establishment on a side street, the front of the building painted black. The undertaker was a skinny, mournful-looking man who fancied himself a jokester. He dressed in black as became his office. It made him look more sallow and unhealthy.

"Hullo, Jeff. What can I do f'you?"

They went into Mayberry's office where Jeff offered the other a cheroot and they lighted up. The large office held a desk and two coffins, both on sawhorses. One was painted black with gilt trim. The other was a plain pine box stained brown. The entire place smelled strongly of chemicals.

Jeff said, "You buried Miz Sobery's first husband?"

The undertaker nodded. "Oh yes. Gave him a nice funeral. Twenty-five-dollar box if I r'member right."

"How did he die?"

"Miz Sobery said it was a fever. He been sick a while and it took him off. We ain't got a doc in town, you know."

"He died natural? No marks on him?"

"Oh yes, not a mark." Mayberry grinned. "You figger she helped him along? No, don't think so. Only mark on him was a birthmark. That's all."

"Well, I'm glad to hear it."

"Talk is, she's going to marry Jerry Titus. That right?"

"Yes, I guess so."

He grinned again. "Is Jerry wonderin' how Mr. Sobery died?"

"Don't go tellin' that around. No, I'm the one who's wondering. I'd take it kind if you was not to say so."

"Oh yes, you got my word on it." He paused. "I wouldn't blame him though, for askin'. Miz Sobery, she's a mighty definite woman. I hope Jerry stays on her good side."

"A pain in the butt, would you say?"

"Yes, I would. I certainly would."

The hotel in Wicker had five rooms; Simon moved into one of them, a tiny cubicle with paper-thin walls. Someone was snoring next door, and it was the middle of the afternoon.

The hotel wasn't much, he thought, and neither was the town. Even the dogs on the street were mangy. The stores straggled along one main street that petered out at one end in a dry wash. The other end drifted off into the prairie. There was no cross-street. It looked poor as a toad.

Simon sat in a creaky chair in the main saloon; it had a dirt floor and smelled of coal oil and tobacco. The beer was warm and tasted a little bitter. There isn't much to like about this town, Simon reflected again. He bought a cigar and wondered if anyone in town played cards—or did they know how?

A few patrons came in as the sun went down and Simon sat in on a desultory game with three others. He won four dollars after nearly two hours, and quit. They glowered at him when he cashed in and got up. He was the big winner.

Simon left the place soon after sunup and rode west to Carreville, the county seat. It was a dreary little town on the high plains, windy, dusty, and unpainted. Alongside the road leading to the town was a wandering creek lined with cottonwood trees and high weeds. Across the creek were half a dozen brown tepees and a few smoke columns. Three small kids were splashing in the water.

Simon arrived at midday and signed for a room in the Carre Hotel. It was the middle of the week, and the clerk said he could have any room in the house.

He ate steak and potatoes in a restaurant and went to sit in the American Bar Saloon, looking for a game. The saloon was an ornate room with a high ceiling and a balcony around two sides, with a stairway at the back. Behind the bar was a large three-piece mirror decorated with gilt paint and flags. A few men were playing cards and a small derby-hatted man was picking a banjo near the piano.

Simon had a beer and got into a game later, when the big room began to babble and hum with laughter and conversation. Several painted women showed up and began to circulate, and the piano player thumped out loud tunes.

Simon had joined three other players, one of them obviously a professional gambler—black suit and red tie, white hands. . . . Simon played a very conservative game, always waiting till he had a fair or good hand before staying. He won a dollar and lost a dollar, and when he was sure the others had him pegged he bluffed and won a good pot. As he pulled in the money he saw the speculative look in the gambler's eyes. He knew the man was wondering whether he'd had the cards or not. Well, let him wonder.

After another hour, when he was about forty dollars ahead, Simon cashed in and left the game. He went to the bar and talked to one of the doxies, then went upstairs with her.

Off the balcony there were half a dozen crib rooms; each had a bunk bed, chair, tiny mirror, and a few nails in the walls to hang clothes on.

The girl said her name was Gypsy. She was dark and possibly Latin, probably older than he. She didn't ask his name. She asked for money at once, went out as she told him to get undressed, returned quickly, and tossed off her gown.

She went about her chores in a passionless, businesslike manner—which he was used to.

As he rolled away she stood up, dressed, and went out and back downstairs. Simon sighed deeply and sat up to reach for his pants. As he pulled on his boots another couple came into the room next door. The man sounded a little drunk, laughing too loud, then swearing. The girl's voice was only a murmur.

They were in the room only a few moments when footsteps approached and the door was slammed open. A third voice yelled that Carmen was his girl, and, "You git the hell out'n here!"

The girl screamed something—and there was a shot.

Simon opened the door and peered out. Two men were struggling in the dark hall and one fell to his knees. The other whipped out a long, glittering knife and was about to plunge it into the other's body—when Simon shot him.

Why the hell did he do that?

Simon saw the fallen man turn and stare at him. The man he'd shot took a step and fell forward on his face. The knife clattered away. The man on the floor got up, looking down at the prone figure, then at Simon. "He was goin' to kill me!" The drunkenness seemed to have left him.

Simon nodded, shoving the Navy into his belt. "I don't like them goddamn knives."

"Don't like 'em neither."

There were noises from downstairs; they had heard the shots. The girl sidled past them.

The man said, "I owe you, friend. But we best get the hell outta here." He pointed down the hall. "Let's go thata-way."

Simon glanced at the body on the floor. Was he an important man in the town? His new friend didn't want to stay and explain, and that might be the reason. He followed the other. They went out a window at the end of the hall, onto a shed, and made a short jump to the ground. It was pitch black but the other seemed to know his way.

"Follow me close. . . ."

The main street was only a few turns away. They hurried between buildings and stopped at the boardwalk, standing in the shadows.

The other said, "You know who that was?"

"No."

"Deputy sheriff named Phelps. Sonofabitch was half drunk." He chuckled. "Well, so was I. But they'll hang us both if they catch us. Where's your horse?"

"In the hotel stable. They don't know me."

"Dozen people saw you go upstairs, and the girl—she'll tell 'em you were there."

That was right. He was in the soup.

The other said, "What's your name?"

"Simon."

"I'm Marty. I'll get my nag and meet you at the stable. Show you how to get outta this burg."

Simon nodded and hurried back to the hotel. Jesus, a deputy! The clerk was asleep. Simon shook him and paid his bill, saying he wanted to get a start toward home.

The clerk grumbled as Simon went up to his room to retrieve his rifle and blanket roll.

He was saddling the horse when Marty showed up. "They millin' around back there. Don't know where to look. But they'll think of the hotel any minute. Come on."

Marty knew the town and its outskirts. He led the way, threading through outhouses and shacks to reach the open prairie. Then they circled the town at a distance and headed southeast.

They were away clear.

The pair rode the rest of the night, putting miles between them and the town. In the first light, Marty was revealed to be a rough-looking, stocky man with a two-day beard. He was dark, with a bristling black mustache and lantern jaw.

When they halted for a breather Marty said, "Well, here's where we part, Simon. 'Less you want to come with me."

"Go with you where?"

Marty indicated eastward with his head. "I'm meetin' up with friends. I was in town there to see a certain girl, but she pulled up stakes, so I went upstairs with Carmen. That stupid deputy thought he owned her—lucky for me you was there."

"You sobered up in a hurry."

Marty laughed shortly. "I figgered he had me when I seen that knife." He fingered a cigar. "They got your name at the hotel?"

Simon swore. He had signed his real name. Damn!

Marty chuckled. "Then they'll get a poster out on you. Maybe you better come along with me."

"Where you bound?"

"A few miles." Marty went to his horse and fiddled with the cinch strap. "Maybe you heard o' me. I'm Marty Webb."

"The outlaw?" Simon was astonished. He was instantly embarrassed at calling the other an outlaw, but Marty grinned.

"Yeh, that's me. Price on my head an' all." He pointed his finger. "Price on yours now too. You comin' with me?"

Simon sighed and nodded.

Chapter Thirty

RACHEL, Leah, Dud, and Jeff went to Pommer for the wedding. Josh stayed behind to run the store and Lili was busy with her drawing. She did not know Titus well anyhow, she said. Roy was off with Amos Mitchell.

Both Rachel and Leah had made new cotton dresses for the occasion; both were folded away in the trap wagon. Old clothes would do for the trip.

Long ago Dud had ordered several silver table pieces from Kansas City for wedding presents. They were carefully wrapped and tied. When they arrived, Leah and Rachel had hated to give them up, but they had nothing else that would do as presents.

Dudley drove the trap wagon, though his wound still itched and made his shoulder stiff. Jeff rode the sorrel with the Hawken across his thighs, but they reached Pommer without seeing anyone.

They pulled the wagon around behind the store. Titus was inside fussing with his shoes, trying to make them shine. Sarah was at home, he told them. Friends would escort her to the church. It was bad luck for him to see her just before the service.

It's bad luck for him to marry her, Jeff thought, but he kept it to himself, with a glance at Dud.

The women brought their clothes in and changed in Titus's office, complaining that his mirror was too small.

Titus was in a black broadcloth suit and blue tie, and he looked like a senator. He was also uneasy and nervous. His first wedding, he said, had been nothing like this. He had simply taken the girl to a justice and married her. But Sarah had been picky about everything.

Neither Jeff nor Dud owned a suit of store clothes; they were both in jeans and worn brown coats. Dud whispered that he hoped Sarah would allow them to attend.

Titus had opened a bottle and taken several stiff ones to keep his

173

courage up. Dud had one with him but Jeff shook his head. Some-one had to stay sober.

When it was time to go Titus looked very pale, and Jeff took his arm. "Are you going to make it?"

Titus's voice was a rumble. "She'll kill me if I don't. . . ."

They walked to the church, with Titus bringing up the rear like a man going to a funeral. It was only a short distance and most of the others were already there, older women who eyed Titus.

Sarah was in a room off the main hall, one woman told the groom. A male cousin would give her away. He was a short, stout man with a ruddy face and pop eyes; he introduced himself as Charles Dobbs. He was in a well-worn brown suit.

The minister was young. The regular clergyman was home in bed with a stomach ailment and this stranger had been pressed into service; he had come from Bowers, he told them. But the older ladies whispered behind their hands that he was much too young to officiate at something as important as a wedding. Sarah had to accept him though, he being the only ordained minister within two days' ride.

He positioned everyone, asking the spectators to find seats. A matronly woman played a small celesta-like instrument, filling the room with high-pitched sounds. Titus took his place in front of the minister, with Jeff holding the ring at his side. Everyone peered around as Sarah came from the room and started toward the front, with Dobbs at her elbow, blinking rapidly.

She was dressed in a light blue gown with a black dotted veil, and carried a handful of pink roses. Jeff thought she was smiling like a cat who has just made a meal of the caged bird. She halted next to Titus, glanced at him, and nodded to the minister, who began his recitation.

It took only a minute, then Titus reached for the ring with shak-ing fingers and managed to get it on her finger. She lifted the veil and turned her head and he kissed her on the cheek. Jeff heard him sigh deeply, like a man who stood on the edge of his own grave. Then she took his arm and they walked to the front of the little church to greet their neighbors.

Jeff looked at Dud, who shrugged. Titus was hooked, legal and deep.

A reception of sorts was held at the bride's home, it being larger than Titus's cramped quarters over the store. The ladies had baked cakes and tarts, and served lemonade that was innocent of spirits.

Titus was doing his best to look happy, Jeff thought, especially when his bride was nearby. But the strain was telling on him.

It was too late to start back home; Jeff had arranged for rooms at the hotel, and they went there as soon as they could slip away. It had been a lovely wedding, so Leah and Rachel thought, though they both knew of Titus's reservations.

"It's been a long time since he was married," Leah said. "He'll get back into the idea of it."

Rachel agreed that he would settle in.

But next morning at the store Titus was miserable. He said to Jeff, "We sat up half the goddamn night talking about money! That woman wants me to account for ever' penny I made since I was twelve!"

"Is it that bad?"

"Hell, I hope she don't find out about that trip I made to Fort Smith six year ago! I had me a time with some of them gals. . . ." He sighed deeply and shook his head, removing his glasses. "Them days is gone forever."

Jeff pressed him. "That's all that happened last night—just talk?"

"That was all," Titus said glumly. "We didn't even sleep in the same bed. Sarah says she can't sleep with anyone because she tosses and turns." He shook his head sadly. "I dunno what I done to deserve this."

"You opened your big mouth," Jeff said, "and mentioned them certain words."

"I admit I was a fool. You think I could kill her and git away with it?"

The town of Pommer had no mayor, but it had a council of sorts composed of the various merchants, one of whom got up in a meeting to suggest the town hold a fair.

It was an idea that caused an immediate response. Any merchant worth his salt could sense that a fair would bring people from miles around, and most of them would have money to spend.

Pommer had never held a fair—nor had any town nearby. So they would organize one by guesswork and memory. Nearly everyone of middle age had been to fairs in other towns. The council appointed a committee, of which Titus was a member. Its job was to organize the event, decide on dates and prizes, and raise the money for the enterprise.

As soon as the decision had been reached, the notice was printed in the newspapers so people could prepare months ahead. Lili read the notice with extreme interest. There would be displays of all kinds, including drawings and paintings. There would even be prizes! She might win as much as fifty dollars!

She went to her father at once, asking to go to Pommer.

He said, "What for?"

"I want Mr. Titus to send away for art materials for me."

"Art materials?"

"I need paints and canvas and better paper."

"Why do you need all this?"

"For the Fair, daddy! They're going to offer prizes!"

"Ahhh. I see. All right. You can go on the next wagon train if your mother will allow it."

Lili grinned. "I've already talked to her."

Jeff hugged his daughter. "You women stick together, don't you?"

Rachel supplied the money and Lili went to Pommer with Jeff. Titus was surprised to see her. "My God! You're a young lady now! What happened to that scrawny little kid with the big mouth I used to see hanging on corral poles?"

Lili laughed. "I guess she grew up a little."

"I guess she did! She certainly did! Well, young madam, what can I do for y'all?"

"She wants art materials," Jeff said. "Not kid paints, real materials like real artists use. Is there any place you can send away for that?"

"Of course. For goodness' sakes! You can send away for most anything these days. Hell, the country ain't as backward as it used to be. We livin' in the age of invention, as the papers like to say." Titus pushed the glasses up on his prominent nose. He glanced around with a finger on his chin. "Let's see. . . . I had that name just t'other day. . . ." He went into the small office and fussed with the papers on his desk. "There's a art store in St. Louis. . . ."

Jeff asked, "Can the things be sent here before the Fair?"

"Here it is!" Titus held up a paper. "Atherton Brothers in St. Louie. They carry ever'thing in art materials. What is it you need, young lady?"

"Can I make out a list?"

"Certainly, certainly. Here's some paper." He glanced at Jeff. "The Fair ain't till next spring. They's plenty of time." He patted a chair. "Sit here, lass, and make out your list."

Jeff and Titus lolled by the black-belly stove. The storekeeper said, "I guess you already heard the news. . . ."

"What news?"

"Remember that Osawatomie Brown feller? Well, he and a bunch

of hotheads captured the United States Arsenal at Harper's Ferry.''
Titus read from a newspaper. " 'Brown proclaimed freedom for
all the slaves in the vicinity. However his band was overpowered
by soldiers led by Colonel Rob't E. Lee and Brown is being held
for trial.' ''

"He captured a military arsenal! The man is crazy."

"That's exactly what they saying." Titus tapped the paper. "But
they also say they going to hang him. And they will. You mark my
words. He's goin' to hang high for ever'one to see. Crazy or not.''

"Who's behind him?"

"The paper says nobody. The whole thing's his idea. He got
maybe twenny people, some negroes, that's all. And the soldiers
captured the whole bunch."

"Slavery again," Jeff said moodily. "No matter what they do,
it won't go away." Jeff looked around. "I thought Sarah was going
to come and work with you in the store."

The other nodded. "She said a lot of things before the weddin'.
Now its different. She says she don't belong in the store." He
smiled. "I'm just as glad."

"Are you still talking at night?"

Titus nodded glumly. "That's the mostest thing we do. She still
got her iron pants on.''

"I thought you said she had some kids."

"She's got two." Titus shrugged. "I dunno how. Maybe she
sent away for them. Maybe there's a store in Kansas City that sells
kids.''

Jeff laughed. "Then the marriage has never been . . . There's a
word for it; Dud would know. But you can tell a judge the facts and
get the marriage thrown out.''

"A name for what?"

"A name that means the marriage ain't really started. Go talk to
the lawyer about it.''

Titus nodded pensively. "I could go over and talk to lawyer
Pierce." He took a long breath. "Of course Sarah would come
after me with a shotgun.''

"That would help your case."

Lili came out of the office with the slip of paper. "Here's the
list, Mr. Titus."

Titus pushed up his specs and read it. "Ummm. You need all
this stuff?''

"Get her what she wants," Jeff said. "Don't argue about it."

"Who arguin'? I was just askin'." He put the paper in his pocket.
"I'll send for all of it today."

"Thanks, Mr. Titus." Lili went out to the street and Titus said, "Well-mannered kid you got there, Jeff."

"She'll do."

"You know, there's a couple ladies here in town that fancies theirselves pretty good artists."

"I didn't know."

"That's why we put drawing and painting on the list for the Fair. So's one of them could win the prizes."

"Politics again?"

"Hell, yes. But I figger to get myself on the judgin' committee." Titus grinned. "Lili's goin' to have a chance."

"Don't you go giving her what she don't deserve."

"You shut your trap, Jeff Becket. If I want to do a fast shuffle, nobody's goin' to stop me. I know as much about dirty politics as anybody in town. I been readin' about Congress all my life."

"I want her to win fair!"

"That's just what I comin' down to. I'll see she gets the fair chance. Them other ladies—they don't know what fair is."

Chapter Thirty-one

LAWYER Elmer Pierce was a wrinkled, dowdy little man, pompous and bald as an egg. He was never seen without store clothes and steel-rimmed specs. He had an office the size of an outhouse, crammed with law books, a desk, two chairs, and a lantern. There was a single grimy window and shelves of folders and papers, and the room smelled of mildew.

He was, however, the only lawyer in Pommer.

"You've been married how long?" he asked Titus.

"Twenty-three days."

"And the marriage has never been consummated?"

"What's that mean?"

"You've never . . . er . . . had relations with your wife?"

"She won't let me sleep with her."

"Hmmm. She allows you to support her, but she allows you no . . . er . . . sexual relations. But you are legally married?"

"I got the papers, yes." Titus handed them over and the lawyer scanned them quickly and nodded.

"Is your wife ill or anything of the sort?"

Titus shook his head. "Hell, no."

"And you have talked to her about this problem?"

"Ever' time I start to she gets up and leaves the room. She says it ain't a fittin' thing for folks to discuss."

"I see. . . ."

"She's a mighty bossy woman, Mr. Pierce."

"Um-hum. She will not discuss it."

"No."

Pierce had not had a divorce case in years. Such things were simply not done among decent folk. But an annulment . . . He said, "I think perhaps three weeks is too short a time to go to court about this matter, Mr. Titus."

"How long do I have to live with this woman?"

179

"You don't have to live with her at all. You can move out—separate. Where are you living now?"

"In her house. She had the house before we were married."

"And where did you live—over the store?"

"Yes."

"Why do you think she married you?"

Titus sighed and shook his head. "I guess she just wanted somebody to support her. And she happened to pick on me."

"Where did you meet, in church?"

"No. She came in the store alla time."

"I see. Well, my advice is to move out. Go back to your quarters over the store."

"She'll yell her fool head off!"

"Let her. From what you've told me, you have one very good rebuttal to anything she does."

"What's a rebuttal?"

"An answer. If she becomes annoying, you can threaten to tell everyone you moved out because she will not sleep with you. Apparently that is a touchy point with her. If you threaten her with it, she may back off."

Titus grinned. "Yeh, that's right."

"And then, when the circuit judge comes to town we can file for an annulment."

"That means I can get shut of her?"

"Yes. I'm sure, if the marriage has never been consummated, the judge will grant an annulment. There has, in effect, been no marriage."

"Good! You do that, Mr. Pierce." Titus stood up. "What I owe you?"

Pierce scratched his chin. "Four dollars will do it."

Titus looked at the other, sighed, and dug into his pocket. If he could shed Sarah, it was worth twice that.

Very little that he owned was at her home. He went there when he knew she'd be away. Sarah and several other ladies gathered for tea and gossip twice a week. Well, he'd give them food for gossip. He and Sarah were through. He packed his clothes in a carpetbag and walked back to the store. He went upstairs, unpacked the bag, and poured himself a large drink. "*Keep* your damned iron pants," he said aloud.

After the debris from Rufe Trotter's saloon had been piled up and burned, Jeff had the land cleared and leveled.

Dud asked, "What're you going to do with it?"

"Is it mine?"

"You burned him out." Dud grinned. "So I guess so. None of us has a deed to his property. We're all here by squatter's right. If you want to squat on it, it's all right with me."

Jeff gazed at the still smoking embers. "Roy will maybe want to get married one of these days. . . . He could build a house there."

"Good idea. You claim the land then?"

"I claim it."

Dud nodded and brought out the chart of the settlement. He crossed off Trotter's name and wrote in Jeff's. "That takes care of it."

Rachel had a faraway look in her eye when he told her what he'd done. "It seems like yesterday that we came here to Eden Creek. . . ."

"Dead Hog Creek, you mean."

She smiled and laid her head on his chest. "And now Roy's almost grown up. . . ."

"Children do that. You can't stop them."

He embraced and kissed her. "It does seem like yesterday. You haven't changed a hair."

She pulled back and frowned at him. "What have you done?"

"What?"

"When you hand out compliments, I get suspicious."

He slapped her butt. "Am I that bad?"

"You take a lot for granted."

"I'm me. Nobody else."

She kissed him. "I know."

It seemed to take forever for Lili's materials to arrive from St. Louis. She counted the days and walked to the way station every time a wagon train came through. Mary Ropers would shake her head sadly. "Nothing today, Lili. . . ."

But the day did come.

A package arrived with her name on it; it was stamped in the corner: ATHERTON BROTHERS. Lili took it and ran home, heart thumping.

She opened the package on the kitchen table. Tubes of oil paint, brushes, canvas, and tablets. She laid them all out, then methodically checked them against her list. Everything was there.

Rachel examined the paint curiously. "Do you know how to use all this?"

"I have an instruction booklet."

"I see."

"And I suppose I'll have to learn by doing."

She spent hours cutting the canvas from the roll and tacking it to the stretchers. Dud supplied her with turpentine and Perly made her a wooden palette. Dudley had a book that showed a drawing of an easel, and from it he and Perly fashioned a tripod that she was delighted with.

Her first oil painting was a landscape of the creek and far meadows. She painted it for nearly a week, changing, discovering what she could do. When it was finished, Rachel hung it in the parlor.

Next she did a painting of her mother sitting by a window knitting. Lili had not intended it to be a portrait, but it looked so much like her mother that everyone exclaimed on seeing it, "That's Rachel!"

Jeff had been away for more than a week; when he returned and saw his daughter's work he was startled. The work was so sophisticated—far different from the little watercolors she'd been doing—that it seemed they must be by another hand.

Dudley praised her to the skies, offering to buy the landscape of the creek. But selling a picture was something she had not thought about. How did one charge for a painting? Dud offered her ten dollars and she happily accepted. She put the money away to buy more canvas and paint.

She spent the rest of the summer and the winter painting, preparing for the Fair. Jerry Titus came out to the creek toward the end of summer and was amazed at the work he saw. He confided to Jeff, "They so much better than the painting ladies in Pommer can do. She's goin' to cause a sensation!"

"Are you a judge of painting?"

Titus drew himself up. "I know what I like! And yes, I'm on the judgin' committee."

He begged the loan of a painting from Lili, to hang in the store. "It'll be on consignment if you want."

"What's that?"

"Consignment means that if I sell it you get the money. Most of it."

She agreed, and he took the painting back with him. It was of horses in a yellow field, and he hung it where everyone could see it upon entering the store.

Roger Parkman was one of the first to see it. He came in to buy tobacco, stared at the picture, and went close to study it.

Then he frowned at Titus. "Where did you get this? Is it a copy?" He sniffed. "The paint is hardly dry."

Titus smiled. "It's on consignment. A friend of mine painted it."

"A friend! You don't mean someone in this town?"

"No."

"An eastern artist then. Someone on vacation?"

"No. She lives in Eden Creek."

"Goddammit, Titus, this is no amateur's work! I studied art for two years at the Blaine Institute. Who're you hiding?"

"I'm not hiding nobody. You want to buy that picture?"

"What're you asking for it?"

"Fifty dollars," Titus said, surprising himself with the ridiculous price.

He was astonished when Parkman at once counted out the bills. "All right. Fifty dollars. Now, who did it? The picture's not signed."

"It's by Lili Becket."

"Becket? The man who runs the freight line?"

"His daughter."

"And she lives in Eden Creek?"

"Yes."

"Give me a bill of sale for this. Does she have more paintings?"

"She's got lots more." Titus wrote out the bill of sale. "She's goin' to enter them at the Fair."

Parkman nodded. He took the painting and departed, with Titus frowning after him. The man was willing to pay fifty dollars! Jesus! Were there more like him?

Roger Parkman rode to Eden Creek the next day. He was thirty-five, with brown hair and mustache, and a rather square face. A banker by trade, he had been sent to Pommer by his bank to make a study of the town and its environs. Would it be feasible to establish a branch bank there? He had decided it would. He had been on the point of returning to Bowers when he'd entered Titus's store.

As he had told the storekeeper, he had studied art and had hoped to become an artist, but his teachers let him down gently. He did not have what it took. Desire was not enough; he did not have the natural talent. He was advised to try another field.

So he had changed schools and studied banking and business and was making a success of it. He told himself that although he was a banker, he had the soul of an artist.

It was a minor consolation.

Seeing that painting—out here in the sticks—was a shock. The painter, Lili Becket, must have inherited buckets of talent from a forebear. Roger Parkman knew talent when he saw it. Like gold, it was where you found it. And Parkman had the feeling he was on the track of gold. If the woman had any sense at all.

When he came face to face with her, he was shocked by her age. He could not believe that this dark-haired young lady was the artist. He sat in the parlor with Lili and her mother and looked at the paintings one by one.

He wanted to buy them all.

He smiled at the girl. "They're too good for the Fair. Do you know the expression 'throwing pearls before swine'?"

Rachel said, "What do you mean, too good for the Fair?"

"Exactly what I say. You'll have no competition there and probably few buyers."

Lili said, "I'd like to enter at least one picture, though."

"Very well. But let me be your agent. I'd like to send these paintings to New York City, to a gallery."

"To New York!" She was startled.

"Yes. It's the center of things. Certainly the center of art in America. But first I want you to check my credentials. Your father will be able to do that. If you decide we can do business, I will take ten percent of any sale, but I will pay for shipping costs and any other fees." He handed her a slip of paper. "Here is my name and the bank I work for."

Lili took the slip and stared at it, seeing a blur. He wanted to be her agent!

"By the way, I bought the painting in Mr. Titus's store in Pommer. He asked fifty dollars for it. I think I got a bargain."

Rachel said, "It was worth more?"

"In the right market, yes, of course. I will get you hundreds of dollars for a painting before I'm through."

Chapter Thirty-two

THEY came to Zack's Place before dark. Simon followed Marty Webb down the gentle grassy slope to several shack-like buildings in the far roll of prairie.

Old Zack ran a trading post; it said so on the front of the building, though Simon could not imagine who would come here to trade. How would anyone know where to find it? Perhaps only an outlaw like Marty.

The trading post occupied the largest building; the others were apparently places to eat and sleep. There were several corrals and privies and a dozen horses at hitchracks and in the corrals.

Marty said, "There's men I got to call on when we go on a big raid. They ain't here now."

They dismounted near the door and went inside. The room smelled of tobacco and lantern oil, among other things. The main room was a bar, with tables and a kitchen at the back. It had a packed dirt floor and was lighted by lanterns hung from the ceiling on wires.

Four men were in the room. As Marty and Simon entered, everyone turned and stared, then they said hello to Marty.

Webb introduced him. "This-here's Simon." He pointed. "Over there's Kid Keefer. That's Hunky next to him and Billy on the other side. Zack's behind the bar, grinnin' like a fool."

Simon raised a hand in greeting. They all looked like hardcases.

Marty removed his hat. "Simon saved my bacon over in Carreville. Y'all treat him good."

The three nodded and the tension seemed to go out of the room. Zack cackled and put a bottle and two glasses on the bar. "Howdy, Marty."

Marty poured out two drinks and pushed one to Simon.

Simon sipped the whiskey, looking round him. He was now a member of an outlaw band.

He sat in on a game with Kid Keefer and Billy. Billy was skinny and small and smiled a lot, a big, toothy smile. Keefer hardly changed expression, playing methodically. Simon had lost two dollars at the end of an hour.

Roger Parkman was easy to check out. John Bowman and Henry Mills both knew his name and passed the information on to Titus.

"He's one of them bankers from up north. They going to build them a bank in Pommer," the storekeeper explained.

"How d'you know that?" Jeff asked.

Titus said, "Because Parkman was at the council meetin' and talked to us. Said he already bought the land. We-all want a bank here. . . . Nearest one's at Bowers, a hunnerd and thirty mile away."

"Parkman wants to be Lili's agent for paintings."

"He does! Damn me! Well, you mark my words, she's going to amount to something. Make us all proud."

"He says he's going to send the paintings to New York to a gallery there."

"I'll be damned. The man sounds like he means business. Lili must be pretty excited."

"She sure is." They were outside the store and went in and sat near the black stove. Jeff put his feet up on the ring. "I spose y'all heard from your bride?"

"Jesus! She come in here callin' me ever' name you ever heard of. She was usin' words that a mule skinner ought to have wrote down. Think she made 'em up. Said I embarrassed her in front of her friends."

"How did you do that?"

"Damned if I know. All I did was pack my bag and git out."

"What're you gonna do now?"

Titus shrugged. "Lawyer Pierce is gonna see the circuit judge when he comes to town and get me an annulment—whatever that is. He says it'll git me free of her."

"Yes, it ought to. You'll have to testify about your wedding night."

"I don't care. That's her problem more'n mine. Hell, I never spent a worse three weeks in my life. And that damn weddin' cost me fifty dollars."

"Well, it'll learn you not to make calf's eyes at ever' pretty woman comes in the store."

Titus sighed. "Ain't you got any work t'do today?"

Jeff laughed and got up. "All right. See you later."

He went out and walked to the freight yard. Sam was tacking up a poster. "Look at this, Jeff."

The poster read WANTED, in large letters, followed by: SIMON CAINE FOR MURDER! There followed a description of Simon. The poster had been put out by officials at Carreville, where it was alleged Simon had shot to death a deputy sheriff.

Jeff made a face. "I'm not surprised."

"It came in this morning with the mail. John Bowman said Caine lived in Eden Creek."

"Yeah, he did. Him and his parents. They both dead now. Simon never did amount to a damn." He went into the office and accepted a cigar from Sam.

Sam said, "I'm going to put on a mud wagon to haul passengers from here to Bowers and back. It'll pay now."

Jeff nodded. "Are you askin' me?"

"No. Just reporting. I know you tried it before."

"Yes, between here and Chandler. It barely broke even."

"We're hauling more passengers, but all men. Some say they'd take their wives along if we had better accomodations."

"What about a Concord?"

"Henry tells me there's one for sale in Bowers. I'll have someone look it over and if it's good, we'll buy it."

Jeff nodded. "Anything else?"

"I guess you heard we're getting a bank here in Pommer."

"Jerry told me."

"Apparently it's true. And they want to build the bank of red brick. There's a brickyard at Bowers, you know. Mr. Parkman wants us to haul bricks for them starting next week."

"You'll be putting on more wagons."

"Yes, have to. I had a session with Parkman. I agreed to put on ten wagons for his job alone."

"Have we got ten wagons?"

"No, but I've got men looking for them and for mules."

Jeff got up and stood at the window, looking out at the yard where the blacksmith was working on a wagon wheel. "It's a job we can save money on."

"What d'you mean?"

Jeff turned. "Who's going to steal bricks? We won't need a guard with each wagon."

Sam snapped his fingers. "That's right. I hadn't got that far. I only talked with Parkman a bit ago."

"We haven't had a holdup attempt in a long time. Why not cut down on guards and send along a few mounted men with each train?"

"We buy the horses?"

"No, hire men with their own, and they care for them. Pay a little extra for the horse."

Sam smiled. "All right. We'll try it."

Amos Mitchell's six wagons plodded into Winship in late afternoon and halted in the freight yard at the edge of town. The Becket Freight Company had a small office, a baggage room, and corrals, just off the main road.

Roy jumped down and stretched. As soon as his wagon was unloaded, his job would be done for the day. He helped put the boxes and bales into the baggage room, then he and Frank Kelly walked down the road to the Half Moon Saloon and had beers, then went next door to the restaurant for supper.

Roy ate broiled chicken and corn bread, with a wedge of lemon pie for dessert. Back in the saloon he and Frank lolled at a table with mugs before them, listening to the piano and singers. The five singers were girls in tights and fluffy dresses, and in between songs they danced on the small stage at the back of the room.

In a little while Frank went to sit in on a card game; a saloon girl drifted by, then came back and sat opposite Roy. "Hullo. You all alone?"

He smiled. "I was, up to a second ago." She looks to be about twenty-five, he thought. It was hard to tell in the poor light.

"You a stranger in town?"

"Yes." He nodded. "Just passing through."

She slid over to the chair next to him and he felt her hand on his thigh. He looked into her smile.

She said, "Why don't you come along with me—we can have some fun."

She was dark, with tight curls about an oval face. Her voice was husky and her touch was warm.

He knew about such girls. He had heard endless talk about them from the other drivers and guards. He had listened and never said a word. He had no experiences to discuss, and he did not want to ask questions that would reveal his innocence.

He glanced at the back of Frank's head. The other was busy with his cards. The girl squeezed his thigh and Roy took a long breath. He remembered many telling about their "first time." Was this his?

Why not? He nodded to the girl. "All right. . . ."

He followed her to the back of the noisy room and through a door that led to a long, dimly lighted hall. The building was larger than it had looked from the street. There were doors along the hall, a few open, most closed. He could hear the murmur of voices.

The girl opened a door; they went in and she lighted a candle. There was a low, built-in bunk bed with a flowered cover over a thin mattress. Against the wall was a chair, beside it a washstand with a basin and pitcher.

She said, "How long you want to stay?"

He hadn't expected the question and looked surprised. "I don't know."

"Give me a dollar then."

He handed it to her and she went out with a tug at his pants. "Take 'em off. . . ."

He removed his boots, wondering where she had gone. She returned as he doffed the pants and dropped them on the chair. She latched the door and pulled the dress off over her head. Beneath, she was naked.

It was the first time he'd ever seen a woman unclothed, and he tried not to look at her as she laughed softly, pulling his chin up.

"Hey—I'm not your mama."

She certainly was not! She pushed him down flat on the bunk and climbed atop him.

For Roy the next moments fled by at dizzying speed. They engaged in a great deal of squirming and rolling about—and then she asked him for another dollar.

He got it out of his pants and she laid it on the chair, then dived at him again. Most of the stories he had heard were about girls who laid in submissive state, hardly moving. This one was a terror, never pausing for a second.

And when she finally crawled off the bunk and slid into the dress, he lay there looking up at her, panting.

She grinned at him. "C'mon, get up. You got to go now."

He agreed. He sat up and reached for his pants.

Chapter Thirty-three

THE new furniture Rachel had ordered arrived from the East, all well padded and crated. Henry Mills brought it to Eden Creek and unloaded it as she watched, biting her lip. It had taken almost a year to get there.

Jeff was in Pommer, so Leah and Dud helped her to uncrate it and carry the furniture inside, all polished wood and soft cushions. They lugged out the old clumsy furniture and piled it in the yard. To Rachel's mind it was fit only for firewood.

She spent hours arranging and rearranging, with Lili's help. Lili had turned her bedroom into a little studio; the walls were covered with paintings. Rachel had hung four of them in the parlor and declared she would not part with two, one being the returned portrait of her knitting by the window.

Roger Parkman returned to Eden Creek in a month and a half, astonished at her productivity. "You have four or five pictures here that will raise eyebrows in New York."

"Are you certain you want to send them there?"

"Of course." He put out his hand. "Do we have an agreement?" She shook his hand and he gave her a paper from an inside pocket. "Here's a contract spelling out what I intend."

She read it quickly and passed it to Rachel. Lili sat down with the paper. What if he was the only one who liked her paintings? Was that possible?

He said, "I'll have these crated and on their way at once. I've written to the Carvajal Galleries—I know the manager. They're expecting the shipment."

"It's all happening so fast."

"My dear Lili, concern yourself only with your paint and canvas. Let me worry about business. Incidentally we must name or number each painting. There must be a way to identify them."

"I have a ledger," Lili said. "I write down the titles I give them."

"Excellent. Let me copy it."

She said, "I still want to enter one or two pictures in the Fair."

He smiled. "All right, if you insist. But do not sell any yourself. Let a potential buyer talk to me."

Lili nodded, smiling.

"I'm your agent. I can probably get more than you can." He shook his finger at her. "This is a blending of business and art. You're the art and I'm the business. You paint and I sell—agreed?"

"Things have suddenly changed," Lili said. "I didn't expect this."

"Changed for the better. You want to sell paintings, don't you?"

Lili nodded slowly. "Yes . . . I must, because it means I can buy more canvas and brushes, and pay back what I've borrowed." She smiled at Rachel.

Rachel said to Roger, "She's a very sensible girl."

"She's more than that," Roger said.

Marty Webb had gone to Carreville to see a particular saloon girl, but he had also gone to have a look at the bank at Hanover, a town only a few miles south and on the far side of a stretch of badlands.

He knew the town. He had spent several years in Hanover as a young man and was familiar with the surrounding countryside as well. It was his plan to take advantage of this knowledge. He would rob the bank, ride at once to the badlands, and lose the posse there. He knew exactly how he would do it and he could not see how the plan could fail—unless something happened in the bank during the holdup.

However, the others, Hunky, Keefer, and Billy, were old and experienced hands at relieving banks of funds. He could depend on them, although Billy was quick on the trigger and had to be watched: Marty had become aware that little smiling Billy was a killer. He enjoyed it.

"The bank should be easy," he told them. "There's a single shotgun guard inside and he looked half asleep when I went in. They've never had a holdup."

He drew a plan of the bank and they discussed what each man would do. Simon listened but did not enter the discussion. He had never been inside a bank in his life.

Marty came to him when the plan was finished. "You'll be our outside man, Sime. You watch the horses. If somebody stampeded them, we'd be caught."

"How long'll y'all be inside?"

"Maybe five minutes. Less if possible. We'll go in as soon as the bank opens in the morning."

He traced the route they would take out of town and into the jumbled hills. With any luck at all they would get away before an outcry was raised. It would take a posse a while to get organized.

"But if somehow we get separated, we meet at Zack's Place. Don't lead nobody here."

It took several days to ride to Hanover. Marty led them by round-about paths, avoiding other travelers. They halted on the outskirts of town at night and Marty went in alone to look it over. When he returned he reported that so far as he could see, nothing had changed. The bank was a crackerbox. They would ride in separately and meet in front of it when it opened for business.

That night, rolled in his blankets on the hard ground, Simon stared into the dark, unable to sleep. A fox barked somewhere near and an owl seemed to answer. The wind felt chilly, and he knew nothing would be the same again. In the morning he would be a bank robber. Once he had cast his lot with Marty there was no turning back.

Marty had told him: "I seen posters up, Sime. You're wanted for the shooting of that deputy."

Of course Marty had thought it a joke. There were a dozen posters out for him, for various crimes. The novelty of seeing his particulars on public exhibit had long since worn off.

Toward morning Simon managed to doze, and then he fell into a deep sleep. Billy woke him at sunup and he rolled out groggily, smelling coffee boiling. Hunky had fixed breakfast and, eating it, Marty was saying, "We all ride in separately and meet at the bank. Don't attract no attention." He stared at Simon. "Try t'look like you come into town to sell a hog."

Simon ate hungrily then saddled up with the others, feeling excitement beginning to build inside him. Billy scraped dirt over the fire and they were ready.

Solemn Kid Keefer went in first, then Marty. Simon was last. The town was quiet, with a long-settled look, boardwalks shaded by overhanging second-story porches. Simon's horse walked on its shadow and Simon got down in front of the bank, a gray stone building, and watched his two companions go inside.

He fiddled with the saddle cinch while gazing round the street, hat pulled low over his eyes. No one was looking his way; very few were on the dusty street.

It was a peaceful morning, cool and dry. How long had they

been in the bank? Marty had said five minutes, or a little longer. . . .
Time was moving by sluggishly. Simon told himself to be calm.
What else could he do?

When he heard the two shots from inside the bank, his head
jerked around and he stared at the door. Then he looked at the
street. Two men several hundred yards away had been talking. Now
they both turned and gazed toward the bank.

Simon swung up into the saddle, feeling nervous and itchy.
Skinny Billy ran out ahead of Marty and climbed on his horse.
Keefer and Hunky followed, both carrying bulging gray sacks.

Mounted, Marty growled, "This way. . . . Come on. . . ."

He headed north out of town as one of the men in the street fired
at them.

Marty spurred his horse to a gallop and in a few moments they
had passed the last house on the street and were on the open road,
with white dust hanging in the air behind them. Simon looked at
the others, wondering who had done the shooting. None looked to
be hurt.

About a mile out of town Marty left the road and headed toward
the hills, which looked gray and gold in the morning light. They
strung out single-file, loping easily, with Simon looking back every
few minutes. No one seemed to be coming after them.

They entered the badlands rather suddenly and slowed to a walk.
For an hour Marty led them in and around, sometimes having them
walk the horses. He did not halt till the sun was high in the brassy sky.

When he stopped he yelled at Billy. "You goddamn fool, Billy—
you just increased the reward out f'us!"

Billy pouted. "He was reachin'. . . ."

"The hell he was! You're just too goddamn quick with that pistol!"

Keefer and Hunky glared at Billy, who bowed his head like a
repentant child. Billy mumbled to himself and hung back, following the others, but in a little while he was smiling again.

They went on, sipping water from the canteens now and again,
and by nightfall they had crossed the badlands. They camped in the
shadow of the hills under box elders. In the morning, on the plains
again, they headed for Zack's Place, where they would divide what
they had taken.

Marty hoped it would be as much as five thousand dollars.

Jerry Titus was one of five persons appointed to the Fair Committee. Their job was to plan it, to raise money for the hundred and
one things that would require funds, and to advertise.

The five decided they would do as all fairs did, offer prizes for baking and home arts, for vegetables and fruits, for hogs and other animals, and for a variety of other crafts. Many of the prizes would be blue or red ribbons, but there would also be cash for certain contests and skills—such as painting. Titus saw to it that the prize for the best painting was put at fifty dollars. He also managed to get himself appointed one of the three judges for the craft contests.

The committee saw to it that a great banner was made that would be stretched across the main street of the town, proclaiming the Fair. It would be put up two weeks in advance. Notices were sent out to all neighboring towns and local weeklies. The Fair would be held for one solid week beginning on the first Saturday in June.

A large plot of land south of town was cleared to be used for the plowing contests, and an oval was laid out for races. Another large plot was rope-fenced to be used by campers, and nearby a row of shacks was built to be rented out to concessionaires.

All this was very expensive. Before even one red cent was taken in, the committee had spent more than four thousand dollars on preparations.

Roy was very interested in the Fair because there would be shooting contests. He spent hours melting lead and making cartridges. During stops with the wagon train he set up targets and practiced offhand shooting with his Navy, usually with Amos Mitchell standing nearby admiringly. Amos was no slouch with a pistol himself, but he admitted he could not hold a candle to this boy.

"I never seen the like of it," Amos told Jeff. "That kid can shoot the ass off'n a honey bee and never touch 'is stinger."

Sam Harris had joined the merchant's council as soon as he knew of it. As a gesture of good will, he agreed to allow the Fair Committee to use some of the firm's wagons to haul lumber and other materials to the fairgrounds. However, he planned to put on several mud wagons to haul passengers to the grounds from town, for fares.

The coming event was the biggest news in the town and its environs—except for the national news, which was heating up. That troublemaker, Osawatomie Brown, who had captured Harper's Ferry, was executed by hanging at Charlestown, Virginia, not long before Christmas.

Jeff read the Baltimore paper in Titus's store. John Brown had handed a note to one of his guards on the day of the execution. It read: "I, John Brown, am now quite certain that the crimes of this guilty land will never be purged away but with blood. I had, as I now think vainly, flattered myself that without very much bloodshed it might be done.''

Titus said, ''The poor sonofabitch had a good opinion of hisself.''

''There's another election comin' up.''

''Yes, and the Democrats is divided. Most of 'em wants Steve Douglas. You mark my words, Douglas will get nominated.''

''Well, a hell of a lot of 'em wants Breckenridge. . . .''

''I don't think he got a chance.''

Jeff said, ''It looks like ever'body and his cousin Charlie is running this time. The Republicans got Will'm Seward. The Constitutional Union Party's got John Bell of Tennessee, and some hayseed from Illinois named Lincoln is in the race.''

''Seward is the man. He can't lose. If the Democrats split the ticket, Seward is a shoo-in. And them dumb Democrats is sure to do the wrong thing.''

''It looks that way,'' Jeff admitted.

He spent an hour with Sam Harris, who wanted to drag the road between Pommer and Eden Creek.

''The government's supposed to do that.''

''The government doesn't know that road exists. It's up to us. We ought to drag it every month. It'd save us maintenance in the long run.''

Jeff said, ''What about the other roads?''

''This one to Eden Creek is the worst. We've had a half dozen breakdowns there.''

They went over the ledgers. Busines was good and improving. Sam said he was thinking of extending the line to Warrentown, about seventy miles northeast of Bowers.

Jeff said, ''You'll be haulin' to Kansas City pretty soon.''

''If it pays,'' Sam said, grinning. ''Only if it pays.''

Chapter Thirty-four

ROGER Parkman selected eight paintings, had them crated, and sent them to the gallery in New York City. Lili chewed her lips, watching the wagons depart. New York was a vast metropolis somewhere over the horizon; she had read about it. She felt completely intimidated and disheartened, despite what Roger had said. They were sure to turn her down.

She knew very well what she was, a backcountry girl with little training or schooling save what she had gleaned from books. They would laugh at her paintings. Roger was being foolish to think they would want them.

She went back to her room and stared at the painting on the easel. It was half-finished, a scene of meadows and hills with horses in the foreground. A bucolic setting, nothing like the grand paintings she had seen in Elinor Locke's books, filled with angels and grand figures in robes.

She sighed deeply—then laughed. She *had* sold one painting. They wouldn't want them in New York, but maybe here, among her own . . . When she exhibited at the Fair maybe enough people would buy paintings to keep her in canvas and paint. She had never thought of becoming a name artist such as Roger envisioned. But of course he was a salesman.

She opened the curtains to let in more light, and got to work.

Now that she had her new furniture Rachel laid out the knives, forks, and spoons they'd been using since they came to Eden Creek. They were all battered and worn and looked very shabby.

At the first opportunity she pulled Jeff into the kitchen and put several forks into his hands. "Look at them."

He smiled and put them down. "Yes, my love. And what will you want next?"

Without hesitation she said, "A sewing machine."

He laughed. "Send Jerry Titus a note. Tell him to get it for you."

* * *

Before the first snowfall the circuit judge appeared in Pommer, along with his bespectacled assistant. The judge was a lean, almost stringy man, dressed in black, with a tall, worn beaver hat. He wore a linen duster over his suit and drove a light wagon that had a square frame welded to it.

He put up at the hotel and arranged with Jerry Titus to use the store as his courtroom, as he always did. His name was Willis Lovitt, and he was known as a fair man who listened to both sides of every question.

Paul Trask, the deputy in Pommer, had a slate of cases waiting, none very important, but all needing to be settled. Jerry Titus's case was the last, and the store was mostly empty by that time.

Judge Lovitt sat at a small table that Titus provided. His assistant, writing everything down, settled nearby.

Lawyer Pierce presented the facts and said, "Mr. Titus has never consummated the marriage, Your Honor. I request an annulment."

The judge looked at Titus in surprise. "Did you want to consummate it?"

"Yes sir, sure."

"Is the woman in question in the court?"

Pierce looked about the store. "No, Your Honor, she is not. I notified her, but her response was not favorable."

"What do you mean, not favorable?"

"She told me to go to hell, Your Honor."

"Ahhh."

"She will not talk to me, Your Honor. She will not talk to Mr. Titus about the problem either."

The judge pointed to Titus. "Swear him in."

The assistant got up, held out a Bible, and Titus put his hand on it, swearing to tell the truth.

Lovitt then said, "Your wife refuses to talk about consummation?"

"Yes, sir."

"Have you ever slept with her?"

"Not once, never."

"Is she ill or distressed in any manner?"

"No, sir. Before we got married she was fine. Now she's crotchety as—er—she won't hardly talk to me at all."

Pierce said, "All she wants is support, Judge."

"Well, that's not right," Lovitt said. "Marriage is a two-way street. If she won't live up to her side of it, then it's no marriage.

The annulment is granted.'' His gavel came down. He looked at the assistant. ''Are we finished here?''

''That's all we got for today.''

Pierce hurried to shake Titus's hand. ''You're a free man. I'll get the papers signed and get you a copy.''

''Thanks. That's a hell of a load off my mind.''

Titus watched the judge and assistant pack up and leave. One of his clerks took the table the judge had been using to the storeroom, and Titus walked out to the street to get some fresh air. He had been a damned idiot to get married to that woman. He had hardly known her.

But he was free of all that now. He felt ten years younger. He walked across the street and down a block, past where they were building the new bank. It was partly constructed, surrounded by a web of scaffolding, with great piles of red bricks unloaded here and there. He entered the Palace Saloon and ordered a whiskey. Now probably everybody in town would find out the reason for his annulment, but he didn't care. He sipped the whiskey and smiled to himself, thinking how Sarah would yell about its being common knowledge. Well, it was her own damn fault. He was free of her and he hoped never to see her again.

He listened to the chatter all around him. A few feet away several were arguing the constant and eternal subject, politics, especially the coming elections. Ordinarily Titus would have joined them, but he finished the drink and walked out into the sun. He was free.

It occurred to him, as he slowly made his way back to the store, that the world was coming down about their ears on account of freedom. On account of slavery. He was not foolish enough to imagine he knew what a slave felt about bondage, but he'd had a tiny taste of another form of it—and it was sour as hell.

There were five of them, and the split gave each man a little less than a thousand dollars. And winter was coming on. They would disband until spring, Marty had told them. He had decided to journey south to San Antonio to spend some of his loot. Who wanted to go along?

Kid Keefer had other plans, and so did smiling Billy. Hunky was content to stay at Zack's Place and be lazy. Simon decided to go with Marty. He wanted to see what a big town looked like.

They packed food in their saddlebags and left one foggy morning; they would all meet again at Zack's in the spring. Marty was in a good mood, cares stripped away. He was not a moody person anyhow, but now he did not have to plan another raid for months. It was a pain in the butt, he told Simon, worrying about who Billy would shoot next.

"One day he's goin' to go up agin somebody who'll shoot first. Them's the odds."

"I guess nobody'll cry much when Billy's put away."

Marty agreed. "Not much."

It took more than a week to make the trip, several hundred miles, and they were both tired and dirty when they arrived. They bought new shirts and pants and took them back to the hotel, where there was a bathhouse. After soaking in copper tubs they tossed out the old duds, then had store shaves and haircuts.

It all made a man feel brand-new. Marty said, "Now we's ready for the girls."

Jeff looked at the chart Dud had been keeping of their little settlement at Eden Creek. There were now twenty-seven homes in the town area, a few shacks and shack-tents, and one canvas shelter owned by a family that had just moved in and as of yet hadn't been able to do better.

Dud's was the only store. He had changed the name over the door from Trading Post to read: GEN'L MERCHANDISE. He would still trade for whatever was offered, but most of his customers bought staples, powder, and necessities. A newcomer to town was planning, he said, to open a dry goods store. Eden Creek could use it. Dud had no area in his few rooms to add stacks of clothes.

Jeff said, "It looks t'me we can definitely call ourselves a town now."

"Certainly we can. Some may laugh at us, but we're growing. By the way, I was down looking at the old Caine house yesterday. It's beginning to fall apart from disuse. We ought to do something about it."

"What'ave you got in mind?"

Dud made a face and ran a hand through his tawny hair. "We agreed some time ago that the property was ours, yours and mine."

"Yes."

"But neither of us needs it. So why don't we sell it, as is, and retain the fields. We can get someone to plow and seed them."

"No objections. Have you got someone in mind?"

"No, but half a dozen have asked me about the place."

Jeff shrugged. "Then do what you think is right."

"Then I'll sell it. What should we ask?"

Jeff made a face. "It's a stone house in fair condition, with a barn and some sheds. Is three hundred dollars too much?"

"I don't think so. All right, three hundred it is."

A mild winter came and ebbed, and the Fair was only a month or two away. Lili had five paintings she was considering as entries. She had decided to enter two. Rachel was adamant about one and Leah another.

She was getting ready to pack the two paintings when Roger Parkman arrived, driving his usual light wagon. He jumped down and doffed his linen duster, grinning at Lili who stood in the door. Did he have news from New York?

He laughed, seeing her face. "You're a success, young lady."

"You mean they liked them?"

He came into the house and greeted Rachel. "The gallery took all eight paintings and, at the time they wrote me, had sold five. I expect the others are gone by now."

Lili ran and hugged him.

He disentangled himself, laughing. He drew out a wallet. "And I have your money here."

Rachel, ever practical, asked, "What did they sell for?"

Roger had a paper. "Two for ninety dollars each, one for ninety-five, two for eighty each."

"Oh my goodness!" Rachel said in a hushed tone.

"That's a total of four hundred and thirty-five dollars, less commissions."

Lili sat down, taking a long breath. She had never allowed herself to dream of such success!

Roger said, "And the gallery wants more."

"They want more paintings?"

"Of course. Your work has touched a chord or a nerve or something. No one else is doing quite the same thing. You are unique, my dear." He beamed at her. "Why do you think I bought your first painting? Because I thought so too."

Lili said, "It's hard for me to believe or understand all this."

"And another thing. The painting I bought has doubled in value. Those in New York will do the same."

Rachel said, "No one else is painting barns and horses in fields?"

Lili laughed. "That's not all I paint, for goodness' sake!"

"No one else is doing what Lili is doing—in quite the same way," Roger said. "That makes all the difference. Her way of painting has caught people's eyes. There is definitely something different—a style—about it." He glanced around. "Have you finished others?"

"I have two for the Fair and three others."

"You insist on entering them at the Fair? The first prize is only fifty dollars, you know. Half of what we will get from New York."

"Yes . . . I want to exhibit them here."

He sighed. "Very well."

"Besides, it's a prize, not a buying price. When the Fair is over you can have the paintings to send."

"Well, that makes me feel better."

"I'll make some lunch," Rachel said.

Chapter Thirty-five

EASY money was easy to squander. "There's more where this came from," Marty said.

Simon lost hundreds at faro; they spent money lavishly on fine suppers and wines—that Simon cared little for. He spent money on painted women and sat in on card games, winning and losing.

And then one night he met Rowan Chace again.

The gambler was dressed as usual, in black with a fancy waistcoat. He was sitting in on a game with four others and was winning. Simon stood opposite and stared at him till Chace looked up.

The gambler smiled. "Hullo, Simon." He did not seem at all surprised to see Caine.

"Hello, Chace." It was as if they had only parted for an hour or two. Simon watched the game for a few minutes then went to the bar. He had no desire to talk to Chace again. He felt he was a different person now. Chace represented something in his past.

He and Marty had made perfunctory changes in their appearances, in hopes that no one would recognize them from the poster descriptions. Simon had put his name down as Simon Cooper. Marty had signed the register as Martin Winter.

One of the hotel clerks was a young student who had once recognized an outlaw who was staying at the hotel under an assumed name—and turned him in. The law had collared the man and the student was paid five hundred dollars. This immense sum would see him through college.

His name was Francis Beckman, he was nineteen, and he had a large collection of wanted posters, supplied him by the local law.

Beckman went through the posters every day. It took him four days to set aside the two posters, one for Marty Webb and one for Simon Caine. He saw the two men every day. They resembled the descriptions and they had the same first names and last initials as the wanted men.

He discussed his find with the local town marshal, who agreed he probably had identified the two. Outlaws did come to town to spend their ill-gotten gains. Webb was worth seven hundred dollars; Simon Caine was worth five hundred. Beckman desperately wanted those rewards.

The marshal went around to the hotel to see for himself. He sat in the lobby and waited for Beckman to point them out. Arresting the two on suspicion could be a problem. What if they were not the wanted men at all? And how would he find out—one way or the other? The Marshal well knew how general the descriptions on wanted posters could be. Most would fit hundreds of men. He had no tintypes of either.

What he needed was a witness who knew them. The trouble with that was, the county probably would not foot the bill to have someone come to identify them.

When the two men came downstairs from their room, Beckman gave the marshal the signal. The marshal followed the pair to a restaurant, and then to a saloon. He sipped beer as he watched the two talking and playing cards. They did not appear to be different from anyone else.

He returned to the hotel and Beckman asked eagerly, "Did you arrest them?"

The marshal shrugged. "What for? They didn't break no laws. Gimme their room key."

Beckman handed him the key. "But you're sure they're the ones on the posters, aren't you?"

"Maybe I am. I'll look through the room."

He went upstairs and searched the room. It had a double bed, a chest of drawers with nothing in it, and a washstand. Evidently the two were wearing all the clothes they owned, except for a couple of heavy jackets piled on a chair. Two empty saddlebags lay on the floor in a corner. He could find no letters with names on them, no writing of any kind.

In the lobby again he shook his head. "I didn't find nothing."

Beckman's face sagged. "Then you're not going to arrest them?"

"If I do, how will I find out their real names? You figger I can beat it out of them?"

Beckman nodded.

The Marshal shook his head and left. He had no hesitation in beating a prisoner when it seemed the only way to get information, but these two might not cooperate. It might take himself and several others to do the trick. The big, black-mustached one looked as if he would turn mean when aroused. There was no telling how good he was at street-fighting. The smaller one had a look of a back-shooter. And both were wanted for murder—if they were Webb and Caine.

Of course the rewards interested him. Was there a way he could cut the clerk, Beckman, out of them? After all, he would be taking all the risks. He hated to think of paying all that money out to a hotel clerk.

The marshal was musing on these matters when a tall stranger entered the office and asked for him. The lawman looked him over; a gambler for sure, from the way he dressed. It was probably the first time a gambler had ever come into the office under his own steam. In his experience, gamblers did not hobnob with lawmen.

The marshal asked curiously, "What can I do f'you?"

Rowan Chace said, "I want to report a desperado."

The marshal almost smiled. "A desperado?"

"He's wanted for murder." Chace took a well-folded poster from his pocket. "This man."

It was the poster concerning Simon Caine.

The marshal pointed to a chair. "What d'you know about him?"

"I know him from a while back. He was in the Garland Saloon last night. He's staying at the Corona Hotel under the name Simon Cooper."

"You know him?"

"Yes. We met months ago up north." Chace took out a thin cigar and rolled it in his fingers. "I'm interested in the reward, Marshal. But I'd rather Simon didn't know I turned him in. He's a dangerous man. He's killed several, he told me."

The marshal nodded. "We can take care o' that." He had the gambler write his name and where he was staying on a slip of paper. Now he had a positive identification on Caine. It was likely that when he arrested Caine the man would turn in Webb. There was little loyalty among criminals.

"D'you know where Caine is now?"

Chace nodded. "He's in the hotel, probably. I just left the saloon this morning and he wasn't there."

"All right. You go back to the saloon and stay there."

The marshal called in three deputies and started for the hotel.

They left the saloon near midnight and Simon told Marty about meeting Rowan Chace. "Didn't expect to ever see him again."

Marty frowned. "He knows you?"

"Sure. . . ."

"He knows your name?"

"Of course. We worked together for a while."

They entered the hotel and went up to the room. Inside Marty said, "You got along with this gambler?"

"Well, it could have been better. He was tight as hell with a dollar. We had some arguments about that."

"Izzat why you parted company?"

Simon shrugged. "He slid out one night without sayin' a word. This is the first time I've seen him since."

Marty stared at the other for a moment. Then he picked up his saddlebags. "Let's go. We're moving."

"What?"

"He's a gambler, you said? I don't trust gamblers. This one knows too much about you. Come on." He put on his heavy coat and went to the door. "Come on."

They went down the back stairs and across the dark yard to the stables, saddled the horses, and rode out slowly, taking back streets. They cut across fields to the road north and saw no one. Lights were out in most houses, honest folk in bed.

Marty had stayed alive by trusting his highly developed sense of danger. If the law got Simon it might get him too. A gambler showing up unexpectedly could mean trouble. Why take a chance?

Their money was getting low anyway. It was time to go.

The next town, only thirty miles away, was Arnett. It wasn't large, but a year ago the telegraph had reached it. As Simon and Marty approached the town, from a mile away, Marty noticed the line of poles. They came into town from a different direction, but there was no mistaking what they were.

He reined in. "They got a damn wire in that town."

Simon frowned. It was light enough to see the poles.

Marty said, "If that gambler turned you in, then they got wires out to ever'where."

"We don't know he turned me in."

"You got to figger he did." Marty grinned. "You worth five hunnerd dollars, boy."

Simon grunted. He wasn't used to looking at it that way.

"Come on. We'll go around the town."

They pointed west and then headed north again. They found a road that headed north and moved along it for several hours, halting on a bare hill.

Looking back, Marty growled. Far in the distance riders could be seen approaching. A film of dust rose, staining the blue sky. "Could be a posse," he said.

"Why would they be comin' this way?"

Marty sniffed at the other's ignorance. "Maybe they got a spyglass. Maybe somebody seen us. You got to figger the law ain't stupid.'' Marty headed off the road at once. "Come on.''

Simon followed, looking back at their plain trail. He yelled at Marty, saying they were leaving tracks, but Marty shook his head. A posse would never catch up to them.

They hurried west for several hours before bending north again, and saw no one. "It prob'ly wan't even a posse,'' Marty decided.

Probably not. But soon after, in the middle of the afternoon, when they turned north, someone fired at them. The bullet ricocheted off a rock ledge and whined away into the sky.

Marty swore, and they spurred the animals into a gallop as more rifle shots followed and sought them out.

"They tryin' to hit the horses,'' Marty muttered.

There were apparently half a dozen men, all eager for reward money. They were tenacious. They had spread out wide so that any deviation of the pursued brought them closer to the pursuers—an old Indian trick.

As darkness approached, Marty turned into a deep, brushy wash. It had a sandy bottom, and they rode along it for a mile or more before dismounting to lead the horses into a niche.

"They'll know we're here some'ers,'' Marty said. "But there ain't enough of them to search ever'where. We'll skin out when they gets tired of lookin'.''

They waited in silence for several hours. Once they heard voices, but no one came close.

"They don't know what the hell t'do,'' Marty whispered.

Simon could see the other's teeth in the darkness as Marty grinned, and he realized the outlaw was enjoying the chase.

An hour later there was the sound of a shot from a mile or so away and Marty chuckled. "Somebody scared up a deer, likely.'' He led out into the wash and found a place to climb the side. Then they mounted and rode eastward, back the way they had come.

Sam Harris bought the Concord coach on John Bowman's recommendation, and promoted Roy to drive it and the six horses. He was the youngest driver in the company. His first act was to pull the coach into the way station south of Bowers and set about painting it the Becket red, a job that took all day while several stood about advising him.

That done he rolled into Hartigan. Rush Hopkins, the agent there, had seven passengers for Pommer, two of them ladies who were delighted to see the Concord.

It was raining lightly as he reached Pommer and halted near the waiting room. Sam had four passengers for Norton. They piled on the baggage and Roy took off in the mist. It was raining hard when they reached Eden Creek and decided to stay the night.

Roy went home at once and spent an hour telling the news he'd picked up, admiring Lili's pictures.

In the morning he went on to Norton.

When he got back to Pommer two days later, Jerry Titus was supervising four men who were stringing a large banner across the street to advertise the Fair.

Roy left the coach in the freight yard and had supper with Titus and Sam. The Fair Committee, Titus said, hoped to entertain as many as three thousand people during its run. If they managed that, the Fair would not only break even but make a few dollars.

Sam thought that a very good possibility. His drivers were posting handbills in every town and way station. Every newspaper for miles around was running ads. Unfortunately, Warrentown, far in the north, was holding a fair at the same time. But it was some two hundred miles away and Titus hoped it would not conflict too much with the attendance in Pommer.

The next morning Roy walked to the fairgrounds. Carpenters were hard at work on the concession shacks, and as soon as they finished one painters slapped whitewash on it. A hundred signs were being made and tacked up. The oval for racing was already completed, and spectator stands were going up, carpenters' hammers beating a steady tattoo. It was all very exciting. The opening was only a few days away.

On the large bulletin boards at the entrance, Roy studied the lists of prize events. Prizes were to be offered for squashes, cabbages, grain, fruit, and livestock. The home arts prizes were for best cake, bread, jellies and jams, fancy needlework and laces—and painting.

He smiled at that. Fifty dollars for best painting. Lili would win it, easy.

The contests were: plowing, a prize for the straightest furrows, and pulling matches by teams. There were always races and shooting contests, pistol and rifle; no fair was complete without them.

On the fairgrounds would be sideshows, medicine shows, and even organ-grinders. Titus had told him that a merry-go-round had been promised but the owners had been enticed to Warrentown at the last moment. Too bad.

Roy glanced at the sky. The weather was kind. It did not promise either rain or wind. Everything seemed to point to the Fair's being a great success.

He went back to the freight yard and talked to Sam. "Let me take the Concord to Eden Creek. I want to bring my mother and sister and some friends to the Fair."

Sam shrugged. "Yes, of course. But try to get a few paying passengers. I'll reserve them cubicles here if you want. The hotel is already full."

"Thanks, Sam."

Roy drove the empty coach, with only four horses, to Eden Creek, and in the morning Rachel, Lili, Leah, Hester, and Josh climbed in with Angus Porter and his wife, Addie, and the two kids, Jason and Faith. Dud rode on top with Roy.

Hester had a large package containing a cake. "It's for the contest," she told them. She held it on her lap the entire trip.

Jeff and Luke met the coach in Pommer and Luke took Hester off to have the cake entered. Roger Parkman was also there, tipping his hat to the ladies. He went away with Lili, carrying the two paintings.

"There are seven paintings already displayed," he said to her. "Wait till you see them."

"Are they good?"

"They're the worst daubs I ever saw." He shuddered and she almost giggled.

One of Titus's clerks took the two paintings and gave her a slip for them. "They'll go in the booth right away, miss."

The booth proved to be a long gallery painted a dull brown. There was a railing five feet along the front to keep the onlookers from touching the paintings. Lili stared at the displayed art and bit her lip.

She whispered to Roger, "It's terrible!"

"It's amateurish," he said. "Wait till they put yours up."

A half dozen of the town ladies were nearby, talking among themselves, eyeing the paintings. Probably, Lili thought, some of them were the artists.

She was studying them when they all turned, gasping, toward the gallery. Lili looked around and saw the same clerk putting her two paintings on display, with her name neatly lettered beside them. The ladies rushed to the railing, gawking at them, and Roger pulled her away.

"I'll be very surprised if any of those daubs are there by nightfall," he said. "I should think they'd be embarrassed to have them seen."

Lili said, "I didn't want to show them up—I shouldn't have entered mine."

"It's done now. The whole town will know who you are. Who was it who said, 'Fame is sometimes thrust upon us'?"

"That's ridiculous. I'm not famous."

"You will be, child."

And Parkman was right. The other seven paintings were withdrawn by evening—only Lili's remained. When Lili met the painting ladies in the fairground they passed her with stony faces.

Luke Tilley was entered in the rifle-shooting contests. He had also bought a fast little mare in Winship and was in the half-mile race. Jeff had entered the pistol-shooting contests, as had Amos Mitchell. "Just to keep you company." Amos thought he might come in second.

Hester's cake was from an old recipe that had been handed down in her family. But when she saw her cake displayed along with two dozen others, she was dejected. The others had fancy ices, some with color and decorations. Hers looked almost dowdy, she said.

But Luke would not let her withdraw it.

The first day at the Fair was exciting and mostly social. People stood in groups everywhere, chatting and gossiping with others not seen in years.

Roy watched the men put up the targets for the next day's shoots. A high mound of earth had been thrown up and tamped to provide a backstop. The paper targets were fastened to wooden frames in front of it. The pistol range was twenty-five yards, the rifle range one hundred.

Roy paced off the pistol range to satisfy himself—it looked too short. But it was not.

Luke Tilley had done the same thing at the rifle range, and found it proper. He had a Sharps model '52 rifle, .52 caliber, and with it he had won a number of shoots.

There was a huge street party in Pommer—it spilled over from the fairgrounds. Guitarists and fiddlers played, and someone joined in with a flute. People danced and stomped in the street, yelling and laughing.

The party lasted until almost eleven o'clock. Then everyone went off to bed.

Chapter Thirty-six

THE next morning Jerry Titus and his judges officially proclaimed Lili Becket's paintings the Best of Fair and awarded her fifty dollars.

A reporter from the Winship *Democrat* tried to pull her aside, but Roger Parkman took his arm and talked to him as the fellow made notes, looking astonished at the things Roger told him.

Later she said to Roger, "You get ten percent of—"

"No," he said firmly. "That's yours. It was not a sale. When the Fair's over I'll send them both east. Buy yourself something with it."

The judging of Household Arts took place just after lunch. Hester, chewing her lower lip, watched the judges make marks on note pads as they went from cake to cake. They examined each, then they sampled them.

Luke stood behind her, hands on her twitching shoulders as Jerry Titus came forward on the raised platform to make the announcement.

Leah, Dud, and Rachel stood next to her and Titus smiled down on them. He said, "The committee is awarding red and blue ribbons, as you know. The red ribbon carries with it a prize of five dollars, the blue ribbon is worth ten."

He beamed at the rapt audience. "We want to thank all the ladies who worked so hard to—"

"Get on with it," someone said.

Titus sighed. "Yes, well, first the red." He consulted a paper. "For second-best cake in the Fair, the judges award the red ribbon and five dollars to Mrs. Millie Smithers."

Everyone clapped and chattered as Mrs. Smithers went forward to claim her prize.

Then Titus held up his hand. "For best cake at the Fair, the judges award the blue ribbon and ten dollars to . . ." He grinned at them. "To Hester Tilley!"

Hester gave a little cry and sagged in Luke's arms. He shook her, saying, "You won! You won!"

"I don't b'lieve it!"

Dud grasped her arm and led her to the platform. "Here's your winner, Jerry."

Titus jumped down and hugged her, then pinned the ribbon to her dress. "That was a damned tasty cake, Hester." He handed her the ten dollars as everyone yelled and clapped.

She looked at Dud. "I never won anything b'fore in my life!"

"Well, you did now."

"Your cake didn't look the best," Titus said, "but it sure'n hell tasted the best."

"Thanks, Mr. Titus." Hester gave the money to Luke. He took it then gave it back to her.

"This's yours. You won it fair'n square."

"But shouldn't we put it away?"

"Yeah, we should. But I want you t'spend it on something you want. They's lots of pretty things here. You go look around, hear?"

She hugged him, sniffling. She *had* seen some wonderful dress material and sew-on laces.

There were three races that afternoon, and Luke won the half-mile with his fast mare. He received fifteen dollars, and later on that night, as they were going to bed, Hester told him part of what she'd done with her money.

"I bet five dollars on you in the race."

He was astounded. "You bet on the race?"

She snuggled up to him. "Uh-huh. I won thirty dollars."

"I'll be damned. . . ." He began laughing.

Marty Webb sat in Zack's Place with a bottle of beer on the table in front of him. He had returned to poor news. Little smiling Billy was dead. As he had predicted, Billy had met someone who had turned out to be slicker with a pistol than he.

Hunky had not left Zack's deadfall and still had most of his money. Kid Keefer walked in soon, and he had spent all his. "Let's go get some, Marty. . . ."

"I'm thinkin' on it."

Simon said, "I know a place where there's no bank."

"What the hell good is that?" Keefer said. "We want a little burg with a easy bank."

Simon shrugged. "If there's no bank, folks have to keep their money with 'em."

"That's right," Marty agreed. "Folks stick it in a mattress or something. What's this place, Sime?"

"It's called Eden Creek. It's where Jeff Becket lives."

"The freight line man?"

"Yeah. He keeps his money in the house. There's a store there too. He got to have a keg fulla money by now. Them two could be as good as a bank."

"Yeah," Marty said, drawing the word out. "I know where that is, Eden Creek. I been there."

"It's just south of Pommer."

"That's right. How many people there—how many guns?"

Simon scratched his chin. "Depends on when you hit the place. Becket is away a lot. . . ."

"What about afterward?" Hunky asked.

"We can go east or west," Simon said. "There's nothing for a hunnerd miles either way . . . maybe more. No roads or trails."

Marty looked around. "They's four of us. You figger that ought to do 'er?"

"As long as Jeff Becket ain't there."

"How can we be sure about that?"

"Send somebody in to ask around."

Marty nodded. "This Becket is bad medicine?"

"The worst."

"All right. Let's go look the place over."

Twenty-five shooters, divided into groups, were entered in the rifle contests. They were shooting at four sets of targets, each smaller than the one before, and contestants were steadily eliminated. Even the first targets were tiny, and half the men had dropped out in the first hour.

Only three remained; Luke Tilley, with his old Sharps, was one of them. All the shooting was done standing. Each shooter was given one minute to fire at his target and step back. Three shots were fired by each contestant, then the judges went forward to examine the targets.

There were three judges led by little, dowdy lawyer Pierce. The three men conferred for five or six minutes, measuring and calculating. Then they finally came back to the shooters and Pierce announced: "The winner is Luke Tilley."

Hester yelled and ran to him. He scooped her up and twirled her about as the crowd laughed. He had won, Pierce said, by the width of half a matchstick.

More than thirty entered the pistol-shooting contests, and it took more than an hour to whittle them down to five men. Amos Mitchell had dropped out after twenty had been eliminated. His hope of second place went dim.

But Jeff was one of the five.

New and smaller targets were put up, and in another half hour only Jeff and one other remained; the man said his name was Pat Waking, and he was cool and deliberate. He had big hands and was squat and broad, with round shoulders and a genial appearance.

Jeff, big and broad, looked like a giant beside him. But after four targets were fired at, they were still even.

"You damn good," Waking said.

"So are you."

Lawyer Pierce said, "Can we make the targets smaller yet?" He looked at both of them.

Waking nodded. "Small's you want."

Jeff agreed.

Pierce and his judges changed the targets and the two fired again. They were still even. The crowd behind them was hushed. Jeff turned and smiled at Dud.

Pierce conferred and announced, "Each man shoots three times. The best group wins."

Jeff reloaded the Navy with linen cartridges. He fired after Waking's shots. The judges went forward and spent long minutes talking and measuring.

This time lawyer Pierce came back and announced: "Winner by a hair—Jeff Becket."

Waking turned and held out his hand. "I ain't been beat in five year. Good shootin', boy."

"Thanks."

Dud shook his hand as the crowd yelled. "An astonishing feat! Congratulations!"

Others pushed and shoved to shake his hand, and it took awhile to work through the well-wishers to find Rachel and Leah. Both complained that their feet hurt, and they demanded supper.

Titus went with them to the hotel dining room, and joined them as they seated themselves. He had just talked with Henry Mills, he said, who had returned from Bowers within the hour with his wagons. There was news from the East. The Democratic Party was divided and had made two nominations, which practically assured the election of a Republican.

"Y'all going to have Seward as president," he told them. "You mark my words. He can't lose."

Jeff asked, "What about Lincoln? He's stronger than folks thought."

"That may be." Titus shrugged. "But not enough people know 'im. And the South don't want him. He's agin slavery."

Leah said, "Can we forget politics for a while?"

"Not while Jerry is around," Jeff said.

Titus chuckled. "Politics is the national pastime. It beats talkin' about chickens."

"Then let's talk about Lili," Leah said. "Roger thinks she has a great future."

"I b'lieve it," Titus said. "She is one in a million—and a damned sensible girl, too."

Dud nodded. "It's hard to comprehend, when you see what she's doing now, that only a few years ago she was a gawky child."

"Genius will out," Titus said firmly. "The good Lord got his finger on her." He cleared his throat. "The Republicans goin' to hold their convention in Chicago. . . ."

Dud laughed and Rachel pulled Jeff's sleeve. "Can we go home tomorrow, husband? All this excitement's too much for me."

"Of course. Have you decided what you want to eat?"

Rachel picked up the menu and frowned at the prices. What an expensive place! Probably because of the Fair. Dinner was fifty cents for each of them! She sighed. She'd be glad to get back to her comfortable home. . . .

Simon and Marty reached the vicinity of Eden Creek and camped in the woods a few miles from the stream. In the morning they rode close to the little settlement that straggled along the creek bank. Simon was surprised at how it had grown during the relatively short time he'd been gone.

The Caines' stone house was now occupied by another family and it had changed a good deal. He felt a considerable annoyance as he stared at the old place. What right did a bunch of strangers have, moving in that way?

Marty asked, "Which one's the Becket house?"

"I'm not sure. Things have changed since I was here last."

Marty grunted and turned his horse toward the creek. A young barefoot boy with a fishpole was sitting by the water. Marty halted by him and they talked for a moment, then the boy rose and pointed.

Marty came back. "Becket's in the big frame house and the Hurleys're in that one, the stone one."

"Dud Hurley owns the general store."

Marty scratched his stubbled chin. "Where you spose he keeps his cash . . . in the house or the store?"

"I dunno. You can't ask a man that."

Marty let out his breath and fished for a cigar.

There was no smoke rising from either the Becket or the Hurley chimneys. Could they be away? The store looked to be closed but it was hard to tell from a distance. Simon pointed out the way station and Marty said he'd ride over there and ask some questions.

"You stay outta sight."

Simon nodded and stepped down to wait.

Marty walked his horse to the station and got down as if he'd been riding all night. He told the man who came to a ticket window that he'd come from Flat Rock in the south.

The man said, "You heading for the Fair?"

"What fair?"

"The one in Pommer. Most folks is there."

"Oh," Marty said quickly. "Think I will. Thanks."

He went back to Simon. "We's in luck. Ever'body is at the fair in Pommer. Le's go get the others."

Roy was not happy about leaving the Fair early, but when his mother asked he hooked up the horses and brought the Concord to the waiting room. The Porters decided to stay till the Fair ended, but Leah and Dud were ready to go. Young Josh begged to stay and was allowed to remain with the Porters. Lili made arrangements with Titus to turn over to Roger Parkman the two displayed paintings. She got into the coach with her mother and the others.

Roy pulled out of the lot, with Jeff riding beside him on the box. The road to Eden Creek had been dragged only a few days before and they made good time, stopping every hour to let everyone get down to walk about a bit.

They approached Eden Creek late in the afternoon and they halted at the way station. Dud jumped down and shaded his eyes, looking toward the store.

Jeff turned his head—and a shot rapped into the Concord!

Jeff jumped to the ground and grabbed Dud, who had started toward the store. "Stay here!" Several horsemen were milling about at the door of the distant store and one of them fired again at the coach.

"They're robbing the store!" Leah yelled.

Jeff trotted into the road with the old Hawken. Halting, he aimed and fired, and one of the horsemen slid down suddenly.

Jeff dropped the rifle in the weeds by the side of the road and ran toward the outlaws with the Navy Colt. Men were shouting and one, a big black-bearded man, galloped his horse toward Jeff, firing a pistol as fast as he could thumb the hammer. Jeff stopped short and fired twice. The man threw up his hands and toppled from the wild-eyed animal. The horse ran off toward the stream and Jeff walked to the downed man. He was dead, with half his head shot away.

The two others remaining had scattered. One was galloping along the street, the other had disappeared behind the houses. Jeff emptied the pistol at the man he could see. He thought the horse swerved, but it continued out of range.

Taking a deep breath, Jeff automatically began reloading the Navy. Roy came up beside him. "Are we going after them?"

Jeff nodded. Dud and Vince Ropers ran to the body in the road. Vince said, "This's the man who came by here yesterday! He said he was going to the Fair."

Dud went through the clothes and came up with a worn leather wallet. "His name was Martin Webb."

"Marty Webb—the outlaw!" Vince cried. "There's a big reward out for him!"

The body near the store entrance was of a slightly older man. There was no identification on him but the initials J H were carved on the butt of his pistol.

Perly Dwyer lay on the floor inside the store. He had been struck on the head and was breathing shallowly. They carried him gently and laid him on a cot.

"Get some ice from the icehouse," Dud said. "We'll put cold compresses on the wound."

"Two got away," Jeff said. He went outside, and Roy came from the corral leading two horses. Jeff picked up the Hawken and mounted the sorrel. Rachel stood in the street and watched them ride away.

They did not catch sight of the outlaws. The two had probably separated, and after several hours Jeff gave it up. There was no telling about owlhoots.

Vince Ropers sent a rider to Pommer and deputy Paul Trask came out to gaze at the bodies before they were buried. He also had information on the man with the initials J. H.

"We know that a man named Hunky rode with Webb. This's probably him. There's a hunnerd-dollar reward on him, too."

Perly was able to talk in another day. The outlaws had taken what cash they found in the store—and had talked about raiding the

Becket home next. He had been hit when he would not tell them where Dud kept his money.

And one of the raiders had been Simon Caine.

Three days later Isaac Closs came to the store riding a big black mule. He dismounted heavily. "Howdy, Dud."

"Howdy, Isaac."

"Heard about the shootin' y'all had over here a few days ago."

Dud nodded. "Bunch came to rob the store. Jeff took care of two of them. . . ."

"I think he took care of one more."

"What?"

"I found 'im in the woods this mornin'. He must been hit when he was ridin' away." Isaac hunched his big shoulders. "It was the feller used to live here."

"Simon? You mean Simon Caine?"

"Yep. What's left of 'im."

Dud looked at the sky and sighed deeply. "All right. Let's go bury him. . . ."

About the Author

ARTHUR MOORE is the author of thirteen westerns including THE
KID FROM RINCON, TRAIL OF THE GATLINGS, THE
STEEL BOX, DEAD OR ALIVE, and MURDER ROAD, pub-
lished by Fawcett Books. He lives in Westlake Village, California.